The Moving F

E. Phillips Oppenheim

Alpha Editions

This edition published in 2023

ISBN : 9789357955867

Design and Setting By
Alpha Editions
www.alphaedis.com
Email - info@alphaedis.com

Contents

PROLOGUE

THE DREAMER

The boy sat with his back to a rock, his knees drawn up and clasped within fingers nervously interlocked. His eyes were fixed upon the great stretch of landscape below, shadowy now, and indistinct, like a rolling plain of patchwork woven by mysterious fingers. Gray mists were floating over the meadows and low-lying lands. Away in the distance they marked the circuitous course of the river, which only an hour ago had shone like a belt of silver in the light of the setting sun. Twilight had fallen with unexpected swiftness. Here and there a light flashed from the isolated farmhouses. On the darkening horizon, a warm glow was reflected in the clouds from the distant town.

The boy, when he had settled down to his vigil, had been alone. From over the brow of the hill, however, had come a few minutes ago a man, dressed in loose shooting clothes, and with a gun under his arm. He came to a standstill by the side of the boy, and stood there watching him for several moments, with a certain faintly amused curiosity shining out of his somewhat supercilious gray eyes. The newcomer was obviously a person of breeding and culture—the sort of person who assumes without question the title of "Gentleman." The boy wore ready-made clothes and hobnailed boots. They remained within a few feet of one another for several moments, without speech.

"My young friend," the newcomer said at last, "you will be late for your tea, or whatever name is given to your evening meal. Did you not hear the bell? It rang nearly half-an-hour ago."

The boy moved his head slightly, but made no attempt to rise.

"It does not matter. I am not hungry."

The newcomer leaned his gun against the rock, and drawing a pipe from the pocket of his shooting-coat, commenced leisurely to fill it. Every now and then he glanced at the boy, who seemed once more to have become unconscious of his presence. He struck a match and lit the tobacco, stooping down for a moment to escape the slight evening breeze. Then he threw the match away, and lounged against the lichen-covered fragment of stone.

"I wonder," he remarked, "why, when you have the whole day in which to come and look at this magnificent view, you should choose to come just at the hour when it has practically been swallowed up."

The boy lifted his head for the first time. His face was a little long, his features irregular but not displeasing, his deep-set eyes seemed unnaturally bright. His cheeks were sunken, his forehead unusually prominent. The whole effect of his personality was a little curious. If he had no claims to be considered good-looking, his face was at least a striking one.

He came to a standstill by the side of the boy.

"I come at this hour," he said slowly, "because the view does not attract me so much at any other time. It is only when the twilight falls that one can see—properly."

The newcomer took his pipe from his mouth.

"You must have marvelous eyesight, my young friend," he remarked. "To me everything seems blurred and uncertain."

"You don't understand!" said the boy impatiently. "I do not come here to see the things that anyone can see at any hour of the day. There is nothing satisfying in that. I come here to look down and see the things which do not really exist. It is easy enough when one is alone," he added, a little pointedly.

The newcomer laughed softly—there was more banter than humor in his mirth.

"So my company displeases you," he remarked. "Do you know that I have the right to tell you to get up, and never to pass through that gate again?"

The boy shrugged his shoulders.

"One place is as good as another," he said.

The man smoked in silence for several moments. Then he withdrew the pipe from his teeth and sighed gently.

"These are indeed democratic days," he said. "You do not know, my young friend, that I am Henry Prestgate Rochester, Esquire, if you please, High Sheriff of this county, Magistrate and Member of Parliament, owner, by the bye, of that rock against which you are leaning, and of most of that country below, which you can or cannot see."

"Really!" the boy answered slowly. "My name is Bertrand Saton, and I am staying at the Convalescent Home down there, a luxury which is costing me exactly eight shillings a week."

"So I concluded," his companion remarked. "May I ask what your occupation is, when in health?"

"It's of no consequence," the boy answered, a little impatiently. "Perhaps I haven't one at all. Whatever it is, as you may imagine, it has not brought me any great success. If you wish me to go——"

"Not at all," Rochester interrupted, with a little protesting gesture.

"I do not wish to remain here on sufferance," the boy continued. "I understood that we were allowed to spend our time upon the hills here."

"That is quite true, I believe," Rochester admitted. "My bailiff sees to those things, and if it amuses you to sit here all night, you are perfectly welcome."

"I shall probably do so."

Rochester watched him curiously for a few seconds.

"Look here," he said, "I will make a bargain with you. You shall have the free run of all my lands for as long as you like, and in return you shall just answer me one question."

The boy turned his head slightly.

"The question?" he asked.

"You shall tell me the things which you see down there," Rochester declared, holding his hand straight out in front of him, pointing downward toward the half-hidden panorama.

The boy shook his head.

"For other people they would not count," he said. "They are for myself only. What I see would be invisible to you."

"A matter of eyesight?" Rochester asked, with raised eyebrows.

"Of imagination," the boy answered. "There is no necessity for you to look outside your own immediate surroundings to see beautiful things, unless you choose deliberately to make your life an ugly thing. With us it is different— with us who work for a living, who dwell in the cities, and who have no power to push back the wheels of life. If we are presumptuous enough to wish to take into our lives anything of the beautiful, anything to help us fight our daily battle against the commonplace, we have to create it for ourselves. That is why I am here just now, and why I was regretting, when I heard your footstep, that one finds it so hard to be alone."

"So I am to be ordered off?" Rochester remarked, smiling.

The boy did not answer. The man did not move. The minutes went by, and the silence remained unbroken. Below, the twilight seemed to be passing into night with unusual rapidity. It was a shapeless world now, a world of black and gray. More lights flashed out every few seconds.

It was the boy who broke the silence at last. He seemed, in some awkward way, to be trying to atone for his former unsociability.

"This is my last night at the Convalescent Home," he said, a little abruptly. "I am cured. To-morrow I am going back to my work in Mechester. For many days I shall see nothing except actual things. I shall know nothing of life except its dreary and material side. That is why I came here with the twilight. That is why I am going to sit here till the night comes—perhaps, even, I shall wait until the dawn. I want one last long rest. I want to carry away with me some absolute impression of life as I would have it. Down there," he added, moving his head slowly, "down there I can see the things I want—the things which, if I could, I would take into my life. I am going to look at them, and think of them, and long for them, until they seem real. I am going to create a concrete memory, and take it away with me."

Rochester looked more than a little puzzled. The boy's speech seemed in no way in keeping with his attire, and the fact of his presence in a charitable home.

"Might one inquire once more," he asked, "what your occupation in Mechester is?"

"It is of no consequence," the boy answered shortly. "It is an occupation that does not count. It does not make for anything in life. One must do something to earn one's daily bread."

"You find my questioning rather a nuisance, I am afraid," Rochester remarked, politely.

"I will not deny it," the boy answered. "I will admit that I wish to be alone. I am hoping that very soon you will be going."

"On the contrary," Rochester replied, smiling, "I am much too interested in your amiable conversation. You see," he added, knocking the ashes from his pipe, and leaning carelessly back against the rock, "I live in a world, every member of which is more or less satisfied. I will be frank with you, and I will admit that I find satisfaction in either man or woman a most reprehensible state. I find a certain relief, therefore, in talking to a person who wants something he hasn't got, or who wants to be something that he isn't."

"Then you can find all the satisfaction you want in talking to me," the boy declared, gloomily. "I am at the opposite pole of life, you see, to those friends of yours. I want everything I haven't got. I am content with nothing that I have."

"For instance?" Rochester asked, suggestively.

"I want freedom from the life of a slave," the boy said. "I want money, the money that gives power. I want the right to shape my own life in my own way, and to my own ends, instead of being forced to remain a miserable, ineffective part of a useless scheme of existence."

"Your desires are perfectly reasonable," Rochester remarked, calmly. "Imagine, if you please—you seem to have plenty of imaginative force—that I am a fairy godfather. I may not look the part, but at least I can live up to it. I will provide the key for your escape. I will set you down in the world you are thirsting to enter. You shall take your place with the others, and run your race."

The boy suddenly abandoned his huddled-up position, and rose to his feet. Against the background of empty air, and in the gathering darkness, he seemed thinner than ever, and smaller.

"I am going," he said shortly. "It may seem amusing to you to make fun of me. I will not stay——"

"Don't be a fool!" Rochester interrupted. "Haven't you heard that I am more than half a madman? I am going to justify my character for eccentricity. You see my house down there—Beauleys, they call it? At twelve o'clock tomorrow, if you come to me, I will give you a sum of money sufficient to keep you for several years. I do not specify the amount at this moment, I shall think it over before you come."

The boy had no words. He simply stared at his chance companion in blank astonishment.

"My offer seems to surprise you," Rochester remarked, pleasantly. "It need not. You can go and tell the whole world of it, if you like, although, as a reputation for sanity is quite a valuable asset, nowadays, I should suggest that you keep your mouth closed. Still, if you do speak of it, no one will be in the least surprised. My friends—I haven't many—call me the most eccentric man in Christendom. My enemies wonder how it is that I keep out of the asylum. Personally, I consider myself a perfectly reasonable mortal. I have whims, and I am not afraid to indulge them. I give you this money on one—or perhaps we had better say two conditions. The first is that you make a *bonâ fide* use of it. When I say that, I mean that you leave immediately your present employment, whatever it may be, and go out into the world with the steadfast purpose of finding for yourself the things which you saw a few minutes ago down in the valley there. You may not find them, but still I pledge you to the search. The second condition is that some day or other you find your way back into this part of the country, and tell me how my experiment has fared."

The boy realized with a little gasp.

"Am I to thank you?" he asked.

"It would be usual but foolish," Rochester answered. "I need no thanks, I deserve none. I yield to a whim, nothing else. I do this thing for my own pleasure. The sum of money which I propose to put into your hands will probably represent to me what a five-shilling piece might to you. This may sound vulgar, but it is true. I think that I need not warn you never to come to me for more. You need not look so horrified. I am quite sure that you would not do that. And there is one thing further."

"Yes?" the boy asked. "Another condition?"

Rochester shook his head.

"No!" he said. "It is not a condition. It is just a little advice. The way through life hasn't been made clear for everyone. You may find yourself brought up in the thorny paths. Take my advice. Don't be content with anything less than success. If you fail, strip off your clothes, and swim out to sea on a sunny day, swim out until your strength fails and you must sink. It is the pleasantest form of oblivion I know of. Don't live on. You are only a nuisance to yourself, and a bad influence to the rest of the world. Succeed, or make your little bow, my young friend. It is the best advice I can give you. Remember that the men who have failed, and who live on, are creatures of the gutter."

"You are right!" the boy muttered. "I have read that somewhere, and it comes home to me. Failure is the one unforgivable sin. If I have to commit every other crime in the decalogue, I will at least avoid that one!"

Rochester shouldered his gun, and prepared to stroll off.

"At twelve o'clock to-morrow, then," he said. "I wouldn't hurry away now, if I were you. Sit down in your old place, and see if there isn't a thread of gold down there in the valley."

The boy obeyed almost mechanically. His heart was beating fast. His back was pressed against the cold rock. The fingers of both hands were nervously buried in the soft turf. Once more his eyes were riveted upon this land of shifting shadows. The whole panorama of life seemed suddenly unveiled before his eyes. More real, more brilliant now were the things upon which he looked. The thread of gold was indeed there!

CHAPTER I

A LETTER PROVES USEFUL

Bertrand Saton leaned against the stone coping of the bridge, and looked downwards, as though watching the seagulls circling round and round, waiting for their usual feast of scraps. The gulls, however, were only his excuse. He stood there, looking hard at the gray, muddy water beneath, trying to make up his mind to this final and inevitable act of despair. He had walked the last hundred yards almost eagerly. He had told himself that he was absolutely and entirely prepared for death. Yet the first sight of that gray, cold-looking river, had chilled him. He felt a new and unaccountable reluctance to quit the world which certainly seemed to have made up its mind that it had no need of him. His thoughts rushed backwards. "Swim out to sea on a sunny day," he repeated to himself slowly. Yes, but this! It was a different thing, this! The longer he looked below, the more he shrank from such a death!

He stood upright with a little shiver, and began—it was not for the first time that day—a searching investigation into the contents of his pocket. The result was uninspiring. There was not an article there which would have fetched the price of a dose of poison. Then his fingers strayed into a breast-pocket which he seldom used, and brought out a letter, unopened, all grimy, and showing signs of having been there for some considerable time. He held it between his fingers, doubtful at first from where it had come. Then suddenly he remembered. He remembered the runaway horses in the Bois, and the strange-looking old woman who had sat in the carriage with grim, drawn lips and pallid face. He remembered the dash into the roadway, the brief, maddening race by the side of the horses, his clutch at the reins, the sense of being dragged along the dusty road. It was, perhaps, the one physically courageous action of his life. The horses were stopped, and the woman's life was saved. He looked at the letter in his hand.

"Why not?" he asked himself softly.

He hesitated, and glanced downward once more toward the river. The sight seemed to decide him. He turned his weary footsteps again westward.

Walking with visible effort, and resting whenever he had a chance, he reached at last the Oxford Street end of Bond Street. Holding the letter in his hand, he made his way, slowly and more painfully than ever, down the right-hand side. People stared at him a little curiously. He was a strange figure, passing through the crowds of well-dressed, sauntering men and women. He was unnaturally thin—the pallor of his cheeks and the gleam in his eyes spoke of starvation. His clothes had been well-cut, but they were almost in rags. His cap had cost him a few pence at a second-hand store.

He made his way toward his destination, looking neither to the right nor to the left. The days had gone when he found it interesting to study the faces of the passers-by, looking out always for adventures, amusing himself with shrewd speculations as to the character and occupation of those who seemed worthy of notice. This was his last quest now—the quest of life or death.

He stopped in front of a certain number, and comparing it with the tattered envelope which he held in his hand, finally entered. The lift-boy, who was lounging in the little hall, looked at him in surprise.

"I want to find Madame Helga," the young man said shortly. "This is number 38, isn't it?"

The boy looked at him doubtfully, and led the way to the lift.

"Third floor," he said. "I'll take you up."

The lift stopped, and Bertrand Saton found in front of him a door upon which was a small brass plate, engraved simply with the name of Helga. He knocked twice, and received no answer. Then, turning the handle, he entered, and stood looking about him with some curiosity.

It was a small room, luxuriously but sombrely furnished. Heavy curtains were drawn more than half-way across the windows, and the room was so dark that at first he was not sure whether it was indeed empty. On a small black oak table in the middle of the rich green carpet, stood a crystal ball. There was nothing else unusual about the apartment, except the absence of any pictures upon the walls, and a faint aromatic odor, as though somewhere dried weeds were being burned.

Some curtains opposite him were suddenly thrust aside. A woman stood there looking at him. She was of middle height, fair, with a complexion which even in that indistinct light he could see owed little of its smoothness to nature. She wore a loose gown which seemed to hang from her shoulders, of some soft green material, drawn around her waist with a girdle. Her eyes were deep-set and penetrating.

"You wish to see me?" she asked.

He held out the note.

"If you are Madame Helga," he answered.

She came a little further into the room, looking at him with a slight frown contracting her pencilled eyebrows. He had no appearance of being a client.

"You have brought a letter, then?" she asked.

"My name is Bertrand Saton," he explained. "This letter was given to me in Paris more than a year ago, by an elderly lady. I have carried it with me all that time. At first it did not seem likely that I should ever need to use it. Unfortunately," he added, a little bitterly, "things have changed."

She took the letter, and tore open the envelope. Its contents consisted only of a few lines, which she read with some appearance of surprise. Then she turned once more to the young man.

"You are the Mr. Bertrand Saton of whom the writer of this letter speaks?" she asked.

He nodded.

"I am," he answered.

She looked him over from head to foot. There was scarcely an inch of his person which did not speak of poverty and starvation.

"You have had trouble," she remarked.

"I have," he admitted.

"The lady who wrote that letter," she said, "is at present in Spain."

He turned to go.

"I am not surprised," he answered. "My star is not exactly in the ascendant just now."

"Don't be too sure," she said. "And whatever you do, don't go away. Sit down if you are tired. You don't seem strong."

"I am not," he admitted. "Would you like," he added, "to know what is the matter with me?"

"It is nothing serious, I hope?"

"I am starving," he declared, simply. "I have eaten nothing for twenty-four hours."

She looked at him for a moment as though doubting his words. Then she moved rapidly to a desk which stood in a corner of the room.

"You are a very foolish person," she said, "to allow yourself to get into such a state, when all the time you had this letter in your pocket. But I forgot," she added, unlocking the desk. "You had not read it. You had better have some money to buy yourself food and clothes, and come here again."

"Food and clothes!" he repeated, vaguely. "I do not understand."

She touched the letter with her forefinger.

"You have a very powerful friend here," she said. "I am told to give you whatever you may be in need of, and to telegraph to her, in whatever part of the world she may be, if ever you should present this letter."

Saton began to laugh softly.

"It is the turn of the wheel," he said. "I am too weak to hear any more. Give me some money, and I will come back. I must eat or I shall faint."

She gave him some notes, and watched him curiously as he staggered out of the room. He forgot the lift, and descended by the stairs, unsteadily, like a drunken person, reeling from the banisters to the wall, and back again. Out in the street, people looked at him curiously as he turned northward toward Oxford Street. His eyes searched the shop-windows. He hurried along like a man feverishly anxious to make use of his last stint of strength. He was in search of food!

CHAPTER II

OLD ACQUAINTANCES

Rochester was walking slowly along the country lane which led from the main road to Beauleys, when the hoot of a motor overtaking him caused him to slacken his pace and draw in close to the hedge-side. The great car swung by, with a covered top upon which was luggage, a chauffeur, immaculate in dark green livery, and inside, two people. Rochester caught a glimpse of them as they passed by—the woman, heavily muffled up notwithstanding the warm afternoon, old and withered; the man, young, with dark, sallow complexion, and thoughtful eyes. They were gone like a flash. Yet Rochester stood for a moment in the road looking after them, before he turned into a field to escape the cloud of dust. The man's face was peculiar, and strangely enough it was familiar. He racked his brains in vain for some clue to its identity— searched every corner of his memory without success. Finally, with a little shrug of his shoulders, he dismissed the subject.

He was soon to be reminded of it, though, for when he reached home, he was told at once that a gentleman was waiting to see him in the study. Then Rochester, with a little gasp of surprise, recalled that likeness which had puzzled him so much. He knew who his visitor was! He walked toward the study, filled with a curious—perhaps, even, an ominous sense of excitement!...

They were face to face in a few seconds. The man was unchanged. The boy alone was altered. Rochester's hair was a little grayer, perhaps, but his face was still smooth. His out-of-door life and that wonderful mouth of his, with its half humorous, half cynical curve, still kept his face young. To the boy had come a change much more marked and evident. He was a boy no longer—not even a youth. He carried himself with the assured bearing of a man of the world. His thick black hair was carefully parted. His clothes bore the stamp of Saville Row. His face was puzzling. His eyes were still the eyes of a dreamer, the eyes of a man who is content to be rather than to do. Yet the rest of his face seemed somehow to have suffered. His cheeks had filled out. His mouth and expression were no longer easy to read. There were things in his face which would have puzzled a physiognomist.

Rochester had entered the library and closed the door behind him. He nodded toward the man who rose slowly to greet him, but ignored his outstretched hand.

"I am sure that I cannot be mistaken," he said. "It is my young friend of the hillside."

"It is he," Saton answered. "I scarcely expected to be remembered."

"One sees so few fresh faces," Rochester murmured. "You have kept the condition, then? I must confess that I am glad to see you. I shall hope that you will have a great deal that is interesting to tell me. At any rate, it is a good sign that you have kept the condition."

"I have kept the condition," Saton answered. "I was never likely to break it. I have wandered up and down the world a good deal during the past five years, and I have met many strange sorts of people, but I have never yet met with philanthropy on such a unique scale as yours."

"Not philanthropy, my young friend," Rochester murmured. "I had but one motive in making you that little gift—curiosity pure and simple."

"Forgive me," Saton remarked. "We will call it a loan, if you do not mind. I am not going to offer you any interest. The five hundred pounds are here."

He handed a little packet across to Rochester, who slipped it carelessly into his pocket.

"This is romance indeed!" he declared, with something of the old banter in his tone. "You are worse than the industrious apprentice. Have I, by chance, the pleasure of speaking to one of the world's masters—a millionaire?"

The young man laughed. His laugh, at any rate, was not unpleasant.

"No!" he said. "I don't suppose that I am even wealthy, as the world reckons wealth. I have succeeded to a certain extent, although I came very, very near to disaster. I have made a little money, and I can make more when it is necessary."

"Your commercial instincts," Rochester remarked, "have not been thoroughly aroused, then?"

The young man smiled.

"Do I need to tell you," he asked, "that great wealth was not among the things I saw that night?"

"That was a marvelous motor-car in which you passed me," remarked the other.

"It belongs to the lady," Saton said, "who brought me down from London."

Rochester nodded.

"It will be interesting to me," he remarked, "later on, to hear something of your adventures. To judge by your appearance, and your repayment of that small amount of money, you have prospered."

"One hates the word," Saton murmured, with a sudden frown upon his forehead. "I suppose I must admit that I have been fortunate to some extent. I am able to repay my debt to you."

"That," Rochester interrupted, "is a trifle. It was not worth considering. In fact I am rather disappointed that you have paid me back."

"I was forced to do it," Saton answered. "One cannot accept alms."

Rochester eyed his visitor a little thoughtfully.

"A platitude merely," he said. "One accepts alms every day, every moment of the day. One goes about the world giving and receiving. It is a small point of view which reckons gold as the only means of exchange."

The young man bowed.

"I am corrected," he said. "Yet you must admit that there is something different in the obligation which is created by money."

"Mine, I fear," Rochester answered, "is not an analytic mind. A blunt regard to truth has always been one of my characteristics. Therefore, at the risk of indelicacy, I am going on to ask you a question. I found you on the hillside, a discontented, miserable youth, and I did for you something which very few sane people would have been inclined even to consider. Years afterwards— it must be nearly seven, isn't it?—you return me my money, and we exchange a few polite platitudes. I notice—or is it that I only seem to notice—on your part an entire lack of gratitude for that eccentric action of mine. The discontented boy has become, presumably, a prosperous citizen of the world. The two are so far apart, perhaps——"

Saton threw out his hands. For the first time, there flashed into his face something of the boy, some trace of that more primitive, more passionate hold upon life. He abandoned his measured tones, his calm, almost studied bearing.

"Gratitude!" he interrupted. "I am not sure that I feel any! In those days I had at least dreams. I am not sure that it was not a devilish experiment of yours to send me out to grope my way amongst the mirages. You were a man of the world then. You knew and understood. You knew how bitter a thing life is, how for one who climbs, a thousand must fall. I am not sure," he repeated, with a little catch in his throat, "that I feel any gratitude."

Rochester nodded thoughtfully. He was not in the least annoyed.

"You interest me," he murmured. "From what you say, I gather that your material prosperity has been somewhat dearly bought."

"There isn't much to be wrung from life," Saton answered bitterly, "that one doesn't pay for."

"A little later on," Rochester said, "it will give me very much pleasure to hear something of your adventures. At present, I fear that I must deny myself that pleasure. My wife has done me the honor to make me one of her somewhat rare visits, and my house is consequently full of guests."

"I will not intrude," the young man answered, rising. "I shall stay in the village for a few days. We may perhaps meet again."

Rochester hesitated for a moment. Then the corners of his mouth twitched. There was humor in this situation, after all, and in the thing which he proposed to himself.

"You must not hurry way," he said. "Come and be introduced to some of my friends."

If Rochester expected any hesitation on the part of his visitor, he was disappointed. The young man seemed to accept the suggestion as the most natural in the world.

"I shall be very glad," he said calmly. "I shall be interested, too, to meet your wife. At the time when I had the pleasure of seeing you before, you were, I believe, unmarried."

Rochester opened the door, and led the way out into the hall without a word.

CHAPTER III

"WHO IS MR. SATON?"

"Really, Henry," Lady Mary Rochester said to her husband, a few minutes before the dinner-gong sounded, "for once you have been positively useful. A new young man is such a godsend, and Charlie Peyton threw us over most abominably. So mean of him, too, after the number of times I had him to dine in Grosvenor Square."

"He's gone to Ostend, I suppose."

Lady Mary nodded.

"So foolish!" she declared. "He hasn't a shilling in the world, and he never wins anything. He might just as well have come down here and made himself agreeable to Lois."

"Matchmaking again?" Rochester asked.

She shook her head.

"What nonsense! Charlie is one of my favorite young men. I am not at all sure that I could spare him, even to Lois. But the poor boy must marry someone! I don't see how else he is to live. By the bye, who is your protégé?"

Rochester, who was lounging in a low chair in his wife's dressing-room, looked thoughtfully at the tip of his patent shoe.

"I haven't the faintest idea," he declared.

His wife frowned, a little impatiently.

"You are so extreme," she protested. "Of course you know something about him. What am I to tell people? They will be sure to ask."

"Make them all happy," Rochester suggested. "Tell Lady Blanche that he is a millionaire from New York, and Lois that he is the latest thing in Spring poets. They probably won't compare notes until to-morrow, so it really doesn't matter."

"I wish you could be serious for five minutes," Lady Mary said. "You really are a trial, Henry. You seem to see everything from some quaint point of view of your own, and to forget all the time that there are a few other people in the world whose eyesight is not so distorted. Sometimes I can't help realizing how fortunate it is that we see so little of one another."

"I can scarcely be expected to agree with you," Rochester answered, with an ironical bow. "I must try and mend my ways, however. To return to the actual subject under discussion, then, I can really tell you very little about this young man."

"You can tell me where he comes from, at any rate," Lady Mary remarked.

Rochester shook his head.

"He comes from the land of mysteries," he declared. "I really am ashamed to be so disappointing, but I only met him once before in my life."

Lady Mary sighed gently.

"It is almost a relief," she said, "to hear you admit that you have seen him before at all. Please tell me where it was that you met," she added, studying the effect of a tiara upon her splendidly coiffured hair.

"I met him," Rochester answered, "sitting with his back to a rock on the top of one of my hills."

"What, you mean here at Beauleys?" Lady Mary asked.

"On Beacon Hill," her husband assented. "It was seven years ago, and as you can gather from his present appearance, he was little more than a boy. He sat there in the twilight, seeing things down in the valley which did not and never had existed—seeing things that never were born, you know—things for which you stretch out your arms, only to find them float away. He was quite young, of course."

Lady Mary turned around.

"Henry!" she exclaimed.

"My dear?"

"You are absolutely the most irritating person I ever attempted to live with!"

"And I have tried so hard to make myself agreeable," he sighed.

"You are one of those uncomfortable people," she declared, "who loathe what they call the obvious, and adore riddles. You would commit any sort of mental gymnastic rather than answer a plain question in a straightforward manner."

"It is perfectly true," he admitted. "You have such insight, my dear Mary."

"I am to take it, then," she continued, "that you know absolutely nothing about your protégé? You know nothing, for instance, about his family, or his means?"

"Absolutely nothing," he admitted. "He has an uncommon name, but I believe that I gathered from him once that his parentage was not particularly exalted."

"At least," she said, with a little sigh, "he is quite presentable. I call him, in fact, remarkably good-looking, and his manners leave nothing to be desired. He has lived abroad, I should think."

"He may have lived anywhere," Rochester admitted.

"Well, I'll have him next me at dinner," she declared. "I daresay I shall find out all about him pretty soon. Come, Henry, I am quite sure that everyone is down. You and I play host and hostess so seldom that we have forgotten our manners."

They descended to the drawing-room, and Lady Mary murmured her apologies. Everyone, however, seemed too absorbed to hear them. They were listening to Saton, who was standing, the centre of a little group, telling stories.

"It was in Buenos Ayres," Rochester heard him conclude, amidst a ripple of laughter. "I can assure you that I saw the incident with my own eyes."

Lois Champneyes—an heiress, pretty, and Rochester's ward—came floating across the room to them. She wore a plain muslin gown, of simpler cut than was usually seen at Lady Mary's house-parties, and her complexion showed no signs whatever of town life. Her hair—it was bright chestnut color, merging in places to golden—was twisted simply in one large coil on the top of her head. She wore no jewelry, and she had very much the appearance of a child just escaped from the schoolroom.

"Mary," she exclaimed, drawing her hostess on one side, "you must send me in with Mr. Saton! He is perfectly charming, and isn't it a lovely name? Do tell me who he is, and whether I may fall in love with him."

Lady Mary nodded.

"My dear child," she said, "I shall do nothing of the sort. You are not nearly old enough to take care of yourself, and we know nothing about this young man at all. Besides, I want him for myself."

"You are the most selfish hostess I ever stayed with," Lois declared, turning away with a little pout. "Never mind! I'll make him talk to me after dinner."

"Is your friend in the diplomatic service?" Lord Penarvon asked Rochester. "He is a most amusing fellow."

"Not at present, at any rate," Rochester answered. "I really forget what he used to do when I met him first. As a matter of fact, I have seen very little of him lately."

A servant announced dinner, and they all trooped across the hall a little informally. It was only a small party, and Lady Mary was a hostess whose ideas were distinctly modern. Conversation at first was nearly altogether general. Saton, without in any way asserting himself, bore at least his part in it. He spoke modestly enough, and yet everything he said seemed to tell. From the first, the dinner was a success.

Rochester found himself listening with a curiosity for which he could not wholly account, to this young man, seated only a few feet away. His presence was so decidedly piquant. It appealed immensely to his sense of humor. Saton's appearance was in every respect irreproachable. His tie was perfectly tied, his collar of the latest shape. His general appearance was that of an exceedingly smart young man about town. The only sign of eccentricity which he displayed was an unobtrusive eyeglass, suspended from his neck by a narrow black ribbon, and which he had only used to study the menu.

Rochester looked at him across the white tablecloth, with its glittering load of silver and glass, its perfumed banks of pink blossoms, and told himself that one at least of his somewhat eccentric experiments had borne strange fruit. He thought of that night upon the hillside, the boy's passionate words, his almost wild desire to realize, to turn into actual life, the fantasies which were then only the creation of his fancy. How far had he realized them, he wondered? What did this alteration in his exterior denote? From a few casual and half-forgotten inquiries, Rochester knew that he was the son, or rather the orphan of working-people in the neighboring town. There was nothing in his blood to make him in any way the social equal of these men and women amongst whom he now sat with such perfect self-possession. Rochester found himself watching for some traces of inferior breeding, some lapse of speech, some signs of an innate lack of refinement. The absence of any of these things puzzled him. Saton was assured, without being over-confident. He spoke of himself only seldom. It was marvelous how often he seemed to avoid the use of the first person. He seemed, too, modestly unconscious of the fact that his conversation was in any way more interesting than the speech of those by whom he was surrounded.

"You seem to have lived," his hostess said to him once, "in so many countries, Mr. Saton. Are you really only as old as you look?"

"How can I answer that," he asked, smiling, "except by telling you that I am twenty-five."

"You must have commenced to live in your perambulator," she declared.

"I have lived nowhere," he answered. "I have visited many places, and travelled through many lands, but life with me has been a search."

"A search?" she murmured, dropping her voice a little, and intimating by the slight movement of her head towards him, that their conversation was to become a tête-á-tête. "Well," she continued, "I suppose that life is that with all of us, only you see with us poor frivolous people, a search means nearly always the same thing—a search for amusement or distraction, whichever you choose to call it."

Saton shrugged his shoulders slightly.

"Different things amuse different people," he remarked. "My search, I will admit, was of a different order."

"It is finished?" she asked.

"It will never be finished," he answered. "The man who finds what he seeks," he added, raising his dark eyes to hers, "as a rule has fixed his ambitions too low."

"Speaking of ambitions, Mr. Saton," Lord Penarvon asked across the table, "are you interested in politics?"

"Not in the least," Saton answered frankly. "There seem to me to be so many other things in life better worth doing than making fugitive laws for a dissatisfied country."

"Tell me," his hostess asked, "what do you yourself consider the things better worth doing?"

Saton hesitated. For the first time, he seemed scarcely at his ease. He glanced across at Rochester, and down at his plate.

"The sciences," he answered, quietly. "There are many torches lit which need strong hands to carry them forward."

Lois leaned across the table. As yet she had scarcely spoken, but she had listened intently to his every word.

"Which of the sciences, Mr. Saton?" she asked, a little breathlessly.

He smiled at her, and hesitated a moment before answering.

"There are so many," he said, "which are equally fascinating, but I think that it is always the least known which is the most attractive. When I spoke, I was really thinking of one which many people would scarcely reckon amongst the orthodox list. I mean occultism."

There was a little murmur of interest. Saton himself, however, deliberately turned the conversation. He reverted to a diplomatic incident which had come to his notice when in Brazil, and asked Lord Penarvon's opinion concerning it.

"By the bye," the latter asked, as their conversation drew toward a close, "how long did you say that you had been in England, Mr. Saton?"

"A very short time," Saton answered, with a faint smile. "I have been something of a wanderer for years."

"And you came from?" Rochester asked, leaning a little forward.

Saton smiled as his eyes met his host's. He hesitated perceptibly.

"I came from the land where the impossible sometimes happens," he answered, lightly, "the land where one dreams in the evening, and is never sure when one wakes in the morning that one's dreams have not become solid things."

Lady Mary sighed.

"Can one get a Cook's ticket?" she asked.

"Can one get there by motor-car, or even flying-machine?" Lois demanded. "I would risk my bones to find my way there."

Saton laughed.

"Unfortunately," he said, "there is a different path for every one of us, and there are no signposts."

Lady Mary sighed as she rose to her feet. She nodded a friendly little farewell to her interesting neighbor.

"Then we may as well go and have some really good bridge," she said, "until you men take it into your heads to come and disturb us."

CHAPTER IV

A QUESTION OF OBLIGATION

Afternoon tea was being served in the hall at Beauleys on the day after Saton's arrival. Saton himself was sitting with Lois Champneyes in a retired corner.

"I was going to ask you," he remarked, as he handed her some cakes, "about Mr. Rochester's marriage. He was a bachelor when I—first met him."

"Were you very intimate in those days?" she asked.

"Not in the least," he answered, with a faint reminiscent smile.

"Then you never heard about the romance of his life?" she asked.

Saton shook his head.

"Never," he declared. "Nor should I ever have associated the word with Mr. Rochester."

She sighed gently.

"I daresay he was very different in those days," she said. "Before the Beauleys property came to him, he was quite poor, and he was very much in love with the dearest woman—Pauline Hambledon. It was impossible for them to marry—her people wouldn't hear of it—so he went abroad, and she married Sir Walter Marrabel! Such a pig! Everyone hated him. Then old Mr. Stephen Rochester died suddenly, without a will, and all this property came to Henry!"

"And then he married, I suppose?" Saton remarked.

"I was going to tell you about that," Lois continued. "Mary was a niece of Stephen Rochester, and a daughter of the Marquis of Haselton, who was absolutely bankrupt when he died. Stephen Rochester adopted her, and then died without leaving her a farthing! So there she was, poor dear, penniless, and Henry had everything. Of course, he had to marry her."

"Why not?" Saton remarked. "She is quite charming."

"Yes! But this is the tantalizing part of it," Lois continued. "They hadn't been married a year when Sir Walter Marrabel died. Pauline is a widow now. She is coming here in a few days. I do hope you will meet her."

"This is quite interesting," Saton murmured. "How do Lady Mary and her husband get on?"

Lois made a little grimace.

"They go different ways most of the time," she answered. "I suppose they're only what people call modern. Isn't that a motor horn?" she cried out, springing to her feet. "I wonder if it's Guerdie!"

"For a man who has been a great lawyer," Lord Penarvon declared, "Guerdon is the most uncertain and unpunctual of men. One never knows when to expect him."

"He was to have arrived yesterday," Lady Mary remarked. "We sent to the station twice."

"I suppose," Rochester said, "that even to gratify the impatience of an expectant house-party, it is not possible to quicken the slow process of the law. If you look at the morning papers, you will see that he was at the Central Criminal Court, trying some case or other, all day yesterday. The man who pleads 'Not Guilty,' and who pays for his defence, expects to be heard out to the bitter end. It is really only natural."

Saton, who had been left alone in his corner, rose suddenly to his feet and came into the circle. He handed his cup to his hostess, and turned toward Rochester.

"You were speaking of judges?" he remarked.

Rochester nodded.

"In a few moments," he said, "you will probably meet the cleverest one we have upon the English bench. Without his robe and wig, some people find him insignificant. Personally, I must confess that I never feel his eyes upon me without a shiver. They say that he never loses sight of a fact or forgets a face."

"And what is the name of this wonderful person?" Saton asked.

"Lord Guerdon," Rochester answered. "Even though you have spent so little time in England of late years, you must have heard of him."

The curtains were suddenly thrown aside, and a footman entered announcing the newly-arrived guest. From the hall beyond came the sound of a departing motor, and the clatter of luggage being brought in. The footman stood on one side.

"Lord Guerdon!" he announced.

Lady Mary held out her hands across the tea-tray. Rochester came a few steps forward. Everyone ceased their conversation to look at the small, spare figure of the man who, clad in a suit of travelling clothes of gray tweed, and cut after a somewhat ancient pattern, insignificant-looking in figure and even in bearing, yet carried something in his clean-shaven, wrinkled face at once impressive and commanding. Everyone seemed to lean forward with a little air of interest, prepared to exchange greetings with him as soon as he had spoken to his host and hostess. Only Saton stood quite still, still as a figure turned suddenly into stone. No one appeared to notice him, to notice the twitching of his fingers, the almost ashen gray of his cheeks—no one except the girl with whom he had been talking, and whose eyes had scarcely left his. He recovered himself quickly. When Rochester turned towards him, a moment or so later, he was almost at his ease.

"You find us all old friends, Guerdon," he said, "except that I have to present to you my friend Mr. Saton. Saton, this is Lord Guerdon, whose caricature you have doubtless admired in many papers, comic and otherwise, and who I am happy to assure you is not nearly so terrible a person as he might seem from behind that ominous iron bar."

Saton held out his hand, but almost immediately withdrawing it, contented himself with a murmured word, and a somewhat low bow. For a second the judge's eyebrows were upraised, his keen eyes seemed to narrow. He made no movement to shake hands.

"I am very glad to meet Mr. Saton," he said slowly. "By the bye," he continued, after a second's pause, "is this our first meeting? I seem to have an idea—your face is somehow familiar to me."

There were few men who could have faced the piercing gaze of those bright brown eyes, set deep in the withered face, without any sign of embarrassment. Yet Saton smiled back pleasantly enough. He was completely at his ease. His face showed only a reasonable amount of pleasure at this encounter with the famous man.

"I am afraid, Lord Guerdon," he said, "that I cannot claim the privilege of any previous acquaintance. Although I am an Englishman, my own country has seen little of me during the last few years."

"Come and have some tea at once," Lady Mary insisted, looking up at the judge. "I want to hear all about this wonderful Clancorry case. Oh, I know you're not supposed to talk about it, but that really doesn't matter down here. You shall have a comfortable chair by my side, and some hot muffins."

Saton went back to his seat by the side of Lois Champneyes, carrying his refilled teacup in his hand. She looked at him a little curiously.

"Tell me," she said, "have you really never met Lord Guerdon before?"

"Never in my life," he answered.

"Did he remind you of anyone?" she asked.

"It is curious that you should ask that," Saton remarked. "In a way he did."

"I thought so," she declared, with a little breath of relief. "That was it, of course. Do you know how you looked when you first heard his name—when he came into the room?"

"I have no idea," he answered. "I only know that when I saw him enter, it gave me almost a shock. He reminded me most strangely of a man who has been dead for many years. I could scarcely take my eyes off him at first."

"I will tell you," she said, "what your look reminded me of. Many years before I was out—in my mother's time—there was a man named Mallory who was tried for murder, the murder of a friend, who everyone knew was his rival. Well, he got off, but only after a long trial, and only by a little weakness in the chain of evidence, which even his friends at the time thought providential. He went abroad for a long time. Then he came into a title and returned to England. He was obliged to take up his position, and people were willing enough to forget the past. He opened his London house, and accepted every invitation which came. At the very first party he went to, he came face to face with the judge who had tried him. My mother was there. I remember she told me how he looked. It was foolish of me, but I thought of it when I saw you just then."

Saton smiled sympathetically.

"And the end of the story?" he asked.

"The man had such a shock," she continued, "that he shut up his house, gave up all his schemes for re-entering life, left England, and never set foot in the country again."

Saton rose to his feet.

"I see that my host is beckoning me," he said. "Will you excuse me for a moment?"

Rochester passed his arm through the younger man's.

"Come into the gun-room for a few minutes," he said. "I want to show you the salmon flies I was speaking of."

Saton smiled a little curiously, and followed his host across the hall and down the long stone passage which led to the back quarters of the house. The gun-room was deserted and empty. Rochester closed the door.

"My young friend," he said, "if you do not object, I should like to have a few minutes of plain speaking with you."

"I should be delighted," Saton answered, seating himself deliberately in a battered old easy-chair.

"Seven years ago," Rochester continued, leaning his elbow against the mantelpiece, "we made a bargain. I sent you out into the world, an egotistical Don Quixote, and I provided you with the means with which you were to turn the windmills into castles. I made one condition—two, in fact. One that you came back. Well, you have kept that. The other was that you told me what it was like to build the castles of bricks and mortar, which in the days when I knew you, you built in fancy only."

"Aren't you a little allegorical?" Saton asked, calmly.

"I admit it," Rochester answered. "I was very nearly, in fact, out of my depth. Tell me, in plain words, what have you done with yourself these seven years?"

"You want me," Saton remarked, "to give an account of my stewardship."

"Put it any way you please," Rochester answered. "The fact remains that though you are a guest in my house, you are a complete stranger to me."

Saton smiled.

"You might have thought of that," he said, "before you asked me here."

Rochester shrugged his shoulders.

"Perhaps," he said, "I preferred to keep up my reputation as an eccentric person. At any rate, you must remember that it was open to me at any moment to ask you the question I have asked you now."

Saton sat perfectly still in his chair, his eyes apparently fixed upon the ground. All the time Rochester was watching him. Was it seven years ago, seven years only, since he had stood by the side of that boy, whose longing eyes had been fixed with almost passionate intensity upon that world of shadows and unseen things? This was a different person. With the swiftness of inspiration itself, he recognised something of the change which had taken place. Saton had fought his battle twice over. He might esteem himself a winner. He might even say that he had proved it. Yet there was another side. This young man with the lined face, and the almost unnatural restraint of manner, might well have taken up the thread of life which the boy had laid down. But there was a difference. The thread might be the same, but it was no longer of gold.

Then Saton raised his eyes, and Rochester, who was watching him intensely, realized with a sudden convincing thrill something which he had felt from the moment when he had stepped into the library and welcomed this unexpected visitor. There was nothing left of gratitude or even kindly feeling in the heart of this young man. There was something else which looked out from his eyes, something else which he did not even trouble to conceal. Rochester knew, from that moment, that he had an enemy.

"There are just two things," Saton said quietly, "of which I should like to remind you. The first is that from the day I left this house with five hundred pounds in bank-notes buttoned up in my pocket, I regarded that sum as a loan. I have always regarded it as a loan, and I have repaid it."

"I do not consider your obligation to me lessened," Rochester remarked coldly. "If it was a loan, it was a loan such as no sane man would have made. You had not a penny in the world, and I did not even know your name. The chances were fifty to one against my ever seeing a penny of my money again."

"I admit that," Saton answered. "Yet I will remind you of your own words— five hundred pounds were no more to you than a crown piece to me. You gave me the money. You gave me little else. You gave me no encouragement, nor word of kindly advice. Go back that seven years, and remember what you said to me when you stood by my side, toying with your gun, and looking at me superciliously, as though I were some sort of curiosity which it amused you to turn inside out.—The one unforgivable thing in life, you said, was failure. Do you remember telling me that if I failed I was to swim out on a sunny day—to swim and swim until the end came? Do you remember telling me that death was sometimes a pleasant thing, but that life after failure was Hell itself?"

Rochester nodded.

"I always had such a clear insight into life," he murmured. "I was perfectly right."

"From your point of view you doubtless were," Saton answered. "You were a cynic and a pessimist, and I find you now unchanged. I went away with your words ringing in my brain. It was the first poisonous thought which had ever entered there, and I never lost it. I said to myself that whatever price I paid for success, success of some sort I would gain. When things went against me, I seemed to hear always those bitter, supercilious words. I could even see the curl of your lips as you looked down upon me, and figured to yourself the only possible result of trusting me, an unfledged, imaginative boy, with the means to carve his way a little further into the world. Failure! I wrote the word out of the dictionary of my life. Sin, crime, ill-doing of any sort if they became necessary—I kept them there. But failure—no! And this was your doing. Now you come to ask me questions. You want to know if I am a fit and proper person to receive in your house. Perhaps I have sinned. Perhaps I have robbed. Perhaps I have proved myself a master in every form of ill-doing. But I have not failed! I have paid you back your five hundred pounds."

"The question of ethics," Rochester remarked, "interests me very little if at all. The only point is that whereas on the hillside you were simply a stray unit of humanity, and the things which we said to one another concerned ourselves only, here matters are a little different. In a thoughtless moment, I asked you to become a guest under my roof. It was, I frankly admit, a mistake. I trust that I need not say more."

"If you will have my things removed to the Inn," Saton said slowly—

"No such extreme measures are necessary," Rochester answered. "You will stay with us until to-morrow morning. After luncheon you will probably find it convenient to terminate your visit as soon as possible."

"I shall be gone," Saton answered, "before any of your guests are up. In case I do not see you again alone, let me ask you a question, or rather a favor."

Rochester bowed slightly.

"There is a house below the Convalescent Home—Blackbird's Nest, they call it," Saton said. "It is empty now—too large for your keepers, too small for a country seat. Will you let it to me?"

Rochester looked at him with uplifted eyebrows.

"Let it to you?" he repeated. "Do you mean to say that after an adventurous career such as I imagine you have had, you think of settling down, at your age, in a neighborhood like this?"

"Scarcely that," Saton answered. "I shall be here only for a few days at a time, at different periods in the year. The one taste which I share in common with the boy whom you knew, is a love for the country, especially this part of it."

"You wish to live there alone?" Rochester asked.

"There is one—other person," Saton answered with some hesitation.

Rochester sighed gently.

"Alas!" he said. "Instinct tells me that that person will turn out to be of the other sex. If only you knew, my young friend, what the morals of this neighborhood are, you would understand how fatal your proposal is."

Something that was almost malign gleamed for a moment in Saton's eyes.

"It is true," he said, "that the person I spoke of is a woman, but as she is at least sixty years old, and can only walk with the help of a stick, I do not think that she would be apt to disturb the moral prejudices of your friends."

"What has she to do with you?" Rochester asked, a little shortly. "Have you found relatives out in the world, or are you married?"

Saton smiled.

"I am not married," he answered, "and as the lady in question is a foreigner, there is no question of any relationship between us. I am, as a matter of fact, her adopted son."

"You can go and see my agent," Rochester answered. "Personally, I shall not interfere. I am to take it for granted, then, I presume, that you have nothing more to tell me concerning yourself?"

"At present, nothing," Saton answered. "Some day, perhaps," he added, rising, "I may tell you everything. You see," he added, "I feel that my life, such as it is, is in some respects dedicated to you, and that you therefore have a certain right to know something of it. But that time has not come yet."

Once more there was a short and somewhat inexplicable pause, and once more Rochester knew that he was in the presence of an enemy. He shrugged his shoulders and turned toward the door.

"Well," he said, "we had better be getting off. Guerdon is a decent fellow, but he always needs looking after. If he is bored for five minutes, he gets sulky. If he is bored for a quarter of an hour, he goes home. You never met Lord Guerdon before, I suppose?" he asked, as he threw open the door.

They were men of nerve, both of them. Neither flinched. Rochester's question had been asked in an absolutely matter-of-fact tone, and Saton's reply was entirely casual. Yet he knew very well that it was only since the coming of the great judge that Rochester had suddenly realized that amongst the guests staying in his house, there was one who might have been any sort of criminal.

"I have seen him in court," Saton remarked, with a slight smile, "and of course I have seen pictures of him everywhere. Do not let me keep you, please. I have some letters to write in my room."

Rochester went back to his guests. His brows were knitted. He was unusually thoughtful. His wife, who was watching him, called him across to the bridge table, where she was dummy.

"Well?" she asked. "What is it?"

Rochester looked down at her. The corners of his mouth slowly unbent.

"Have you ever heard," he whispered in her ear, "of the legend of the Frankenstein?"

CHAPTER V

A MORNING WALK

"My dear Henry," Lady Mary said, a few days later, swinging round in her chair from the writing-table, "whatever in this world induced you to encourage that extraordinary person Bertrand Saton to settle down in this part of the world?"

Rochester continued for a moment to gaze out of the window across the Park, with expressionless face.

"My dear Mary," he said, "I did not encourage him to do anything of the sort."

"You let him Blackbird's Nest," she reminded him.

"I had scarcely a reasonable excuse for refusing to let it," Rochester answered. "I did not suggest that he should take it. I merely referred him to my agents. He went to see old Bland the very next morning, and the thing was arranged."

"I think," Lady Mary said deliberately, "that it is one of those cases where you should have exercised a little more discrimination. This is a small neighborhood, and I find it irritating to be continually running up against people whom I dislike."

"You dislike Saton?" Rochester remarked, nonchalantly.

"Dislike is perhaps a strong word," his wife answered. "I distrust him. I disbelieve in him. And I dislike exceedingly the friendship between him and Lois."

Rochester shrugged his shoulders.

"Does it amount to a friendship?" he asked.

"What else?" his wife answered. "It was obvious that she was interested in him when he was staying here, and twice since I have met them walking together. I hate mysterious people. They tell me that he has made Blackbird's Nest look like a museum inside, and there is the most awful old woman, with white hair and black eyes, who never leaves his side, they say, when he is at home."

"She is," Rochester remarked, "I presume, of an age to disarm scandal?"

"She looks as old as Methuselah," his wife answered, "but what does the man want with such a creature at all?"

"She may be an elderly relative," Rochester suggested.

"Relative? Why, she calls herself the Comtesse somebody!" Lady Mary declared. "I do wish you would tell me, Henry, exactly what you know and what you do not know about this young man."

"What I do know is simple enough," he answered. "What I do not know would, I begin to believe, fill a volume."

"Then you had better go and see him, and readjust matters," she declared, a little sharply. "I want Lois to marry well, and she mustn't have her head turned by this young man."

Rochester strolled through the open French-window into the flower-garden. He pulled a low basket chair out into the sun, close to a bed of pink and white hyacinths. A man-servant, seeing him, brought out the morning papers, which had just arrived, but Rochester waved them away.

"Fancy reading the newspapers on a morning like this!" he murmured, half to himself. "The person who would welcome the intrusion of a world of vulgar facts into an æsthetically perfect half-hour, deserves—well, deserves to be the sort of person he must be. Take the papers away, Groves," he added, as the man stood by, a little embarrassed. "Take them to Lord Penarvon or Mr. Hinckley."

The man bowed and withdrew. Rochester half closed his eyes, but opened them again almost immediately. A white clad figure was passing down the path on the other side of the lawn. He roused himself to a sitting posture.

"Lois!" he called out. "Lois!"

She waved her hand, but did not stop. He rose to his feet and called again. She paused with a reluctance which was indifferently concealed.

"I am going down to the village," she said.

He crossed the lawn towards her.

"I will be a model host," he said, "and come with you. It is always the function of the model host, is it not, to neglect the whole of the rest of the guests, and attach himself to the one most charming?"

She shook her head at him.

"I dare not risk being so unpopular," she declared. "Really, don't bother to come. It is such a very short distance."

"That decides me," he answered, falling into step with her. "A short walk is exactly what I want. For the last few days I have been oppressed with a horrible fear. I am afraid of growing fat!"

She looked at his long slim figure, and laughed derisively.

"You will have to find another reason for this sudden desire for exercise," she remarked.

"Do I need to find one?" he answered, laughing down into her pretty face.

She shook her head.

"This is all very well," she said, "but I quite understand that it is my last morning. I know what will happen this afternoon, and I really do not think that I shall allow you to come past that gate."

"Why not?" he asked earnestly.

"You know very well that Pauline is coming," she answered.

The change in his face was too slight for her to notice it, but there was a change. His lips moved as though he were repeating the name to himself.

"And why should Pauline's coming affect the situation?" he asked.

She shook her head.

"You say nice things to me," she declared, looking at him reproachfully, "but only when Pauline isn't here. We all know that directly she comes we are no longer any of us human beings. I wish I were intelligent."

"Don't!" he begged. "Don't wish anything so foolish. Intelligence is the greatest curse of the day. Few people possess it, it is true, but those few spend most of their time wishing they were fools."

"Am I a fool?" she asked.

"Of course," he answered. "All pretty and charming people are fools."

"And Pauline?" she asked.

"Pauline, unfortunately, is amongst the cursed," he answered.

"That, I suppose," she remarked, "is what brings you so close together."

"It is a bond of common suffering," he declared. "By the bye, who is this ferocious-looking person?"

It was Saton who had suddenly turned the corner, and whose expression had certainly darkened for a moment as he came face to face with the two. He was correctly enough dressed in gray tweeds and thick walking boots, but somehow or other his sallow face and dark, plentiful hair, seemed to go oddly with his country clothes.

Rochester glanced at his companion, and he distinctly saw a little grimace. Saton would have passed on, for Rochester's nod was of the slightest, but Lois insisted upon stopping.

"Mr. Saton," she said, "I have been hearing all sorts of wonderful things about your house. When are you going to ask us all to tea to see your curiosities?"

Saton looked into Rochester's immovable face.

"Whenever you choose to come," he answered calmly. "I am nearly always at home in the afternoon, or rather I shall be after next Thursday," he added, as an afterthought. "I am going to town this evening."

"Going away?" she asked, a little blankly.

"I have to go up to London," he answered, "but it is only for two days."

There was a short, uneasy silence. Rochester purposely avoided speech. He understood the situation exactly. They had something to say to one another, and wished him away.

"You won't be able to send me that book, then?" she asked.

"I will leave it at the house this afternoon, if I may," he answered, half looking toward Rochester.

Rochester made no sign. Saton raised his cap and passed on.

"Wonderful syringa bush, that," Rochester remarked, pointing with his stick.

"Wonderful!" Lois answered.

"Quite an ideal village, mine," he continued. "You see there are crocuses growing out even in the roadway."

"Very pretty!" she answered.

"You are not by any chance annoyed with me?"

"I did not think you were very civil to that poor young man."

"Naturally," he answered. "I didn't mean to be civil. I am one of those simple folk who are always annoyed by the incomprehensible. I do not understand Mr. Bertrand Saton. I do not quite understand, either, why you should find him an interesting companion for your morning walks."

"You are a hateful person!" she declared, as he held open the gate which led back to the Park.

"I intend to remain so," he answered drily.

The sound of footsteps coming along the path which they had just quitted, attracted his attention momentarily. He turned round. Lois, too, hesitated.

"I beg your pardon, sir," the newcomer said, "but can you tell me whereabouts in this neighborhood I can find a house called Blackbird's Nest? A Mr. Bertrand Saton lives there, I believe."

Rochester hesitated for a few seconds. He looked at the woman, summing her up with swift comprehension. Lois, by his side, stared at her in surprise. She was inclined to be stout, and her face was flushed with walking, notwithstanding an obviously recent use of the powder-puff. A mass of copper-colored hair was untidily arranged underneath a large black hat. Her clothes were fashionable in cut, but cheap in quality. She wore openwork stockings and high-heeled shoes, which had already suffered from walking along the dusty roads. While she waited for an answer to her question, she drew a handkerchief from her pocket, and the perfume of the violet scented hedge by the side of which they stood, was no longer a thing apparent.

Rochester, whose hatred of perfumes was one of his few weaknesses, drew back a step involuntarily.

"If you pass through the village," he said, "Blackbird's Nest is the second house upon the right-hand side. It lies a little way back from the road, but you cannot miss it."

"I am sure I am very much obliged," the lady answered. "If I had known it was as far as this, I'd have waited till I could have found a carriage. The porter at the station told me that it was just a step."

Rochester raised his cap and turned away. Lois walked soberly by his side for several moments.

"I wonder," she said softly, "what a person like that could want with Mr. Saton."

Rochester shrugged his shoulders.

"We know nothing of Saton or his life," he answered. "He has wandered up and down the world, and I daresay he has made some queer acquaintances."

"But his taste," Lois persisted, "is so perfect. I cannot understand his permitting a creature like that to even come near him."

Rochester smiled.

"One does strange things under compulsion," he remarked. "I see that they have been rolling the putting greens. Shall we go and challenge Penarvon and Mrs. Hinckley to a round at golf?"

She glanced once more over her shoulder toward the village—perhaps beyond.

"If you like," she answered, resignedly.

CHAPTER VI

PAULINE MARRABEL

The words which passed between Pauline Marrabel and her host at the railway station were words which the whole world might have heard and remained unedified. The first part of their drive homeward, even, passed in complete silence. Yet if their faces told the story, Rochester was with the woman he loved. He had driven a small pony-cart to the station. There was no room, even, for a groom behind. They sat side by side, jogging on through the green country lanes, until they came to the long hill which led to the higher country. The luggage cart and the omnibus, with her maid and the groom who had driven down with Rochester, passed them soon after they had left the station. They were alone in the country lane, alone behind a fat pony, who had ideas of his own as to what was the proper pace to travel on a warm spring afternoon.

More than once he looked at her. Her oval face was almost devoid of color. There were rings underneath her large soft eyes. Her dark hair was brushed simply back from her forehead. Her travelling clothes were of the plainest. Yet she was always beautiful—more so than ever just now, perhaps, when the slight hardness had gone from her mouth, and the strain had passed from her features.

Rochester, too, was curiously altered by the change in the curve of his lips. There was a new smile there, a new light in his eyes as they jogged on between the honeysuckle-wreathed hedges. Their silence was even curiously protracted, but underneath the holland apron his left hand was clasping hers.

"How are things with you?" she asked softly.

"About the same," he answered. "We make the best of it, you know. Mary amuses herself easily enough. She has what she wanted—a home, and I have someone to entertain my guests. I believe that we are considered quite a model couple."

Pauline sighed.

"Henry," she said, "it is beautiful to be here, to be here with you. The days will not seem long enough."

Rochester, so apt of speech, seemed curiously tongue-tied. His fingers pressed hers. He made no answer. She leaned a little forward and looked into his face.

"Wonderful person!" she declared. "Never a line or a wrinkle!"

He smiled.

"I live quietly," he said. "I am out of doors all day. Excitement of any sort has not touched my life for many years. Sometimes I feel that this perfect health is a torture. Sometimes I am afraid of never growing old."

She laughed very softly—a dear, familiar sound it was to him. He turned his head to watch the curve of the lips that he loved, the faint contraction of her eyebrows as the smile spread.

"You dear man!" she murmured. "To look at you makes me feel quite *passée*."

"The *Daily Telegraph* should reassure you," he answered. "I read this morning that the most beautiful woman at the Opera last night was Lady Marrabel."

"The *Daily Telegraph* man is such a delightful creature," she answered. "I do not like reporters, but I fancy that I must once have been civil to this one by mistake. Henry, you have had the road shortened. I am perfectly certain of it. We cannot be there."

"I am afraid it is the sad truth," he answered. "You see they are all having tea upon the lawn."

He touched the pony with his whip, and turning off the main avenue, drew up at the bottom of one of the lawns, before a sunk fence. A servant came hurrying down to the pony's head, and together Pauline and he made their way across the short green turf to where Lady Mary was dispensing tea. Rochester's face suddenly darkened. Seated next to his wife, with Lois on the other side of him, was Saton!

Lady Mary rose to welcome her guest, and Rochester exchanged greetings with some callers who had just arrived. To Saton he merely nodded, but when a little later Lois rose, and announced that she was going to show Mr. Saton the orchid houses, he intervened lazily.

"We will all go," he said. "Lady Penarvon is interested in orchids, and I am sure that Pauline would like to see the houses."

"I am interested in everything belonging to this delightful place," she declared, rising.

Lois frowned slightly. Saton's face remained inscrutable. In the general exodus Rochester found himself for a moment behind with his wife.

"Did you encourage that young man to stay to tea?" he asked. "I thought you disliked him so much."

Lady Mary sighed. She was a gentle, fluffy little creature, who had a new whim every few minutes.

"I am so changeable," she declared. "I detested him yesterday. He wore such an ugly tie, and he would monopolize Lois. This afternoon I found him most interesting. I believe he knows all about the future, if one could only get him to tell us things."

"Really!" Rochester remarked politely.

"He has been talking in a most interesting fashion," continued Lady Mary.

"Has he been telling you all your fortunes?"

"You put it so crudely, my dear Henry," his wife declared. "Of course he doesn't tell fortunes! Only he's the sort of person that if one really wanted to know anything, I believe his advice would be better than most peoples'. Perhaps he will talk to us about it after dinner."

"What, is he dining here?" Rochester asked.

"I have asked him to," Lady Mary answered, complacently. "We are short of young men, as you know, and really this afternoon he quite fascinated us all. The dear Duchess is so difficult and heavy to entertain, but she quite woke up when he began to talk. Lady Penarvon just told me that she thought he was wonderful."

"He seems to have the knack of interesting women," Rochester remarked.

"And therefore, I suppose," Lady Mary said, "you men will all hate him. Never mind, I have changed my opinion entirely. I think that he is going to be an acquisition to the neighborhood, and I am going to study occultism."

Rochester turned away with a barely concealed grimace. He went up to Lois, calmly usurping Saton's place.

"My dear Lois," he said, as they fell behind a few paces, "so your latest young man has been charming everybody."

"He is nice, isn't he?" she answered, turning to him a little impulsively.

"Marvelously!" Rochester answered. "Hatefully so! Has he told you anything, by the bye, about himself?"

She shook her head.

"Nothing that I can remember," she answered. "He is so clever," she added, enthusiastically, "and he has explained all sorts of wonderful things to me. If one had only brains," she continued, with a little sigh, "there is so much to learn."

Rochester picked a great red rose and handed it to her.

"My dear child," he said, "there is nothing in knowledge so beautiful as that flower. By the bye," he added, raising his voice to Saton, who was just ahead, "I thought you were going to London to-day."

"I have put off my visit until to-morrow," Saton answered. "Your wife has been kind enough to ask me to dine."

Rochester nodded. He carefully avoided endorsing the invitation.

"By the bye," he remarked, "we had the pleasure of directing a lady in distress to your house this morning."

Saton paused for a moment before he answered.

"I am very much obliged to you," he said.

He offered no explanation. Rochester, with a little shrug of the shoulders, rejoined Pauline. Lady Mary was called away to receive some visitors, and for the first time Lois and Saton were alone.

"Mr. Rochester has taken a dislike to me," he said quietly.

Lois was distressed.

"I wonder why," she said. "As a rule he is so indifferent to people."

Saton shook his head a little sadly.

"I cannot tell," he answered. "Certainly I cannot think of anything I have done to offend him. But I am nearly always unfortunate. The people whom I would like to have care about me, as a rule don't."

"There are exceptions," she murmured.

She met his eyes, and looked away. He smiled softly to himself. Women had looked away from him before like that!

"Fortunately," he continued, "Lady Mary seems to be a little more gracious. It was very kind of her to ask me to dine to-night."

"She is always so interested," Lois said, "in things which she does not understand. You talked so well this afternoon, Mr. Saton. I am afraid I could not follow you, but it sounded very brilliant and very wonderful."

"One speaks convincingly," he said, "when one really feels. Some day, remember," he continued, "we are going to have a long, long talk. We are going to begin at the beginning, and you are going to let me help you to understand how many wonderful things there are in life which scarcely any of us ever even think about. I wonder——"

"Well?" she asked, looking up at him.

"Will they let me take you down to dinner?"

She shook her head doubtfully.

"I am afraid not," she said. "I am almost certain to go in with Captain Vandermere."

He sighed.

"After all," he said, "perhaps I had better have taken that train to town."

CHAPTER VII

AN UNWELCOME VISITOR

Saton was only a few minutes being whirled down the avenue of Beauleys and up along the narrow country lane, wreathed with honeysuckle and wild roses, to Blackbird's Nest. He leaned back in the great car, his unseeing eyes travelling over the quiet landscape. There was something out of keeping, a little uncanny, even, in the flight of the motor-car with its solitary passenger along the country lane, past the hay carts, and the villagers resting after their long day's toil. The man who leaned back amongst the cushions, with his pale, drawn face, and dark, melancholy eyes, seemed to them like a creature from another world, even as the vehicle in which he travelled, so swift and luxurious, filled them with wonder. Saton heard nothing of their respectful good-nights. He saw nothing of their dotted hats and curious, wondering glances. He was thinking with a considerable amount of uneasiness of the interview which probably lay before him.

The car turned in at the rude gates, and climbed the rough road which led to Saton's temporary abode. A servant met him at the door as he descended, a gray-haired, elderly man, irreproachably attired, whose manner denoted at once the well-trained servant.

"There is a lady here, sir," he said—"she arrived some hours ago—who has been waiting to see you. You will find her in the morning-room."

Saton took off his hat, and moved slowly down the little hall.

"I trust that I did not make a mistake, sir, in allowing her to wait?" the man asked. "She assured me that she was intimately known to you."

"You were quite right, Parkins," Saton answered. "I think I know who she is, but I was scarcely expecting her to-day."

He opened the door of the morning-room and closed it quickly. The woman rose up from the couch, where she had apparently been asleep, and looked at him.

"At last!" she exclaimed. "Bertrand, do you know that I have been here since the morning?"

"How was I to know?" he answered. "You sent no word that you were coming. I certainly did not expect you."

"Are you glad?" she asked, a little abruptly.

"I am always glad to see you, Violet," he said, putting his arm around her waist and kissing her. "All the same, I am not sure that your coming here is altogether wise."

"I waited as long as I could," she answered. "You didn't come to me. You scarcely even answered my letters. I couldn't bear it any longer. I had to come and see you. Bertrand, you haven't forgotten? Tell me that you haven't forgotten."

He sat down by her side. She was a young woman, and though her face was a little hardened by the constant use of cosmetics, she was still well enough looking.

"My dear Violet," he said, "of course I have not forgotten. Only don't you see how unwise it is of you to come down here? If she were to know——"

"She will not know," the girl interrupted. "She is safe in London, and will be there for a week."

"The servants here might tell her that you have been," he suggested.

"You will have to see to it that they don't," she said. "Bertrand, I am so unhappy. When are you coming back?"

"Very soon," he answered.

"We can spend the evening together, can't we?" she asked, looking at him anxiously. "My train doesn't go back until nine."

"That is just what we cannot do," he answered. "You did not tell me that you were coming, and I have to go out to dinner to-night."

"To dinner? Here?" she repeated. "You have soon made friends." And her face darkened.

"I stayed here when I was a boy," he answered. "There is someone living here who knew me then."

"Can't you put it off, Bertrand?" she begged. "It is five weeks since I have seen you. Every day I have hoped that you would run up, if it was only for an hour. Bertrand dear, don't go to this dinner. Can't we have something here, and go for a walk in the country before my train goes, or sit in your study and talk? There are so many things I want to ask you about our future."

He took her hand and leaned towards her.

"My dear Violet," he said, "you must be reasonable. I dare not offend these people with whom I have promised to dine, and apart from that, I think it is very unwise that I should spend any time at all here with you. You know what sort of a person it is whom we both have to consider. She would turn us both into the street and treat it all as a jest, if it pleased her. I tell you frankly, Violet, I have been too near starvation once to care about facing it again. I am going to send you back to the station in the car now. You can catch a train to London almost at once."

Her face grew suddenly hard. She looked older. The light which had flashed into her face at his coming, was gone. One saw now the irregularities of her complexion, the over-red lips.

"You dismiss me," she said, in a low tone. "I have come all this way, have waited all this time, and you throw me a kiss out of pity, and you tell me to go home as fast as I can. Bertrand, you did not talk like this a few months ago. You did not talk like this when you asked me to marry you!"

"Nor shall I talk like it," he answered, "when we meet once more in London, and have another of our cosy little dinners. But frankly, you are doing an absolutely unwise thing in staying here. These people are not my servants. They are hers. They are beyond my bribing. Violet," he added, dropping his voice a little, and drawing her into his arms, "don't be foolish, dear. Don't run the risk of bringing disaster upon both of us. You wouldn't care to have to do without her now. Nor should I. It was a little thoughtless of you to come, dear. Do follow my advice now, and I will try and make it up to you very soon. I shall certainly be in London next week."

She rested in his arms for a moment with half closed eyes, as though content with his words and his embrace. Yet, as she disengaged herself, she sighed a little. She was willing to deceive herself—she was anxious to do so—but always the doubt remained!

"Very well, Bertrand," she said, "I will go."

"You will just catch a fast train to London," he said, more cheerfully. "You will change at Mechester, and you will find a dining-car there. Have you plenty of money?"

"Plenty, thank you," she answered.

He walked with her out into the hall.

"Madame will be so sorry," he said, "to have missed you. The telegram must have been a complete misunderstanding. Till next week, then."

He handed her into the car, and raising her fingers to his lips, kissed them gallantly.

"To the station, William," he ordered the chauffeur, "and then get back for me as quickly as you can."

The car swung off. Saton stood watching it with darkening face. There was some pity in his heart for this somewhat *passée* young person, who had been kind to him during those first few weeks of his re-entering into life. He recognised the fact that his swift progress was unfortunate for her. He even sat for a moment or two smoking a cigarette in his very luxurious dressing-room, fingering the gold-topped bottles of his dressing-case, and wondering what would be the most effectual and least painful means of coming to an understanding with her!

CHAPTER VIII

AN INSTANCE OF OCCULTISM

The guests at Beauleys were all grouped together in the hall after dinner, the men, and some of the women, smoking cigarettes. Coffee and liqueurs were being served from the great oak sideboard. Lord Guerdon and his host had drawn a little apart from the others, at the former's instigation.

"Your friend Saton—extraordinary name, by the bye—seems to have struck upon an interesting theme of conversation," the judge remarked, a little drily, glancing across to where Saton stood, surrounded by most of the other guests.

"He has travelled a great deal," Rochester said, "and he seems to be one of that extravagant sort of persons who imbibe more or less the ideas of every country. Chiefly froth, I should imagine, but it gives him plenty to talk about."

The judge nodded thoughtfully.

"His face," he declared, "still puzzles me a little. Sometimes I am sure that I have seen it before. At others, I find it quite unfamiliar."

Rochester, who was watching Pauline, shrugged his shoulders.

"We may as well hear what the fellow is talking about," he remarked. "Let us join the adoring throng." ...

"I will tell you one thing which I have realized in the course of my travels," Saton was saying as they drew near. "Amongst all the nations of the world, we English are at once the most ignorant, and the slowest to receive a new thing. In the exact sciences, we are perhaps just able to hold our own, but when it comes to the great unexplored fields, the average English person turns away with a shrug of the shoulders. 'I do not believe!' he says stolidly, and that is sufficient. He does not believe! Since the birth of Time there has been no more pitiful cry than that."

"One might easily be convinced that the fellow is in earnest," Rochester whispered.

The judge laid his hand upon his host's shoulder. There was a curious gleam in those deep-set eyes.

"Let him go on," he said. "This is interesting. I begin to remember."

"We all have a hobby, I suppose," Saton continued. "Mine has always been the study of the least understood of the sciences—I mean occultism. I, too, was prejudiced at first. I saw wonderful things in India, and my British instincts rose up like a wall. I did not believe. I refused to believe my eyes. In Egypt, and on the west coast of Africa, I had the chance of learning new things, and again I refused. But there came a time when even I was impressed. Then I began to study. I began to see that some of those things which we accept as being wonderful, and from which we turn away with a shrug of the shoulders, are capable of explanation—are submissive, in fact, to natural laws. There is not a doubt that in the generations to come, people will smile upon us, and pity us for our colossal stupidity."

"No wise person, my dear Mr. Saton," Mrs. Hinckley remarked, "would deny that there is yet a great deal to learn in life. But tell us exactly to what you refer?"

Saton raised his dark eyes and looked steadfastly at her.

"I mean, madam," he said, "the apprehension of things happening in the present in other parts, the apprehension of things about to happen in the future. Our brain we realize, and our muscles, but there is a subtler part of ourselves, of which we are as ignorant to-day as our forefathers were of electricity."

Lady Mary drew a little sigh.

"This is so fascinating," she said. "Do you really believe, then, that it is possible to foretell the future?"

"Why not?" Saton answered quietly. "The world is governed by laws just as inevitable as the physical laws which govern the seasons. It is only a matter of apprehension, a deliberate schooling of ourselves into the necessary temperament."

"Then all these people in Bond Street—these crystal gazers and fortune-tellers—" Lois began eagerly.

"They are charlatans, and stand in the way of progress," Saton declared, fiercely. "They have not the faintest glimmering of the truth, and they turn what should be the greatest of the sciences into buffoonery. To the real student it is never possible to answer questions to foretell specific things. On the other hand, it is as sure as the coming of night itself that there are times when a person who has studied these matters even so slightly as I myself, can feel the coming of events."

"Give us an instance," Lady Mary begged. "Tell us of something that is going to happen."

Saton moved a little back. His face was unnaturally pale.

"No!" he answered. "Don't ask me that. Remember, this is not a game. It might even happen that I should tell you something terrifying. I am sorry that I've talked like this," he went on, a little wildly. "I am sorry that I came here to-night. Before I came I felt it coming. If you will excuse me, Lady Mary——"

She held out her hands and refused to accept his adieux.

"You shall not go!" she declared. "There is something in your mind. You could tell us something if you would."

Saton looked around, as one genuinely anxious to escape. On the outskirts of the circle he saw Rochester, smiling faintly, half amused, half contemptuous, and by his side the parchment-like face of Lord Guerdon, whose eyes seemed riveted upon his.

"My dear Saton," Rochester said, "pray don't disappoint us of our thrill, after all this most effective preliminary. You believe that you possess a gift which we none of us share. Give us a proof of it. No one here is afraid to hear the truth. Is it one specific thing you could tell?"

"One specific thing," Saton answered quickly, "about to happen to one person, and one person only."

"Is it a man or a woman?" Rochester asked.

"A man!" was the quick reply.

Rochester glanced carelessly around the little circle.

"Come," he said, "the women can have their thrill. There is nothing to fear. Penarvon here has all the pluck in the world. Hinckley is a V.C. Captain Vandermere is a soldier, and I will answer for it that he has no nerves. Guerdon and I, I am sure, are safe. Let us hear your gruesome prophecy, my dear Saton, and if it comes true, we will form a little society, and you shall be our apostle. We will study occultism in place of bridge. We will be the founders of a new cult."

Saton pushed them away from him. His face was almost ghastly.

"It is not fair, this," he cried. "You do not know what you are asking. Can't you feel it, any of you others, as I do?" he exclaimed, looking a little wildly around. "There is something else in the room, something else besides you warm and living people. Be still, all of you."

There was a moment's breathless silence. Some papers on the table rustled. A picture on the wall shook. Lady Mary sat down in a chair. Lois gave a little scream.

"There is a slight draught," Rochester remarked, calmly.

"It is no draught," Saton answered. "You want the truth and you shall have it. See, there are five men present."—He counted rapidly with his forefinger. "One of them will be dead before we leave this room."

Rochester strolled over to the sideboard, and helped himself to a cigarette.

"Come," he said, "this is going a little too far! Look at the cheeks of these ladies, Saton. A little melodrama is all very well, but you are too good an actor. Hinckley, and all of you," he said, looking around, "I propose that we end the strain. Let us go into the billiard-room and have a pool. I presume that the spell will then be broken."

Lady Mary shrieked.

"Don't move, any of you!" she cried. "I am afraid!"

Rochester laughed softly, and crossed the floor with firm footsteps. He stood on the threshold of the door leading to the billiard-room.

"Come," he said, "I am indeed between life and death, for I have one foot in one room and one in the other. Come, you others, and seek safety too."

The women also rose. There was a rush for the door, a swish of draperies, a little sob from Lois, who was terrified. Saton remained standing alone. He had not moved. His eyes were fixed upon the figure of the judge, who also lingered. They two were left in the centre of the hall.

"Come, Guerdon," Rochester cried. "You and I will take the lot on."

Guerdon did not move. He motioned to Saton slightly.

"Young man," he said, "we have met before. I said so when you first came in. My memory is improving."

Saton leaned forward.

"Some water, quick, and brandy," Rochester cried.

"Be careful, judge," he said.

"Be careful be d—d!" the judge answered. "Rochester, come here. God in Heaven!"

His left hand went suddenly to his throat. He almost tore away the collar and primly arranged tie. Rochester was by his side in a second, and saved him from falling. His face was white to the lips. A shriek from the women rang through the hall, and came echoing back again from the black rafters.

"Some water quick, and brandy," Rochester cried, tearing open the shirt from the man he was supporting. "Send for a doctor, someone. Penarvon, you see to that. Let them take the motor. Keep those d—d women quiet!"

The judge opened his eyes.

"I remember him," he faltered.

"Drink some of this, old fellow," Rochester said. "You'll be better in a moment."

The judge's eyes were closed again. He had suddenly become a dead weight on Rochester's arm. Vandermere, who had done amateur doctoring at the war, brought a pillow for his head. They cut off more of his clothes. They tried by every means to keep a flicker of life in him until the doctor came. Only Rochester knew it was useless. He had seen the shadow of death pass across the gray, stricken face.

CHAPTER IX

A SENTIMENTAL TALK

Lois opened the gate and stole into the lane with the air of a guilty child. She gave a little gasp as she came face to face with Saton, and picking up her skirts, seemed for a moment about to fly. He stood quite still—his face was sad—almost reproachful. She dropped her skirt and came slowly, doubtfully towards him.

"I have come," she said. "I was forced to come. Oh, Mr. Saton! How could you?"

His features were wan. There were lines under his dark eyes. He was looking thin and nervous. His voice, too, had lost some of its pleasant qualities

"My dear young lady," he said, "my dear Lois, what do you mean? You don't suppose—you can't—that it was through me in any way that—that thing happened?"

"Oh, I don't know!" she faltered, with white lips. "It was all so horrible. You pointed to him, and your eyes when you looked at him seemed to shine as though they were on fire. I saw him shrink away, and the color leave his cheeks. It was horrible!"

"But, Lois," he protested, "you cannot imagine that by looking at a man I could help to kill him? I can't explain what happened. As yet there are things in the world which no one can explain. This is one of them. I know a little more than most people. It is partly temperament, perhaps—partly study, but it is surely true that I can sometimes feel things coming. From the first moment I looked into Guerdon's face at dinner-time, I knew what was going to happen. Out there in the hall I felt it. Once before in South America, I saw a man shoot himself. I tell you that I was certain of what he was going to do before I knew that he had even a revolver in his pocket. It comes to me, the knowledge of these things. I cannot be blamed for it. Some day I shall write the first text-book that has ever been written of a new science. I shall evolve the first few rudimentary laws, and after that the thing will go easily. Every generation will add to them. But, Lois, because I am the first, because I have seen a little further into the world than others, you are not going to look at me as though I were a murderer!"

She drew a little breath, a breath of relief. Her hand fell upon his arm.

"No!" she said. "I have been foolish. It is absurd to imagine that you could have brought that about by just wishing for it."

"Why, even, should I have wished for it?" he asked. "Lord Guerdon was a stranger to me. As an acquaintance I found him pleasant enough. I had no grudge against him."

She drew him a little way on down the lane.

"I must only stay for a few minutes," she said. "If we walk down here we shall meet nobody. Do you know what Mr. Rochester has suggested?"

"No!" Saton answered. "What?"

"He says that Lord Guerdon had always been uneasily conscious of having seen you somewhere before. He says that at the very moment when he was stricken down, he seemed to remember!"

"That does not seem to me to be important," Saton remarked.

"Can't you understand?" she continued. "Mr. Rochester seems to think that Lord Guerdon had seen you somewhere under disgraceful circumstances. There! I've got it out now," she added, with a wan little smile. "That is why he feels sure that somehow or other you did your best to help him toward death."

"And the others?" Saton asked.

"Oh, it hasn't been talked about!" she answered. "Everyone has left the house, you know. I only knew this through Mary."

Saton smiled scornfully.

"My dear girl," he said, "I know for a fact that Lord Guerdon was suffering from acute heart disease. He went about always with a letter in his pocket giving directions as to what should become of him if he were to die suddenly."

"Is that really true?" she asked. "Oh, I am glad! Lord Penarvon said so, but no one else seemed sure."

"There is no need, even for an inquest," Saton continued. "I went to see the doctor this morning, and he told me so. I am very, very sorry," he went on, taking her hand in his, "that such a thing should happen to spoil the memory of these few days. They have been wonderful days, Lois."

She drew her hand quietly away.

"Yes!" she admitted. "They have been wonderful in many ways."

"For you," he continued, walking a little more slowly, and with his hands clasped behind him, "they have been, perhaps, just a tiny little leaf out of the book of your life. To me I fancy they have been something different. You see I have been a wanderer all my days. I have had no home, and I have had few friends. All the time I have had to fight, and there seems to have been no time for the gentler things, for the things that really make for happiness. Perhaps," he continued, reflectively, "that is why I find it sometimes a little difficult to talk to you. You are so young and fresh and wonderful. Your feet are scarcely yet upon the threshold of the life whose scars I am bearing."

"I am not so very young," Lois said, "nor are you so very old."

"And yet," he answered, looking into her face, "there is a great gulf between us, a gulf, perhaps, of more than years. Miss Lois, I am not going to ask you too much, but I would like to ask you one thing. Have these days meant just a little to you also?"

She raised her eyes and looked him frankly in the face. They were honest brown eyes, a little clouded just now with some reflection of the vague trouble which was stirring in her heart.

"I will answer you frankly," she said, "Yes, they have meant something to me! And yet, listen. I am going to say something unkind. There is something—I don't know what it is—between us, which troubles me. Oh, I know that you are much cleverer than other men, and I would not have you different! Yet there is something else. Would you be very angry, I wonder, if I told the truth?"

"No!" he assured her. "Go on, please."

"I feel sometimes," she continued, "as though I could not trust you. There, don't be angry," she went on, laying her fingers on his arm. "I know how horrid it sounds, but it is there in my heart, and it is because I would like to believe, it is because I want there to be nothing between us of distrust, that I have told you."

They walked slowly on, side by side. His face was turned a little from hers. She was bending forward, as though anxious to catch a glimpse of his expression. Through the case hardening of years, her voice for a moment seemed to have found its way back into the heart of the boy, to have brought him at least a momentary twinge as he realized, with a passing regret, the abstract beauty of the more simple ways in life. Those few minutes were effective enough. They helped his pose. The regret passed. A shadow of pain took its place. He came to a standstill and took her hands in his.

"Dear little girl," he said, "perhaps you are right. I am not altogether honest. I am not in the least like the sort of man who ought to look at you and feel towards you as I have looked and felt during these wonderful days. But all of us have our weak spots, you know. I think that you found mine. Good-bye, little girl!"

She would have called him back, but he had no idea of lending himself to anything so inartistic. With head thrown back, he left the footpath and climbed the hill round which they had been walking. Not once did he look behind. Not once did he turn his head till he stood on the top of the rock-strewn eminence, his figure clearly outlined against the blue sky. Then he straightened himself and turned round, thinking all the time how wonderfully effective his profile must seem in that deep, soft light, if she should have the sense to look.

She did look. She was standing very nearly where he had left her. She was waving her handkerchief, beckoning him to come down. He raised his hand above his head as though in farewell, and turned slowly away. As soon as he was quite sure that he was out of sight, he took his cigarette case from his pocket and began to smoke!

CHAPTER X

THE SCENE CHANGES

Saton left the country on the following afternoon, arrived at St. Pancras soon after five, and drove at once to a large, roomy house on the north side of Regent's Park. He was admitted by a trim parlormaid—Parkins had been left behind to superintend the removal from Blackbird's Nest—and he found himself asking his first question with a certain amount of temerity.

"Madame is in?" he inquired.

"Madame is in the drawing-room," the maid answered.

"Alone?" Saton asked.

"Quite alone, sir."

Saton ascended the stairs and entered the drawing-room, which was on the first floor, unannounced. At the further end of the apartment a woman was sitting, her hands folded in front of her, her eyes fixed upon the wall. Saton advanced with outstretched hands.

"At last!" he exclaimed.

The woman made no reply. Her silence while he crossed a considerable space of carpet, would have been embarrassing to a less accomplished *poseur*. She was tall, dressed in a gown of plain black silk, and her brown, withered face seemed one of those which defy alike time and its reckoning. Her white hair was drawn back from her forehead, and tied in a loose knot at the back of her head. Her mouth was cruel. Her eyes were hard and brilliant. There was not an atom of softness, or of human weakness of any sort, to be traced in any one of her features. Around her neck she wore a scarf of brilliant red, the ends of which were fastened with a great topaz.

Saton bent over her affectionately. He kissed her upon the forehead, and remained with his arm resting upon her shoulder. She did not return his embrace in any way.

"So you've come back," she said, speaking with a sharpness which would have been unpleasant but for the slight foreign accent.

"As you see," he answered. "I left this afternoon, and came straight here."

"That woman Helga has been down there. What did she want?" she demanded.

Saton shrugged his shoulders slightly, and turning away, fetched a chair, which he brought close to her side.

"I am afraid," he said bluntly, "that she came to see me."

The woman's eyes flashed.

"Ah!" she exclaimed. "Go on."

Saton took her hand, and held it between his. It was dry and withered, but the nails were exquisitely manicured, and the fingers were aflame with jewels.

"Dear Rachael," he said, "you must remember that when I was alone in London waiting to hear from you, I naturally saw a good deal of Helga. She was kind to me, and she was the means by which your letters and messages reached me. I am afraid," he continued, thoughtfully, "that I was so happy, in those days, to have found anyone who was kind and talked decently to me, that I may have misled her. There has been a little trouble once or twice since. I have tried to be pleasant and friendly with her. She seems—forgive me if it sounds conceited—she seems to want more."

"Hussy!" the old lady declared. "She shall go."

"Don't send her away," he begged, replacing her hand gently on her lap. "I daresay it was entirely my fault."

The woman looked at him, and a cruel smile parted her lips.

"I have no doubt it was," she said. "You are like that, you know, Bertrand. Still, one must have discipline. She asked for a day's holiday to go into the country to see her relatives, and I find her going to see you behind my back. It cannot be permitted."

"It will not happen again," he assured her. "I feel myself so much to blame."

"I have no doubt," she said, "that you are entirely to blame, but that is not the question. Unfortunately, there are other things to be considered, or she would have been sent packing before now. Tell me, Bertrand, what kept you down in the country these last few days?"

"I wanted a rest," he answered. "I have to read my paper to-night, you know, and I was tired."

"You have been spending your time alone?"

"No!" he answered, with scarcely a second's hesitation. "I have been once or twice to Beauleys."

"To see your friend Henry Rochester, I suppose?" she asked.

Saton's face darkened.

"No!" he answered. "I would not move a step to see him. I hate him, and I think he knows it."

"Who were the ladies of the party?" the woman asked. "Their names one by one, mind. Begin with the eldest."

"Lady Penarvon."

"I know. Go on," she said.

"Mrs. Hinckley."

"Go on."

"Miss Lois Champneyes."

"Young?" the woman asked.

"Yes!"

"Pretty?"

"Yes!"

"A victim?"

Saton frowned.

"There was also," he continued, "my hostess, Lady Mary Rochester."

"A silly, fluffy little woman," Madame declared. "Did she flirt?"

"Not with me, at any rate," Saton answered.

"Too experienced," Madame remarked. "Perhaps too good a judge of your sex. Who else?"

"Lady Marrabel."

"A very beautiful woman, I have heard," Madame remarked. "Also young, I believe. Also, I presume, a victim."

"It is not kind of you," Saton protested. "These women were staying in the house. One has to make oneself agreeable to them."

"Someone else was staying in the house," Madame continued, fixing her brilliant eyes upon his face. "Someone else, I see, died there."

"You mean Lord Guerdon?" Saton muttered, softly.

"He died there," she said, nodding. "Bertrand, did he—did he recognise you?"

"He would have done," Saton said slowly, "if he had not died. He was just beginning to remember."

She looked at him curiously for several minutes.

"Well," she said, "I ask no questions. Perhaps it is wiser not. But remember this, Bertrand, I know something of the world, and the men and women who live in it. You are a born deceiver of women. It is the rôle which nature meant you to play. You can turn them, if you will, inside out. Perhaps you think you do the same with me. Let that go. And remember this. Have as little to do with men as possible. Your very strength with women would be your very weakness with men. Remember, I have warned you."

"You don't flatter me," he said, a little unpleasantly.

"Bah!" she answered. "Why should you and I play with words? We know one another for what we are. Give me your hands."

He held them out. She took them suddenly in hers and drew him towards her.

"Kiss me!" she commanded.

He obeyed at once. Then she thrust him away.

"I go with you to this conversazione to-night," she said. "It is well that we should sometimes be seen together. I shall let it be known that you are my adopted son."

"That is as you will," he said, with secret satisfaction.

"Why not?" she declared. "I never had a son, but I'm foolish enough to care for you quite as much as I could for any child of my own. Go and get ready. We dine at seven.—No! come back."

She placed her long, clawlike fingers upon his shoulders, and kissed him on both cheeks. She held him tightly by the arms, as though there was something else she would have said—her lips a little parted, her eyes brilliant.

"Go and get ready," she said abruptly. "Look your prettiest. You have a chance to make friends to-night."

CHAPTER XI

A BUSY EVENING

The conversazione was, in its way, a brilliant gathering. There were present scientists, men of letters, artists, with a very fair sprinkling of society people, always anxious to absorb any new sensation. One saw there amongst the white-haired men, passing backwards and forwards, or talking together in little knots, professors whose names were famous throughout Europe.

A very great man indeed brought Saton up to Pauline with a little word of explanation.

"I am sure," he said to her—she was one of his oldest friends—"that you will be glad to meet the gentleman whose brilliant paper has interested us all so much. This is Lady Marrabel, Saton, whose father was professor at Oxford before your day."

The great man passed on. Pauline's first impulse had been to hold out her hand, but she had immediately withdrawn it. Saton contented himself with a grave bow.

"I am afraid, Lady Marrabel," he said, "that you are prejudiced against me."

"I think not," she answered. "Naturally, seeing you so suddenly brought into my mind the terrible occurrence of only a few days ago."

"An occurrence," he declared, "which no one could regret so greatly as myself. But apart from that, Lady Marrabel, I am afraid that you are not prepared to do me justice. You look at me through Rochester's eyes, and I am quite sure that all his days Rochester will believe that I am more or less of a charlatan."

"Your paper was very wonderful, Mr. Saton," she said slowly. "I am convinced that Mr. Rochester would have admitted that himself if he had been here."

"He might," Saton said. "He might have admitted that much, with a supercilious smile and a little shrug of the shoulders. Rochester is a clever man, I believe, but he is absolutely insular. There is a belt of prejudice around him, to the hardening of which centuries have come and gone. You are not, you cannot be like that," he continued with conviction. "There is truth in these things. I am not an ignorant mountebank, posing as a Messiah of science. Look at the men and women who are here to-night. They know a little. They understand a little. They are only eager to see a little further through the shadows. I do not ask you to become a convert. I ask you only to believe that I speak of the things in which I have faith."

"I am quite sure that you do," she answered, with a marked access of cordiality in her tone. "Believe me, it was not from any distrust of that sort that I perhaps looked strangely at you when you came up. You must remember that it is a very short time since our last meeting. One does not often come face to face with a tragedy like that."

"You are right," he answered. "It was awful. Yet you saw how they drove me on. I spoke what I felt and knew. It is not often that those things come to one, but that there was death in the room that night I knew as surely as I am sitting with you here now. They goaded me on to speak of it. I could not help it."

"It was very terrible and very wonderful," she said, looking at him with troubled eyes. "They say that Lady Mary is still suffering from the shock."

"It might have happened at any moment," he reminded her. "The man had heart disease. He had had his warning. He knew very well that the end might come at any moment."

"That is true, I suppose," she admitted. "The medical examination seemed to account easily enough for his death. Yet there was something uncanny about it."

"The party broke up the next day, I suppose," he continued. "I have been down in the country, but I have heard nothing."

"We left before the funeral, of course," she answered.

"Fortunately for me," he remarked, "I had important things to think of. I had to prepare this paper. The invitation to read it came quite unexpectedly. I have been in London for so short a time, indeed, that I scarcely expected the honor of being asked to take any share in a meeting so important as this."

"I do not see why you should be surprised," she said.

"You certainly seem to have gone as far in the study of occultism as any of those others."

He looked at her thoughtfully.

"You yourself should read a little about these things," he said—"read a little and think a little. You would find very much to interest you."

"I am sure of it," she answered, almost humbly. "Will you come and see me one day, and talk about it? I live at Number 17, Cadogan Street."

"I will come with pleasure," he answered, rising. "Will you forgive me if I leave you now? There is a man just leaving with whom I must speak."

He passed away, and left the room with a little thrill of satisfaction. He had contrived to impress the one woman whom he was anxious to impress! Children like little Lois Champneyes and those others, were easy. This woman he knew at once was something different. Besides, she was a friend of Rochester's, and that meant something to him.

He walked along Regent Street to the end, and crossing the road, entered a large café. Here he sat before one of the marble-topped tables, and ordered some coffee. In a few minutes he was joined by another man, who handed his coat and hat to the waiter, and sat down with the air of one who was expected. Saton nodded, a little curtly.

"Will you take anything?" he asked.

"A bottle of beer and a cigar," the newcomer ordered. "A shilling cigar, I think, to-night. It will run to it."

"Anything special?" Saton asked.

"Things in general are about the same as usual," his companion answered. "They did a little better in Oxford Street and Regent Street, but Violet had a dull day in Bond Street. I have closed up the Egyptian place in the Arcade—'Ayesha' we called it. The police are always suspicious of a woman's name, and I had a hint from a detective I know."

Saton nodded.

"You have something else to tell me, haven't you?" he asked.

"Yes!" the other answered. "We had a very important client in Bond Street this afternoon, one of those whose names you gave me."

Saton leaned across the table.

"Who was it?" he asked.

"Lady Mary Rochester of Beauleys," the other answered—"got a town house, and a big country place down in Mechestershire."

Something flashed for a moment in Saton's eyes, but he said nothing. His companion commenced to draw leisurely a sheet of paper from his breast coat pocket. He was fair and middle-aged, respectably dressed, and with the air of a prosperous city merchant. His eyes were a little small, and his cheeks inclined to be fat, or he would have been reasonably good-looking.

"Lady Mary called without giving her name," he continued, "but we knew her, of course, by our picture gallery. She called professedly to amuse herself. She was told the usual sorts of things, with a few additions thrown in from our knowledge of her. She seemed very much impressed, and in the end she came to a specific inquiry."

"Go on," said Saton.

"The specific inquiry was briefly this," the man continued. "She gave herself away the moment she opened her mouth. She behaved, in fact, like a farmer's daughter asking questions of a gipsy girl. She showed us the photograph of a man, whom we also recognised, and wanted to know the usual sort of rubbish—whether he was really fond of her, whether he would be true to her if she married him."

"Married him?" Saton repeated.

"She posed as a widow," the other man reminded him.

"What was the reply?"

"Violet was clever," the man remarked, with a slow smile. "She saw at once that this was a case where something might be done. She asked for three days, and for a letter from the man. She said that it was a case in which a sight of his handwriting, and a close study of it, would help them to give an absolutely truthful answer."

"She agreed?" Saton asked.

The other nodded, and produced a letter from his pocket.

"She handed one over at once," he said. "It isn't particularly compromising, perhaps, but it's full of the usual sort of rot. She's coming for it on Tuesday."

Saton smiled as he thrust it into his pocketbook.

"I will put this into Dorrington's hands at once," he said. "This has been very well managed, Huntley. I will have a liqueur, and you shall have some more beer."

"Don't mind if I do," Mr. Huntley assented cheerfully. "It's thirsty weather."

They summoned a waiter, and Saton lit a cigarette.

"You've been amongst the big pots to-night," Huntley remarked, looking at him.

Saton nodded.

"I have been keeping our end up," he said, "in the legitimate branch of our profession. You needn't grin like that," he added, a little irritably. "There is a legitimate side, and a very wonderful side, only a brain like yours is not capable of assimilating it. You should have heard my paper to-night upon self-directed mesmeric waves."

The man shook his head, and laughed complacently.

"It's not in my way," he answered. "Our business is good enough as it is."

"You are a fool," Saton said, a little contemptuously. "You can't see that but for the legitimate side there would be no business at all. Unless there was a glimmer of truth at the bottom of the well, unless there existed somewhere a prototype, Madame Helga, and Omega, and Naomi might sit in their empty temples from morning till night. People know, or are beginning to know, that there are forces abroad beyond the control of the ordinary commonplace mortal. They are willing to take it for granted that those who declare themselves able to do so, are able to govern them."

He broke off a little abruptly. Huntley's unsympathetic face, with the big cigar in the corner of his mouth, choked the flow of his words.

"Never mind," he said. "This isn't interesting to you, of course. As you say, the business side is the more important. I will see you at the hotel to-morrow night. Considering where I have been this evening, it is scarcely wise for us to be seen together."

Huntley took the hint, finished his drink, and departed. Saton sat for a few more minutes alone. Then he too went out into the street, and walked slowly homewards. He let himself into the house in Regent's Park with his latchkey, and went thoughtfully upstairs. The room was still brilliantly illuminated, and the woman who was sitting over the fire, turned round to greet him.

"Well?" she asked.

Saton divested himself of his hat and coat. Madame's black eyes were still fixed upon him. He came slowly across towards her.

"Well?" she repeated.

"You were there," he reminded her. "I saw you sitting almost in the front row. What did you think of it?"

She shrugged her shoulders.

"What does it matter what I think of it? Tell me about the others."

"My paper was pronounced everywhere to be a great success," he declared. "Many of the cleverest men in London were there. They listened to every syllable."

Madame nodded.

"Why trouble to teach them?" she asked, a little scornfully. "What of Huntley? Have you seen him? How have they done to-day?"

"It goes well," he answered. "It always goes well."

She moved her head slowly.

"Yet to-night you are not thinking of it," she said. "For many nights you have not counted your earnings. You are thinking of other things," she declared harshly. "Don't look away from me. Look into my eyes."

"It is true," he answered. "To-night I have been with clever men. I have measured my wits against theirs. I have pushed into their consciousness things which they were unwilling to believe. I have made them believe. There were many people there who felt, I believe, for the first time, that they were ignorant."

The woman looked at him scornfully. There was no softening in her face, and yet she had taken his hand in hers and held it.

"What do we gain by that?" she asked harshly. "What we want is gold, gold all the time. You ought to know that, you, who have been so near to starvation. Are you a fool that you don't realize it?"

"I am not a fool," Saton answered calmly, "but there is another side to the whole matter. A meeting such as to-night's gives an immense fillip on the part of society to what they are pleased to call the supernatural. It is only the fear of ridicule which keeps half the people in the world from flooding our branches, every one of them eager to have their fortunes told. A night like to-night is a great help. Clever men, men who are believed in, have accepted the principle that there are laws which govern the future so surely as the past in its turn has been governed. One needs only to apprehend those laws, to reduce them to intelligible formulæ. It is an exact study, an exact science. This is the doctrine which I have preached. When people once believe it, what is to keep them from coming in their thousands to those who know more than they do?"

The woman shook her head derisively.

"No need to wait for those days," she answered. "The world is packed full of fools now. No need to wrestle with nature, to wear oneself inside out to give them truth. Give them any rubbish. Give them what they seem to want. It is enough so long as they bring the gold. How much was taken to-day altogether?"

Saton passed on to her the papers which the man Huntley had given him in the café.

"There is the account," he said. "You see it grows larger every day."

"What becomes of the money?" she asked.

"It is paid into the bank, and the banker's receipt comes to me each morning. There is no chance for fraud. I must make some more investments soon. Our balance grows and grows."

The woman's eyes glittered.

"Bring me some money to-morrow," she begged, grasping his other hand. "I like to have it here in my hands. Money and you, Bertrand, my son—they are all I care for. Banks and investments are well enough. I like money. Kiss me, Bertrand."

He laughed tolerantly, and kissed her cheek.

"My dear Rachael," he said, "you have already bagsful of gold about the place."

"They are safe," she assured him, "absolutely safe. They never leave my person. I feel them as I sit. I sleep with them at night. I am going to bed now. Bertrand!"

"Well?" he asked.

She pointed to him with long forefinger, a forefinger aflame with jewels.

"Look! We play with no fortune-telling here. What is there in your face? What is there in your life you are not telling me of? Is it a woman?"

"There are many women in my life," he answered. "You know that."

"I do," she answered. "Poor fools! Play with them all you will, but remember—the one whom you choose must have gold!"

He nodded.

"I am not likely to forget," he said.

She left the room with a farewell caress. There was something almost tigress-like about the way in which her arms wound themselves around him—some gleam of the terrified victim in his eyes, as he felt her touch. Then she left the room. Saton sank back into an easy-chair, and gazed steadfastly into the fire through half-closed eyes.

CHAPTER XII

A CALL ON LADY MARRABEL

Saton, after the reading of his paper before the members of the London Psychical Society, established a certain vogue of which he was not slow to avail himself. His picture appeared in several illustrated papers. His name was freely mentioned as being one of the most brilliant apostles of the younger school of occultism. He subscribed to a newspaper cutting agency, and he read every word that was written about himself. Whenever he got a chance, he made friends with the press. Everything that he could possibly do to obtain a certain position in a certain place, he sedulously attempted. He was always carefully dressed, and he was quite conscious of the fact that his clothes were of correct pattern and cut. His ties were properly subdued in tone. His gloves and hat were immaculate.

Yet all the time he lacked confidence in himself. The word charlatan clung to him like a pestilential memory. His hair was cropped close to his head. He had shaved off his moustache. He imitated almost slavishly the attire and bearing of those young men of fashion with whom he was brought into contact. Yet he was somehow conscious of a difference. The women seemed never to notice it—the men always. Was it jealousy, he wondered, which made them, even the most unintelligent, treat him with a certain tolerance, as though he were a person not quite of themselves, whom they scarcely understood, but were willing to make the best of?

With women it was different always. His encounter with Pauline Marrabel at the conversazione had given him the keenest pleasure. He had at once fixed a day sometime ahead upon which he would take to her the books he had spoken of. The day had arrived at last, but he had first another engagement. Early in the afternoon he turned into Kensington Gardens, and walked up and down the broad path, glancing every now and then toward one of the entrances. He saw at last the person for whom he was waiting.

Lois, in a plain white muslin gown, and a big hat gay with flowers, came blithely towards him, a little Pomeranian under one arm, and a parasol in the other hand.

"I do hope I'm not too dreadfully late!" she exclaimed, setting the dog down, and taking his hand a little shyly. "It seems such an age since I saw you last. Where can we go and talk?"

"You are not frightened at me any more, then?"

"Of course not," she answered. "We spoke about that at Beauleys. I do not want to think any more of that evening. It is over and done with. What a clever person you are becoming!" she went on. "I saw your name one day last week in the *Morning Post*. You read a paper before no end of clever men. And do you know that your photograph is in two or three of the illustrated papers this week?"

His cheeks flushed with pleasure. He was unreasonably glad that she appreciated these things. His vanity, which had been a trifle ruffled by some incident earlier in the day, was effectually soothed.

"These things," he said, "are absolutely valueless to me except so far as they testify to the importance of my work. Before long," he went on, "I think that there will be many other people like you, Miss Lois. They will believe that there is a little more in life than their dull eyes can see. You were one of those who understood from the first. But there are not many."

She sighed.

"I don't think I am a bit clever," she admitted.

"Cleverness," he answered, "is not a matter of erudition. It is a matter of instinct, of capacity for grasping new truths. You have that capacity, dear Lois, and I am glad that you are here. It is good to be with you again."

"You really are the most wonderful person," she declared, poking at her little dog with the end of her fluffy parasol. "You make me feel as though I were something quite important, and you know I am really a very unformed, very unintelligent young person. That is what my last governess said."

"Cat!" he answered laughing. "I can see her now. She wore a *pince-nez* and a bicycling skirt. I am sure of it. Come and sit down here, and I will prove to you how much cleverer I am than that ancient relic." ...

They parted at the gates, an hour or so later. Saton resented a little her evident desire to leave him there, and her half frightened refusal of his invitation to lunch, but he consoled himself by taking his mid-day meal alone at *Prince's*, where several people pointed him out to others, and he was aware that he was the object of a good deal of respectful interest.

Later in the day, with several books under his arm, he rang the bell at 17, Cadogan Street. He was committed now to the enterprise, which had never been out of his thoughts since the night of the conversazione.

Pauline kept him waiting for nearly a quarter of an hour. When at last she entered, he found himself lost in admiration of the marvelous simplicity of her muslin gown and her perfect figure. There was about her some sort of exquisite perfection, a delicacy of outline and detail almost cameolike, and impossible of reproduction.

She welcomed him kindly, but without any enthusiasm. He felt from the first that he still had prejudices to conquer. He sat down by her side and commenced his task. Very wisely, he eliminated altogether the personal note from his talk. He showed her the books which he had brought, and he talked of them fluently and well. She became more and more interested. It was scarcely possible that she could refrain from showing it, for he spoke of the things which he knew, and things which the citizens of the world in every age have found fascinating. He seemed to her to have gone a little further into the great mysterious shadowland than anyone else—to have come a little nearer reading the great riddle. She was a good listener, and she interrupted him only once.

"But tell me this," she asked, towards the close of one of his arguments. "This apprehension which you say one must cultivate, to be able—how is it you put it?—to throw out feelers for the things which our ordinary senses cannot grasp—isn't it a matter largely of temperament?"

"One finds it difficult or easy to acquire," he answered, "according to one's temperament. A nervous, magnetic person, who is not afraid of solitude, of solitary thought, of taking the truth to his heart and wrestling with it—that person is, of course, always nearer the truth than the person of phlegmatic temperament, who has to struggle ever so hard to be conscious of anything not actually within the sphere of his physical apprehension. These things in our generation will have a great effect. In centuries to come, they will become less and less apparent. We move rapidly," he went on, "and I am still a young man. Before I die, it is my ambition to leave behind me the first text-book on this new science, the first real and logical attempt to enunciate absolute laws."

"It is all very wonderful," she said, sighing gently. "Do you think that I shall understand any more about it when I have read these books?"

"I am sure that you will," he answered. "You have intelligence. You have sensibility. You are not afraid to believe—that is the trouble with most people."

"Answer me one question," she begged. "All these fortune-telling people who have sprung up round Bond Street—I mean the palmists and crystal-gazers, and people like that—do they proceed upon any knowledge whatever, or are they all absolute humbugs?"

"To the best of my belief," he answered fervently, "every one of them. Personally, I haven't very much information, but it has not come under my notice that there is a single one of these people who even attempts to probe the future scientifically or even intelligently, according to the demands made upon them. They impose as much as they can upon the credulity of their clients. I consider that their existence is absolutely the worst possible thing for us who are endeavouring to gain a foothold in the scientific world. Your friend Mr. Rochester, you know, called me a charlatan."

"Mr. Rochester is never unjust," she answered quietly. "Some day, perhaps, he will take that word back."

He tried to give their conversation a more personal note, but he found her elusive. She accepted an invitation, however, to be present at a lecture which he was giving before another learned society during the following week. With that he felt that he ought to be content. Nevertheless, he left her a little dissatisfied. He was perfectly well aware that the magnetism which he was usually able to exert over her sex had so far availed him nothing with her. Her eyes met his freely, but without any response to the things which he was striving to express. She had seemed interested all the time, but she had dismissed him without regret. He walked homewards a little thoughtfully. If only she were a little like Lois!

As he passed the entrance to the Park, an electric brougham was suddenly pulled up, and a lady leaned forward towards him. He stepped up to her side, hat in hand. It was Lady Mary Rochester. She was exquisitely gowned and hatted, with a great white veil which floated gracefully around her picture-hat, and she welcomed him with a brilliant smile.

"My dear Mr. Saton," she exclaimed, "what a fortunate meeting! Only a few minutes ago I was thinking of you."

"I am very much flattered," he answered.

"I mean it," she declared. "I wonder whether you could spare me a few minutes. I don't mean here," she added. "One can scarcely talk, driving. Come in after dinner, if you have nothing to do, just for half-an-hour. My husband is down in the country, and I am not going out until eleven."

"I shall be very pleased," he answered, a little mechanically, for he found the situation not altogether an easy one to grasp.

"Don't forget," she said. "Number 10, Berkeley Square," with a look of relief.

The electric brougham rolled on, and Saton crossed the road thoughtfully. Then a sudden smile lightened his features. He realized all at once what it was that Lady Mary wanted from him.

Rachael was waiting for him when he returned. She was seated before the table, her head resting upon her hands, her eyes fixed upon the little piles of gold and notes which she had arranged in front of her. She watched him come in and take off his hat and coat, in silence.

"Well?" she asked. "How do things go to-day?"

"I have not the reports yet," he answered. "It is too early. I shall have them later."

"What have you been doing?" she asked.

"I walked with a girl, Lois Champneyes, in Kensington Gardens most of the morning, and I called upon a woman—Lady Marrabel—this afternoon," he answered.

Rachael nodded.

"Safe companions for you," she muttered. "Remember what I always tell you. You are of the breed that can make fools of women. A man might find you out."

He turned an angry face upon her.

"What is there to find out?" he demanded. "I am not an impostor. I am a man of science. I have proved it. Your fortune-telling temples are all very well, and the money they bring is welcome enough. But nevertheless, I am not the vulgar adventurer that you sometimes suggest."

The woman laughed, laughed silently and yet heartily, but she never spoke. She looked away from him presently, and drawing the pile of gold and notes nearer to her, began to recount them with her left hand. Her right she held out to him, slowly drawing him towards her.

CHAPTER XIII

LADY MARY'S DILEMMA

Lady Mary's boudoir was certainly the most luxurious apartment of its sort into which Saton had ever been admitted. There were great bowls of red roses upon the small ormolu table and on the mantelpiece. Several exquisite etchings hung upon the lavender walls. The furniture was all French. Every available space seemed occupied with costly knick-knacks and curios. Photographs of beautiful women, men in court dress and uniform, nearly all of them signed, were scattered about on every available inch of space, and there was also that subtle air of femininity about the apartment, to which he was unaccustomed, and which went to his head like wine. It was evident that only privileged visitors were received there, for apart from the air of intimacy which seemed somehow to pervade the place, there were several articles of apparel, and a pair of slippers lying upon the hearthrug.

Lady Mary herself came rustling in to him a few minutes after his arrival, gorgeous in a wonderful shimmering gown, which seemed to hang straight from her shoulders—the very latest creation in the way of tea-gowns.

"I know you will forgive my receiving you like this," she said, holding out her hand. "To tell you the truth, I dined here absolutely alone, and I thought that I would not dress till afterwards. I am going on to the ball at Huntingford House, and it is always less trouble to go straight from one's maid. You have had coffee? Yes? Then sit down at the end of this couch, please, and tell me whether you think you can help me."

Saton was not altogether at his ease. The brilliancy of his surroundings, the easy charm of the woman, were a little disconcerting. And she was Rochester's wife, the wife of the man whom he hated! That in itself was a thing to be always kept in mind. Never before had she seemed so desirable.

"If you will tell me in what way I can be of service, Lady Mary," he began——

She turned towards him pathetically.

"Really," she said, "I scarcely know why I asked for your help, except that you seem to me so much cleverer than most of the men I know."

"I am afraid you over-rate my abilities," he said, with a slight deprecating smile. "But at any rate, please be sure of one thing. You could not have asked the advice of anyone more anxious to serve you."

"How kind you are!" she murmured. "I am going to make a confession, and you will see, after all, that the trouble I am in has something to do with you. You remember that night at Beauleys?"

"Yes!" he answered.

"We won't talk about it," she continued. "We mustn't talk about it. Only it gave me foolish thoughts. From being utterly incredulous or indifferent, I went to the other extreme. I became, I suppose, absolutely foolish. I went to one of those stupid women in Bond Street."

"You went to have your fortune told?" he asked.

She nodded.

"Oh, I suppose so!" she said. "I asked her a lot of things, and she looked into a crystal globe and told me what she saw. It was quite interesting, but unfortunately I went a little further than I meant to. I asked her some ridiculous questions about—a friend of mine."

He smiled sympathetically.

"Well," he said, "this all seems rather like a waste of time, but I scarcely see how it would be likely to land you in a difficulty."

"But it has," she answered. "That is what I want to explain to you. The woman insisted upon having a letter in the handwriting of the person I asked questions about, and I foolishly gave her one that was in my pocket. When I asked for it back again, the day afterwards, she said she had mislaid it."

"But was the letter of any importance?" he asked.

"There wasn't much in it, of course," she answered, "but it was a private letter."

"It is infamous!" he declared. "I should give information to the police at once."

She held out her hands—tiny little white hands, ringless and soft.

"My dear man," she exclaimed, "how can I? Give information to the police, indeed! What, go and admit before a magistrate that I had been to a fortune-teller, especially," she added, looking down, "on such an errand?"

He drew a little nearer to her.

"I beg your pardon," he answered. "I was thoughtless. That, of course, is not possible. Tell me the name and the address of the person to whom you went."

"The woman's name was Helga," she answered, "and it was in the upper end of Bond Street. Daisy Knowles told me about the place. Heaps of people I know have been."

"And the letter?" he asked. "Tell me, if you can, what is its precise significance?"

"It was a letter from Charlie Peyton," she answered—"Major Peyton, in the Guards, you know. There wasn't anything in it that mattered really, but I shall not have a moment's peace until it is returned to me."

"Have you told me everything?" he asked.

"No!" she admitted.

"Perhaps it would be as well," he murmured.

She produced a letter from the bosom of her gown.

"I received this last night," she said.

He glanced it rapidly through. The form of it was well known to him

"*Dear Madam,*

"*A letter addressed to you, and in the handwriting of a certain Major Charles Peyton, has come into our hands within the last few hours. It is dated from the Army and Navy Club, and its postmark is June 1st. The contents are probably well-known to you.*

"*It is our wish to return same into your hands at once, but we may say that it was handed to us in trust by a gentleman who is indebted to us for a considerable sum of money and he spoke of this document, which we did not inspect at the time, as being a probable form of security.*

"*Perhaps your ladyship can suggest some means by which we might be able to hand over the letter to you without breaking faith with our friend.*

"*Sincerely yours,*
"*Jacobson & Co.—Agents.*

"*17, Charing Cross Road.*"

"A distinct attempt at blackmail!" Saton exclaimed, indignantly.

"Isn't it wicked?" Lady Mary replied, looking at him appealingly. "But how am I to deal with it? What am I to do? I don't wish to correspond with these people, and I daren't tell Henry a thing about it."

"Naturally," he answered. "My dear Lady Mary, there are two courses open to you. First, you can take this letter to the police, when you will get your own letter back without paying a penny, and these rascals will be prosecuted. The only disadvantage attached to this course is that your name will appear in the papers, and the letter will be made public."

"You must see," she declared, "that that is an absolute impossibility. My husband would be furious with me, and so would Major Peyton. Please suggest something else."

"Then, on the other hand," he continued, "the only alternative course is to make the best bargain you can with the scoundrels who are responsible for this."

"But how can I?" she asked plaintively. "I cannot go to see these people, nor can I have them come here. I don't know how much money they want. You know I haven't a penny of my own, and although my husband is generous enough, he likes to know what I want money for. I have spent my allowance for the whole of the year already. I believe I am even in debt."

Saton hesitated for several moments. Lady Mary watched him all the time anxiously.

"If you will allow me," he said, "I will take this letter away with me, and see these people on your behalf. I have no doubt that I can make much better terms with them than you could."

She drew a little sigh of relief.

"That is just what I was hoping you would propose," she declared, handing it over to him. "It is so good of you, Mr. Saton. I feel there are so few people I could trust in a matter like this. You will be very careful, won't you?"

"I will be very careful," he answered.

"And when you have the letter," she continued, "you will bring it straight back to me?"

"Of course," he promised, "only first I must find out what their terms are. They will probably begin by suggesting an extravagant sum. Tell me how far you are prepared to go?"

"You think I shall have to pay a great deal of money, then?" she asked, anxiously.

"That depends entirely," he answered, "upon what you call a great deal of money."

"I might manage two hundred pounds," she said, doubtfully.

He smiled.

"I am afraid," he said, "that Messrs. Jacobson & Co., or whatever their name is, will expect more than that."

"It is so unlucky," she murmured. "I have just paid a huge dressmaker's bill, and I have lost at bridge every night for a week. Do the best you can for me, dear Mr. Saton."

He leaned towards her, but he was too great an artist not to realize that her feeling for him was one of pure indifference. He was to be made use of, if possible—to be dazzled a little, perhaps, but nothing more.

"I will do the best I can," he said, rising, as he saw her eyes travel towards the clock, "but I am afraid—I don't want to frighten you—but I am afraid that you will have to find at least five hundred pounds."

"If I must, I must," she answered, with a sigh. "I shall have to owe money everywhere, or else tell Henry that I have lost it at bridge. This is so good of you, Mr. Saton."

"If I can serve you," he concluded, holding her hand for a moment in his, "it will be a pleasure, even though the circumstances are so unfortunate."

"I shall esteem the service none the less," she answered, smiling at him. "Come and see me directly you know anything. I shall be so anxious."

Saton made his way to the café at the end of Regent Street. This time he had to wait a little longer, but in the end the man who had met him there before appeared. He came in smoking a huge cigar, and with his silk hat a little on one side.

"A splendid day!" he declared. "Nearly double yesterday's receipts. The papers are all here."

Saton nodded, taking them up and glancing them rapidly through.

"Do you know where I can find Dorrington?" he said. "I want that letter—the Peyton letter, you know."

Huntley nodded.

"I've got it in my pocket," he said. "I was keeping it until to-morrow."

Saton held out his hand.

"I'll take it," he said. "I can arrange terms for this matter myself."

Huntley looked at him in surprise.

"It isn't often," he remarked, "that you care to interfere with this side of the game. Sure you're not running any risk? We can't do without our professor, you know."

Saton shivered a little.

"No! I am running no risk," he said. "It happens that I have a chance of settling this fairly well."

He had a few more instructions to give. Afterwards he left the place. The night outside was close, and he was conscious of a certain breathlessness, a certain impatient desire for air. He turned down toward the Embankment, and sat on one of the seats, looking out at the sky signs and colored advertisements on the other side of the river, and down lower, where the tall black buildings lost their outline in the growing dusk.

His thoughts travelled backwards. It seemed to him that once more he sat upon the hillside and built for himself dream houses, saw himself fighting a splendid battle, gathering into his life all the great joys, the mysterious emotions which one may wrest from fate. Once more he thrilled with the subtle pleasure of imagined triumphs. Then the note of reality had come. Rochester's voice sounded in his ears. His dreams were to become true. The sword was to be put into his hand. The strength was to be given him. The treasure-houses of the world were to fly open at his touch. And then once more he seemed to hear Rochester's voice, cold and penetrating. "*Anything but failure! If you fail, swim out on a sunny day, and wait until the waves creep over your neck, over your head, and you sink! The men who fail are the creatures of the gutter!*"

Saton gripped the sides of his seat. He felt himself suddenly choking. He rose and turned away.

"It would have been better! It would have been better!" he muttered to himself.

CHAPTER XIV

PETTY WORRIES

Saton threw down the letter which he had been reading, with a little exclamation of impatience. It was from a man whom, on the strength of an acquaintance which had certainly bordered upon friendship, he had asked to propose him at a certain well-known club.

"My dear Mr. Saton," it ran, "I was sent for to-day by the Committee here upon the question of your candidature for the club. They asked me a good many questions, which I answered to the best of my ability, but you know they are a very old-fashioned lot, and I think it would perhaps be wisest if I were to withdraw your name for the present. This I propose to do unless I hear from you to the contrary.

"Sincerely yours,
"Gordon Chambers."

Saton felt his cheeks flush as he thrust the letter to the bottom of the little pile which stood in front of him. It was one more of the little annoyances to which somehow or other he seemed at regular intervals to be subjected. Latterly, things had begun to expand with him. He had persuaded Madame to give up the old-fashioned house in Regent's Park, and they had moved into a maisonette in Mayfair—a little white-fronted house, with boxes full of scarlet geraniums, a second man-servant to open the door, and an electric brougham in place of the somewhat antiquated carriage, which the Countess had brought with her from abroad. His banking account was entirely satisfactory. There were many men and women who were only too pleased to welcome him at their houses. And yet he was at all times subject to such an occurrence as this.

His lips were twisted in an unpleasant smile as he frowned down upon the tablecloth.

"It is always like it!" he muttered. "One climbs a little, and then the stings come."

Madame entered the room, and took her place at the other end of the breakfast table. She leaned upon her stick as she walked, and her face seemed more than ever lined in the early morning sunlight. She wore a dress of some soft black material, unrelieved by any patch of color, against which her cheeks were almost ghastly in their pallor.

"The stings, Bertrand? What are they?" she asked, pouring herself out some coffee.

Saton shrugged his shoulders.

"Nothing that you would understand," he answered coldly. "I mean that you would not understand its significance. Nothing, perhaps, that I ought not to be prepared for."

She looked across the table at him with cold expressionless eyes. To see these two together in their moments of intimacy, no one would ever imagine that her love for this boy—he was nothing more when chance had thrown him in her way—had been the only real passion of her later days.

"You do not know," she said, "what I understand or what I do not understand. Tell me what it is that worries you in that letter."

He pushed it away from him impatiently.

"I asked a friend—a man named Chambers—to put me up for a club I wanted to join," he said. "He promised to do his best. I have just received a letter advising me to withdraw. The committee would not elect me."

"What club is it?" she asked.

"The 'Wanderers'," he answered. "The social qualification is not very stringent. I imagined that they would elect me."

The woman looked at him as one seeking to understand some creature of an alien world.

"You attach importance," she asked, "to such an incident as this? You?"

"Not real importance, perhaps," he answered, "only you must remember that these are the small things that annoy. They amount to nothing really. I know that. And yet they sting!"

"Do not dwell upon the small things, then," she said coldly. "It is well, for all our sakes, that you should occupy some position in the social world, but it is also well that you should remember that your position there is not worth a snap of the fingers as against the great things which you and I know of. What do these people matter, with their strange ideas of birth and position, their little social distinctions, which remind one of nothing so much as Swift's famous satire? You are losing your sense of proportion, my dear Bertrand. Go into your study for an hour this morning, and think. Listen to the voices of the greater life. Remember that all these small happenings are of less account than the flight of a bird on a summer's day."

"You are right," he answered, with a little sigh, "and yet you must remember that you and I can scarcely look at things from the same standpoint. They do not affect you in the slightest. They cannot fail to remind me that I am after all an outcast, rescued from shipwreck by one strange turn in the wheel of chance."

She looked at him with penetrating eyes.

"Something is happening to you, Bertrand," she said. "It may be that it is your sense of proportion which is at fault. It may be that your head is a little turned by the greatness of the task which it has fallen to your lot to carry out. It is true that you are a young man, and that I am an old woman. And yet, remember! We are both of us little live atoms in the great world. The only things which can appeal to us in a different manner are the everyday things which should not count, which should not count for a single moment," she added, with a sudden tremor in her tone.

"You are right, of course," he answered, "and yet, Rachael, you must remember this. You have finished with the world. I am compelled to live in it."

"If you are," she rejoined, "is that any reason, Bertrand, why you should pause to listen to the voices whose cry is meaningless? Think! Remember the blind folly of it all. A decade, a cycle of years, and the men who pass you in Pall Mall, and the women who smile at you from their carriages, will be dead and gone. You—you may become the Emperor of Time itself. Remember that!"

"And in the meantime, one has to live."

"Keep your head in the clouds," she said. "Make use of these people, but always remember that in the light of what may come, they are only the dirt beneath your feet. Remember that you may be the first of all the ages to solve the great secret—the secret of carrying your consciousness beyond the grave."

"Life is short," he said, "and the task is great."

"Too great for cowards," she answered. "Yet look at me. Do I despair? I am seventy-one years old. I have no fear of death. I have learnt enough at least to help me into the grave. That will do, Bertrand. Go on with your breakfast, and burn that letter."

He tore it in half, and went to the sideboard to help himself from one of the dishes. When he returned, Madame was drumming thoughtfully upon the tablecloth with her long fingers.

"Bertrand," she said.

He looked toward her curiously. There was a new note, a new expression in the way she had pronounced his name.

"The girl, the little fair fool of a girl with money—Lois Champneyes you called her—where is she?"

"She is in London," he answered.

"With the Rochesters?"

"Yes!"

Rachael frowned.

"You find it difficult to see her, then?" she remarked, thoughtfully.

"I can see her whenever I choose to," he answered.

"You must marry her," Rachael said. "The girl will serve your purpose as well as another. She is rich, and she is a fool."

"She is not of age," Saton said drily, "and Mr. Rochester is her guardian."

"She will be of age very soon," Rachael answered, "and the money is sure."

"Do we need it?" he asked, a little impatiently. "We are making now far more than we can spend."

"We need money all the time," she answered. "At present, things prosper. Yet a change might come—a change in the laws, a campaign in the press—anything. Even the truth might leak out."

Saton rose from his place, and going once more to the sideboard, took up and lit a long Russian cigarette. He returned with the box, and laid it before Rachael.

"If the truth should leak out," he said, "that would be the end of us in this country. We have had one escape. I do not mean to find myself in the prisoner's dock a second time."

"There is no fear of that," she answered. "The whole business is so arranged that neither you nor I would be connected with it. Besides, we have rearranged things. We are within the pale of the law now. To return to what I was saying about this girl."

"There is no hurry," he said. "Marriage does not interest me."

"Marriage for its own sake, perhaps, no," she answered, "and yet money you must have. No man has ever succeeded in any great work without it. If a pauper proclaims a theory, he is laughed to scorn. He is called a charlatan and an impostor. If a rich man speaks of the same thing, his words are listened to as one who stirs the world. There is a change in you, Bertrand," she continued. "You have avoided this girl lately. You have avoided, even, your work. What is it?"

"Who knows?" he answered, lightly. "The weather, perhaps—the moon—one's humor. I will walk this morning in Kensington Gardens. Perhaps I shall see Lois."

He left the house half-an-hour later, after dictating some letters to a newly installed secretary. He accepted a carefully brushed hat from a well-trained and perfectly respectful servant, who placed also in his hands his stick and gloves. He descended a few immaculate steps and turned westward, frowning thoughtfully. The matter with him! He knew well enough. He had taken his fate into his hands, played his cards boldly enough, but Fate was beginning to get her own back.

He turned not toward Kensington Gardens, but towards Cadogan Street. He rang the bell at one of the most pretentious houses, and asked for Lady Marrabel. The butler was doubtful whether she would be inclined to receive anyone at that hour. He was shown into a morning-room and kept waiting for some time. Then she came in, serene as usual, with a faint note of inquiry in her upraised eyebrows and the tone of her voice as she welcomed him.

"I must apologize," he began, a little nervously. "I have no right to come at such an hour. I heard this morning that Max Naudheim will be in London before the end of the week, and I wondered whether you would care to meet him."

"Of course I should," she answered, "only I hope that he is more comprehensible than his book."

"I have never met him myself," Saton answered, "but I know that he has a letter to me. He will come to my house, I believe, and if he follows out his usual custom, he will scarcely leave it while he stays in England. I shall ask a few people to talk one night. I cannot attempt anything conventional. It does not seem to me to be an occasion for anything of the sort. If you will come, I will let you know the night and the time."

She hesitated for a moment.

"And if you should come," he continued, "even though it be the evening, please wear an old dress and hat. Naudheim himself seldom appears in a collar. Any social gathering of any sort is loathsome to him. He will talk only amongst those whom he believes are his friends."

"I will come, of course," Pauline answered. "It is good of you to think of me."

"He may speak to you," Saton continued. "He takes curious fancies sometimes to address a perfect stranger, and talk to them intimately. Remember that though he lives in Switzerland, and has a German name, he is really an Englishman. Nothing annoys him more than to be spoken to in any other language."

"I will remember," Pauline said.

There was a moment's silence. Saton felt that he was expected to go. Yet there was something in her manner which he could not altogether understand, some nervousness, which seemed absolutely foreign to her usual demeanour. He took up his hat reluctantly.

"You are busy to-day?" he asked.

"I am always busy," she answered. "Perhaps it is because I am so lazy. I never do anything, so there is always so much to do."

He made the plunge, speaking without any of his usual confidence—hurriedly, almost indistinctly.

"Won't you come and have some luncheon with me at the Berkeley, or anywhere you please? I feel like talking to-day. I feel that I am a little nearer the first law. I want to speak of it to someone."

She hesitated, and he saw her fingers twitch.

"Thank you," she said, "I am afraid I can't. If you like, you can come and have luncheon here. I have one or two people coming in."

"Thank you," he said. "I shall be glad to come. About half-past one, I suppose?"

"From that to two," she answered. "My friends drop in at any time."

He passed out into the street, not altogether satisfied with his visit, and yet not dissatisfied. He had an instinctive feeling that in some degree her demeanour towards him was changed. What it meant he could not wholly tell. She no longer met his eyes with that look of careless, slightly contemptuous interest. Yet when he tried to find encouragement from the fact, he felt that he lacked all his usual confidence. He realized with a little impulse of annoyance that in the presence of this woman, whom he was more anxious to impress than anyone else in the world, he was subject to sudden lapses of self-confidence, to a certain self-depreciation, which irritated him. Was it, he wondered, because he was always fancying that she looked at him out of Rochester's eyes?

A cab drove past him, and stopped before the house which he had just left. He looked behind, with a sudden feeling of almost passionate jealousy. It was Rochester, who had driven by him unseen, and who was now mounting the steps to her house.

CHAPTER XV

ROCHESTER IS INDIGNANT

Rochester accepted his wife's offer of a lift in her victoria after the luncheon party in Cadogan Street.

"Mary," he said, as soon as the horses had started, "I cannot imagine why you were so civil to that insufferable bounder Saton."

She looked at him thoughtfully.

"Is he an insufferable bounder?" she asked.

"I find him so," Rochester answered, deliberately. "He dresses like other men, he walks and moves like other men, he speaks like other men, and all the time I know that he is acting. He plays the game well, but it is a game. The man is a bounder, and you will all of you find it out some day."

"Don't you think, perhaps," his wife remarked, "that you are prejudiced because you have some knowledge of his antecedents?"

"Not in the least," Rochester answered. "The fetish of birth has never appealed to me. I find as many gentlefolk amongst my tenants and servants, as at the parties to which I have the honor of escorting you. It isn't that at all. It's a matter of insight. Some day you will all of you find it out."

"All of us, I presume," Lady Mary said, "includes Pauline."

Rochester nodded.

"Pauline has disappointed me," he said. "Never before have I known her instinct at fault. She must know—in her heart she must know that there is something wrong about the fellow. And yet she receives him at her house, and treats him with a consideration which, frankly, shall we say, annoys me?"

"One might remind you," Lady Mary remarked, "that it is you who are responsible for this young man's introduction amongst our friends."

"It is true," Rochester answered. "I regret it bitterly. I regret it more than ever to-day."

"Because of Pauline?" Lady Mary asked.

"Because of Pauline, and for one other reason," Rochester answered, lowering his voice, and turning a little in his seat towards his wife. "Mary, I was unfortunate enough to hear a sentence which passed between you and this person in the hall. I would have shut my ears if I could, but it was not possible. Am I to understand that you have made use of him in some way?"

Lady Mary gasped. This was a thunderbolt to descend at her feet without a second's warning!

"As a matter of fact," she said slowly, "he has done me a service."

Rochester's face darkened.

"I should be interested," he said, "to know the circumstances."

Lady Mary was not a coward, and she realized that there was nothing for it but the absolute truth. Her husband's eyes were fixed upon her, filled with an expression which she very seldom saw in them. After all, she had little enough to fear. Their relations were scarcely such that he could assume the position of a jealous husband.

"I suppose that you will laugh at me, Henry," she said. "Perhaps you will be angry. However, one must amuse oneself. Frankly, I think that all this talk that is going on about occultism, and being able to read the future, and to find new laws for the government of the will, has perhaps turned my brain a little. Anyhow, I went to one of those Bond Street people, and asked them a few questions."

"You mean to one of these crystal-gazers or fortune-tellers?" he asked.

"Precisely," she answered. "No doubt you think that I am mad, but if you had any idea of the women in our own set who have done the same thing, I think you would be astonished. Well, whilst I was there I chanced to drop, or leave behind—it scarcely concerns you to know which—a letter written to me by a very dear friend. One of my perfectly harmless love affairs, you know, Henry, but men do make such idiots of themselves when they have pen and paper to do it with."

Rochester moved a little uneasily in his place.

"May I inquire——" he began.

"No, I shouldn't!" she interrupted. "You know very well, my dear Henry, the exact terms upon which we have both found married life endurable. If I choose to receive foolish letters from foolish men, it concerns you no more than your silent adoration of Pauline Marrabel does me. You understand?"

"I understand," he answered quietly. "Go on."

"Well," she continued, "a few days afterwards I had just about as terrifying a specimen of a blackmailing letter as you can possibly imagine."

"From these people?" Rochester asked.

"No! From a firm who called themselves agents, and said that the letter had come into their possession, had been deposited with them, in fact, by someone who owed them some money," Lady Mary answered. "Of course, I was frightened to death. I don't know what made me think of Bertrand Saton as the best person to consult, but anyhow I did. He took the matter up for me, paid over some money on my account, and recovered the letter."

"The sum of money being?"

"Five hundred pounds," Lady Mary answered, with a sigh. "It was a great deal, but the letter—well, the letter was certainly very foolish."

Rochester was silent for several moments.

"Do you know," he asked at length, "what the natural inference to me seems—the inference, I mean, of what you have just told me?"

"You are not going to say anything disagreeable?" she asked, looking at him through the lace fringe of her parasol.

"Not in the least," he answered. "I was not thinking of the personal side of the affair—so far as you and I are concerned, I have accepted your declaration. I claim no jurisdiction over your correspondence. I mean as regards Saton."

"No! What?" she asked.

"It seems to me highly possible," he declared, "that Saton was in league with these blackmailers, whoever they may have been. Any ordinary man whom you had consulted would have settled the matter in a very different way."

"I was quite satisfied," Lady Mary answered. "I thought it was really very kind of him to take the trouble."

"Indeed!" Rochester remarked drily. "I must say, Mary, that I gave you credit for greater perspicuity. The man is an intriguer. Naturally, he was only too anxious to be of service to so charming a lady."

Lady Mary raised her eyebrows, but did not answer.

"I might add," Rochester continued, "that however satisfactory our present relations may seem to you, I still claim the privilege of being able to assist my wife in any difficulty in which she may find herself."

"You are very kind," she murmured.

"Further," Rochester said, "I resent the interference of any third party in such a matter. You will remember this?"

"I will remember it," Lady Mary said. "Still, the circumstances being as they are, you can scarcely blame me for having been civil to him to-day. Besides, you must admit that he is clever."

"Clever! Oh! I've no doubt that he is clever enough," Rochester answered, impatiently. "Nowadays, all you women seem as though you can only be attracted by something freakish—brains, or peculiar gifts of some sort."

Lady Mary laughed lightly.

"My dear Henry," she said, "you are not exactly a fool yourself, are you? And then you must remember this. Bertrand Saton's cleverness is the sort of cleverness which appeals to women. We can't help our natures, I suppose, and we are always attracted by the mysterious. We are always wanting to know something which other people don't know, something of what lies behind the curtain."

"It is a very dangerous curiosity," Rochester said. "You are liable to become the prey of any adventurer with a plausible manner, who has learned to talk glibly about the things which he doesn't understand. I'll get out here, if I may," he added, "and take a short cut across the Park to my club. Mary, if you want to oblige me, for Heaven's sake don't run this fellow! He gets on my nerves. I hate the sight of him."

Lady Mary turned towards her husband with a faint, curious smile as the carriage drew up.

"You had better talk to Pauline," she said. "He is more in her line than mine."

Rochester walked across the Park a little gloomily. His wife's last words were ringing in his ears. For the first time since he could remember, a little cloud had loomed over his few short hours with Pauline. She had resented some contemptuous speech of his, and as though to mark her sense of his lack of generosity, she had encouraged Saton to talk, encouraged him to talk until the other conversation had died away, and the whole room had listened to this exponent of what he declared to be a new science. The fellow was a *poseur* and an impostor, Rochester told himself vigorously. He knew, he was absolutely convinced that he was not honest.

He sat down on a seat for a few minutes, and his thoughts somehow wandered back to that night when he had strolled over the hills and found a lonely boy gazing downward through the tree tops to the fading landscape. He remembered his own whimsical generosity, the feelings with which he had made his offer. He remembered, too, the conditions which he had made. With a sudden swift anger, he realized that those conditions had not been kept. Saton had told him little or nothing of his doings out in the world, of his struggles and his failures, of the growth of this new enthusiasm, if indeed it was an enthusiasm. He had hinted at strange adventures, but he had spoken of nothing definite. He had not kept his word.

Rochester rose to his feet with a little exclamation.

"He shall tell me!" he muttered to himself, "or I will expose him, if I have to turn detective and follow him round the world."

He swung round again across the Park toward Mayfair, and rang the bell at Saton's new house. Mr. Saton was not at home, he was informed, but was expected back at any moment. Rochester accepted an invitation to wait, and was shown into a room which at first he thought empty. Then someone rose from an old-fashioned easy-chair, set back amongst the shadows. Rachael peered forward, leaning upon her stick, and shading her eyes as though from the sun.

"Who is that?" she asked. "Who are you?"

Rochester bowed, and introduced himself. As yet he could see very little of the person who had spoken. The blinds, and even the curtains of the room, were close drawn. It was one of Rachael's strange fancies on certain days to sit in the darkness. Suddenly, however, she leaned forward and touched the knob of the electric light.

"My name is Rochester," he said. "I called to see Mr. Saton for a few minutes. They asked me to wait."

"I am the Comtesse de Vestignes," Rachael said slowly, "and Bertrand Saton is my adopted son. He will be back in a few moments. Draw your chair up close to me. I should like to talk, if you do not mind this light. I have been resting, and my eyes are tired."

Rochester obeyed, and seated himself by her side with a curious little thrill of interest. It seemed to him that she was like the mummy of some ancient goddess, the shadowy presentment of days long past. She had the withered appearance of great age, and yet the dignity which refuses to yield to time.

"Come nearer," she said. "I am no longer a young woman, and I am a little deaf."

"You must tell me if you do not hear me," Rochester said. "My voice is generally thought to be a clear one. I am very much interested in this young man. Suppose, while we wait, you tell me a few things about him. You have no objection?"

Rachael laughed softly.

"I wonder," she said, "what it is that you expect to hear from me."

CHAPTER XVI

PLAIN SPEAKING

From the depths of her chair, Rachael for several moments sat and subjected her visitor to a close and merciless scrutiny.

"So you," she said at last, "were the fairy godfather. You were the man who trusted a nameless boy with five hundred pounds, because his vaporings amused you. You pushed him out into the world, you bade him go and seek his fortune."

"I was that infernal fool!" Rochester muttered.

The woman nodded.

"Yes, a fool!" she said. "No one but a fool would do such a thing. And yet great things have come of it."

Rochester shrugged his shoulders. He was not prepared to admit that Bertrand Saton was in any sense great.

"My adopted son," she continued, "is very wonderful. Egypt had its soothsayers thousands of years ago. This century, too, may have its prophet. Bertrand gains power every day. He is beginning to understand."

"You, too," Rochester asked politely, "are perhaps a student of the occult?"

"Whatever I am," she answered scornfully, "I am not one of those who because their two feet are planted upon the earth, and their head reaches six feet towards the sky, are prepared to declare that there is no universe save the earth upon which they stand, no sky save the sky toward which they look—nothing in life which their eyes will not show them, or which their hands may not touch."

Rochester smiled faintly.

"Materialism is an easy faith and a safe one," he said. "Imagination is very distorting."

"For you who feel like that," she answered, "the way through life is simple enough. We others can only pity."

"Comtesse," Rochester said, "such an attitude is perfectly reasonable. It is only when you attempt to convert that we are obliged to fall back upon our readiest weapons."

"You are one of those," she said, looking at him keenly, "who do not wish to understand more than you understand at present, who have no desire to gain the knowledge of hidden things."

"You are right, Comtesse," Rochester answered, with a smile. "I am one of those pig-headed individuals."

"It is the Saxon race," she muttered, "who have kept back the progress of the world for centuries."

"We have kept it backward, perhaps," he answered, "but wholesome."

"You think always of your bodies," she said.

"They were entrusted to us, madam, to look after," he answered.

She smiled grimly.

"You are not such a fool," she said, "as my adopted son would have me believe. You have spared me at least that hideous Latin quotation which has done so much harm to your race."

"Out of respect to you," he declared, "I avoided it. It was really a little too obvious."

"Come," she said, "you are a type of man I have not met with for years. You are strong and vigorous and healthy. You have color upon your cheeks, and strength in your tone and movements. In any show of your kind, you should certainly be entitled to a prize."

Rochester laughed, at first softly, and then heartily.

"My dear lady," he said, "forgive me. I can assure you that although my inclinations do not prompt me to sit at your son's feet and accept his mythical sayings as the words of a god, I am really not a fool. I will even go so far as this. I will even admit the possibility that a serious and religious study of occultism might result in benefit to all of us. The chief point where you and I differ is with regard to your adopted son. You believe in him, apparently. I don't!"

"Then why are you here?" she asked. "What do you want with him? Do you come as an enemy?"

Rochester was spared the necessity of making any answer. He heard the door open, and the woman's eyes glittered as they turned toward it.

"Bertrand is here himself," she said. "You can settle your business with him."

Rochester rose to his feet. Saton had just entered, closing the door behind him. Prepared for Rochester's presence by the servants, he greeted him calmly enough.

"This is an unexpected honor," he said, bowing. "I did not imagine that we should meet again so soon."

"Nor I," Rochester answered. "Where can we talk?"

"Here as well as anywhere," Saton answered, going up to Rachael, and lifting her hand for a moment to his lips. "From this lady, whose acquaintance I presume you have made, I have no secrets."

Rochester glanced from one to the other—the woman, sitting erect and severe in her chair, the young man bending affectionately over her. Yes, he was right! There was something about the two hard to explain, yet apparent to him as he sat there, which seemed in some way to remove them out of direct kinship with the ordinary people of the world. Was it, he wondered, with a sudden swift intuition, a touch of insularity, a sign of narrowness, that he should find himself so utterly repelled by this foreign note in their temperaments? Was his disapproval, after all, but a mark of snobbishness, the snobbishness which, to use a mundane parallel, takes objection to the shape of an unfashionable collar, or the cut of a country-made coat? There were other races upon the world beside the race of aristocrats. There was an aristocracy of brains, of genius, of character. Yet he reasoned against his inspiration. Nothing could make him believe that the boy who had held out his hands so eagerly toward the fire of life, had not ended by gathering to himself experiences and a cult of living from which any ordinary mortal would have shrunk.

"I am quite content," Rochester said, "to say what I have to say before this lady, especially if she knows your history. I have come here to tell you this. I have been your sponsor, perhaps your unwilling sponsor, into the society and to the friends amongst whom you spend your time. I am not satisfied with my sponsorship. That you came of humble parentage, although you never allude to the fact, goes for nothing. That you may be forgiven. But there are seven years of your past the knowledge of which is a pledge to me. I have come to insist upon your fulfilment of it. For seven years you disappeared. Where were you? How did you blossom into prosperity? How is it that you, the professor of a new cult, whose first work is as yet unpublished, find yourself enabled to live in luxury like this? You had no godmother then. Who is this lady? Why do you call her your godmother? She is nothing of the sort. You and I know that—you and I and she. There are things about you, Saton, which I find it hard to understand. I want to understand them for the sake of my friends."

"And if you do not?" Saton asked calmly.

"Well, it must be open war," Rochester declared.

"I should say that it amounted to that now," Saton answered.

"Scarcely," Rochester declared, "for if it had been open war I should have asked you before now to tell me where it was that you and Lord Guerdon had met. Remember I heard the words trembling upon his lips, and I saw your face!"

Saton did not move, nor did he speak for a moment. His cheeks were a little pale, but he gave no sign of being moved. The woman's face was like the face of a sphinx, withered and emotionless. Her eyes were fixed upon Saton's.

"You have spoken to me before somewhat in this strain, sir," Saton said. "What I said to you then, I repeat. The account between us is ruled out. You lent or gave me a sum of money, and I returned it. As to gratitude," he went on, "that I may or may not feel. I leave you to judge. You can ask yourself, if you will, whether that action of yours came from an impulse of generosity, or was merely the gratification of a cynical whim."

"My motives are beside the question," Rochester answered. "Do I understand that you decline to give me any account of yourself?"

"I see no reason," Saton said coldly, "why I should gratify your curiosity."

"There is no reason," Rochester admitted. "It is simply a matter of policy. Frankly, I mistrust you. There are points about your behaviour, ever since in a foolish moment I asked you to stay at Beauleys, which I do not understand. I do not understand Lord Guerdon's sudden recognition of you, and even suddener death. I do not understand why it has amused you to fill the head of my young ward, Lois Champneyes, with foolish thoughts. I do not understand why you should stand between my wife and the writers of a blackmailing letter. I do not ask you for any explanation. I simply tell you that these things present themselves as enigmas to me. You have declared your position. I declare mine. What you will not tell me I shall make it my business to discover."

The Comtesse leaned a little forward. Her face was still unchanged, her tone scornful.

"It is I who will answer you," she said. "My adopted son—for he is my adopted son if I choose to make him so—will explain nothing. He has, in fact, nothing more to say to you. You and he are quits so far as regards obligations. Your paths in life lie apart. You are one of the self-centred, sedentary loiterers by the way. For him," she added, throwing out suddenly her brown, withered hand, aflame with jewels, "there lie different things. Something he knows; something he has learned; much there is yet for him to learn. He will go on his way, undisturbed by you or any friends of yours. As for his means, your question is an impertinence. Ask at Rothschilds concerning the Comtesse de Vestignes, and remember that what belongs to me belongs to him. Measure your wits against his, to-day, to-morrow, or any time you choose, and the end is certain. Show your patron out, Bertrand. He has amused me for a little time, but I am tired."

Rochester rose to his feet.

"Madam," he said, "I am sorry to have fatigued you. For the rest," he added, with a note of irony in his tone, "I suppose I must accept your challenge. I feel that I am measuring myself and my poor powers against all sorts of nameless gifts. And yet," he added, as he followed Saton towards the door, "the world goes round, and the things which happened yesterday repeat themselves to-morrow. Your new science should teach you, at least, not to gamble against certainties."

He passed out of the room, and Saton returned slowly to where Rachael was sitting. Her eyes sought his inquiringly. They read the anguish in his face.

"You are afraid," she muttered.

"I am afraid," he admitted. "Given an inversion of their relative positions, I feel like Faust befriended by Mephistopheles. I felt it when he stood by my side on the hilltop, seven years ago. I felt it when he thrust that money into my hand, and bade me go and see what I could make of life, bade me go, without a word of kindness, without a touch of his fingers, without a sentence of encouragement, with no admonitory words save that one single diatribe against failure. You know what he told me? 'Go out,' he said, 'and try your luck. Go out along the road which your eyes have watched fading into the mists. But remember this. For men there is no such thing as failure. One may swim too far out to sea on a sunny day. One may trifle with a loaded revolver, or drink in one's sleep the draught from which one does not awake. But for men, there is no failure.'"

The woman nodded.

"Well," she said harshly, "you remembered that. You did not fail. Who dares to say that you have failed!"

Saton threw himself into the easy-chair drawn apart from hers. His head fell forward into his hands. The woman rested her head upon her fingers, and watched him through the shadows.

CHAPTER XVII

THE GREAT NAUDHEIM

Naudheim had finished his address, and stood talking with his host.

"Do you mind," Saton asked, "if I introduce some of these people to you? You know many of them by name."

Naudheim shook his head. He was a tall man, with gray, unkempt hair, and long, wizened face. He wore a black suit of clothes, of ancient cut, and a stock which had literally belonged to his grandfather.

"No!" he said vigorously. "I will be introduced to no one. Why should I? I have spoken to them of the things which make life for us. I have told them my thoughts. What need is there of introduction? I shake hands with no one. I leave that, and silly speeches, and banquets, to my enemies, the professors. These are not my ways."

"It shall be as you wish, of course," Saton replied. "You are very fortunate to be able to live and work alone. Here we have to adapt ourself in some way to the customs of the people with whom we are forced to come into daily contact."

Naudheim suddenly abandoned that far-away look of his, his habit of seeing through the person with whom he was talking. He looked into Saton's face steadily, almost fiercely.

"Young man," he said, "you talk like a fool. Now listen to me. These are my parting words! There is stuff in you. You know a little. You could be taught much more. And above all, you have the temperament. Temperament is a wonderful thing," he added. "And yet, with all these gifts, you make me feel as though I would like to take you by the collar and lift you up in my arms—yes, I am strong though I am thin—and throw you out of that window, and see you lie there, because you are a fool!"

"Go on," Saton said, his face growing a little pale.

"Oh, you know it!" Naudheim declared. "You feel it in your blood. You know it in your heart. You truckle to these people, you play at living their life, and you forget, if ever you knew, that our great mistress has never yet opened her arms save to those who have sought her single-hearted and with a single purpose. You are a dallier, philanderer. You will end your days wearing your fashionable clothes. They may make you a professor here. You will talk learnedly. You will write a book. And when you die, people will say a great man has gone. Listen! You listen to me now with only half your ears, but listen once more. The time may come. The light may burn in your heart, the truth may fill your soul. Then come to me. Come to me, young man, and

I will make bone and sinew of your flabby limbs. I will take you in my hands and I will teach you the way to the stars."

Silently, and without a glance on either side of him, Naudheim left the room, amidst a silence which was almost an instinctive thing—the realization, perhaps, of the strange nature of this man, who from a stern sense of duty had left his hermit's life for a few days, to speak with his fellow-workers.

It had been in some respects a very curious function, this. It was neither meeting nor reception. There was neither host nor hostess, except that Saton had shaken hands with a few, and from his place by the side of Naudheim had indicated the turn of those who wished to speak. Their visitor's peculiarities were well-known to all of them. He had left them abruptly, not from any sense of discourtesy, but because he had not the slightest idea of, or sympathy with, the manners of civilized people. He had given them something to think about. He had no desire to hear their criticisms. After he had gone, the doors were held open. There was no one to bid them stay, and so they went, in little groups of twos and threes, a curious, heterogeneous crowd, with the stamp upon their features or clothes or bearing, which somehow or other is always found upon those who are seekers for new things. Sallow, dissatisfied-looking men; women whose faces spoke, many of them, of a joyless life; people of overtrained minds; and here and there a strong, zealous, brilliant student of the last of the sciences left for solution.

Pauline would have gone with the others, but Saton touched her hand. Half unwillingly she lingered behind until they were alone in the darkened room. He went to the window and threw it wide open. The scent of the flowers in the window-boxes and a little wave of the soft west wind came stealing in. She threw her head back with an exclamation of relief.

"Ah!" she said. "This is good."

"You found the room close?" he asked.

Pauline sank into the window-seat. She rested her delicate oval face upon her fingers, and looked away toward the deep green foliage of the trees outside.

"I did not notice it," she said, "and yet, somehow or other the whole atmosphere seemed stifling. Naudheim is great," she went on. "Oh, he is a great man, of course. He said wonderful things in a convincing way. He made one gasp."

"This afternoon," Saton declared slowly, "marks an epoch. What Naudheim said was remarkable because of what he left unsaid. Couldn't you feel that? Didn't you understand? If that man had ambitions, he could startle even this matter-of-fact world of ours. He could shake it to its very base."

She shivered a little. Her fingers were idly tapping the window-sill. Her thoughtful eyes were clouded with trouble. He stood over her, absorbed in the charm of her presence, the sensuous charm of watching her slim, exquisite figure, the poise of her head, the delicate coloring of her cheeks, the tremulous human lips, which seemed somehow to humanize the spirituality of her expression. They had talked so much that day of a new science. Saton felt his heart sink as he realized that he was the victim of a greater thing than science could teach. It was madness!—sheer, irredeemable madness! But it was in his blood. It was there to be reckoned with.

"It is all very wonderful," she continued thoughtfully. "And yet, can you understand what I mean when I say that it makes me feel a trifle hysterical? It is as though something had been poured into one which was too great, too much for our capacity. It is all true, I believe, but I don't want it to come."

"Why not?" he asked.

"Oh! It seems somehow," she answered, "as though the whole balance of life would be disturbed. Of course, I know that it is feasible enough. For thousands of years men and women lived upon the earth, and never dreamed that all around them existed a great force which only needed a little humoring, a little understanding, to do the work of all the world. Oh, it is easy to understand that we too carry with us some psychical force corresponding to this! One feels it so often. Premonitions come and go. We can't tell why, but they are there, and they are true. One feels that sense at work at strange times. Experiments have already shown us that it exists. But I wonder what sort of a place the world will be when once it has yielded itself to law."

"There has never been a time," Saton said thoughtfully, "when knowledge has not been for the good of man."

She shook her head.

"I wonder," she said, "whether we realize what is for our good. Knowledge, development, culture, may reach their zenith and pass beyond. We may become debauched with the surfeit of these things. The end and aim of life is happiness."

"The end and aim of life," he contradicted her, "is knowledge."

She laughed.

"I am a woman, you see," she said thoughtfully.

"And am I not a man?" he whispered.

She turned her head and looked at him. The trouble in her eyes deepened. She felt the color coming and going in her cheeks. His eyes seemed to stir things in her against which her whole physical self rebelled. She rose abruptly to her feet.

"I must go," she said. "I have a thousand things to do this evening."

"To play at, you mean," he corrected her. "You don't really do very much, do you? The women don't in your world."

"You are polite," she answered lightly. "Please to show me the way out."

"In a moment," he said.

She was inclined to rebel. They had moved a little from the window, and were standing in a darker part of the room. She felt his fingers upon her wrist. She would have given the world to have been able to wrench it away, but she could not. She stood there submissively, her breath coming quickly, her eyes compelled to meet his.

"Stay for a moment longer," he begged. "I want to talk to you for a little while about this."

"There is no time now," she said hurriedly. "It is an inexhaustible subject."

"Inexhaustible indeed," he answered, with an enigmatic laugh.

She read his thoughts. She knew very well what was in his mind, what was almost on his lips, and she struggled to be free of him.

"Mr. Saton," she said, "I am sorry—but you must really let me go."

He did not move.

"It is very hard to let you go," he murmured. "Can't you—don't you realize a little that it is always hard for me to see you go—to see you leave the world where we have at least interests in common, to go back to a life of which I know so little, a life in which I have so small a part, a life which is scarcely worthy of you, Pauline?"

Again she felt a sort of physical impotence. She struggled desperately against the loss of nerve power which kept her there. She would have given anything in the world to have left him, to have run out of the room with a little shriek, out into the streets and squares she knew so well, to breathe the air she had known all her life, to escape from this unknown emotion. She told herself that she hated the man whose will kept her there. She was sure of it. And yet—!

"I do not understand you," she said, "and I must, I really must go. Can't you see that just now, at any rate, I don't want to understand?" she added, fighting all the time for her words. "I want to go. Please do not keep me here against my will. Do you understand? Let me go, and I will be grateful to you."

Somehow the strain seemed suddenly lightened. He was only a very ordinary, rather doubtful sort of person—a harmless but necessary part of interesting things. He had moved toward the door, which he was holding open for her to pass through.

"Thank you so much," she said, with genuine relief in her tone. "I have stayed an unconscionable time, and I found your Master delightful."

"You will come again?" he said softly. "I want to explain a little further what Naudheim was saying. I can take you a little further, even, than he did to-day."

"You must come and see me," she answered lightly. "Remember that after all the world has conventions."

He stepped back on to the doorstep after he had handed her into her carriage. She threw herself back amongst the cushions with something that was like a sob of relief. She had sensations which she could not analyze—a curious feeling of having escaped, and yet coupled with it a sense of something new and strange in her life, something of which she was a little afraid, and yet from which she would not willingly have parted. She told herself that she detested the house which she had left, detested the thought of that darkened room. Nevertheless, she was forced to look back. He was standing in the open doorway, from which the butler had discreetly retired, and meeting her eyes he bowed once more. She tried to smile unconcernedly, but failed. She looked away with scarcely a return of his greeting.

"Home!" she told the man. "Drive quickly."

Almost before her own door she met Rochester. The sight of him was somehow or other an immense relief to her. She fell back again in the world which she knew. She stopped the carriage and called to him.

"Come and drive with me a little way," she begged. "I am stifled. I want some fresh air. I want to talk to you. Oh, come, please!"

Rochester took the vacant seat by her side at once.

"What is it?" he asked gravely. "Tell me. You have had bad news?"

She shook her head.

"No!" she said. "I am afraid—that is all!"

CHAPTER XVIII

ROCHESTER'S ULTIMATUM

The Park into which they turned was almost deserted. Pauline stopped the carriage and got out.

"Come and walk with me a little way," she said to Rochester. "We will go and sit amongst that wilderness of empty chairs. I want to talk. I must talk to someone. We shall be quite alone there."

Rochester walked by her side, puzzled. He had never seen her like this.

"I suppose I am hysterical," she said, clutching at his arm for a moment as they passed along the walk. "There, even that does me good. It's good to feel—oh, I don't know what I'm talking about!" she exclaimed.

"Where have you been this afternoon?" he asked gravely.

"To hear that awful man Naudheim," she answered. "Henry, I wish I'd never been. I wish to Heaven you'd never asked Bertrand Saton to Beauleys."

Rochester's face grew darker.

"I wish I'd wrung the fellow's neck the first day I saw him," he declared, bitterly. "But after all, Pauline, you don't take this sort of person seriously?"

"I wish I didn't," she answered.

"He's an infernal charlatan," Rochester declared. "I'm convinced of it, and I mean to expose him."

She shook her head.

"You can call him what you like," she said, "but there is Naudheim behind him. There is no one in Europe who would dare to call Naudheim a charlatan."

"He is a wonderful man, but he is mad," Rochester said.

"No, he is not mad," she said. "It is we who are mad, to listen a little, to think a little, to play a little with the thoughts he gives us."

"I know of Naudheim only by reputation," Rochester said. "And so far as regards Saton, nothing will convince me that he is not an impostor."

She sighed.

"There may be something of the charlatan in his methods," she said, "but there is something else. Henry, why can't we be content with the things that we know and see and feel?"

He smiled bitterly.

"I am," he answered. "I thank God that I have none of that insane desire for probing and dissecting nature to discover things which we are not fit yet to understand, if, even, they do exist. It's a sort of spiritual vivisection, Pauline, and it can bring nothing but disquiet and unhappiness. Grant for a moment that Naudheim, and that even this bounder Saton, are honest, what possible good can it do you or me to hang upon their lips, to become their disciples?"

"Oh, I don't know!" she answered. "Yet it's hideously fascinating, Henry hideously! And the man himself—Bertrand Saton. I can't tell what there is about him. I only know——"

She broke off in the middle of her sentence. Rochester caught her by the wrist.

"Pauline," he said, "for God's sake, don't tell me that that fellow has dared to make love to you."

"I don't know," she answered. "Sometimes I hate the very sight of him. Sometimes I feel almost as you do. And at others, well, I can't explain it. It isn't any use trying."

"Pauline," he said, "you see for yourself the state to which you have been reduced this afternoon. Tell me, is there happiness in being associated with any science or any form of knowledge the study of which upsets you so completely? There are better things in life. Forget this wretched little man, and his melodramatic talk."

"If only I could!" she murmured.

They sat side by side in silence. Strong man though he was, Rochester was struggling fiercely with the wave of passionate anger which had swept in upon him. For years he had treated this woman as his dearest friend. The love which was a part of his life lay deep down in his heart, a thing with the seal of silence set upon it, zealously treasured, in its very voicelessness a splendid oblation to the man's chivalry. And now this unmentionable creature, this Frankenstein of his own creation, the boy whom he had pitchforked into life, had dared to be guilty of this unspeakable sacrilege. It was hard, indeed, for Rochester to maintain his self-control.

"Pauline," he said, "I cannot stand by and see your life wrecked. You are too sane, too reasonable a woman to become the prey of such a pitiful adventurer. Won't you listen to me for a moment?"

"Indeed I am listening," she faltered.

"Give yourself a chance," he begged. "Leave England this week—to-morrow, if you can. Go right away from here. You have friends in Rome. I heard your cousin ask you not long ago to pay her a visit at her villa on the Adriatic. Start to-morrow, and I promise that you will come back a sane woman. You will be able to laugh at Saton, to see through the fellow, and to realise what a tissue of shams he's built of. You will be able to feel a reasonable interest in anything Naudheim has to say. Just now you are unnerved, these men have frightened you. Believe me that your greatest and most effectual safety lies in flight."

A sudden hope lit up her face. She turned towards him eagerly. She was going to consent—he felt it, he was almost conscious of the words trembling upon her lips. Already his own personal regrets at her absence were beginning to cloud his joy. Then her whole expression changed. Something of the look settled upon her features which he had seen when first she had stopped the carriage. Her lips were parted, her eyes distended. She looked nervously around as though she were afraid that some one was following them.

"I cannot do that, Henry," she said. "In a way it would be a relief, but it is impossible. I cannot, indeed."

She led the way to the carriage. They walked in absolute silence for nearly a minute. He felt that he had lost a great part of his influence over her and he was bitter.

"Tell me why you almost consented," he asked, abruptly, "and then changed your mind? In your heart you must know that it is for your good."

"I only know," she answered, slowly, "that at first I longed to say yes, and now, when I come to think of it, I see that it is impossible."

"You are going to allow yourself, then, to be the prey of these morbid fancies? You are going to treat this creature as a human being of your own order? You are going to let him work upon your imagination?"

"It is no use," she said wearily. "For the present, I cannot talk any more about it. I do not understand myself at all."

They stood for a moment by the carriage.

"We shall meet to-night," he reminded her.

She gave him a doubtful little smile.

"You are really coming to the Wintertons?" she asked.

"I have promised," he answered. "Caroline has bribed me. I am going to take you in to dinner."

"Will you drive home with me now?" she asked.

He shook his head.

"I have another call to make," he said, a little grimly.

Saton was still in the half darkened library, sitting with his back turned to the light, and his eyes fixed with a curious stare into vacancy, when the door opened, and Rochester entered unannounced. Saton rose at once to his feet, but the interrogative words died away upon his lips. Rochester's fair, sunburnt face was grim with angry purpose. He had the air of a man stirred to the very depths. He came only a little way into the room, and he took up his position with his back to the door.

"My young friend," he said, "it is not many hours since you and I came to an understanding of a sort. I am here to add a few words to it."

Saton said nothing. He stood immovable, waiting.

"Whatever your game in life may be," Rochester continued, "you can play it, for all I care, to the end. But there is one thing which I forbid. I have come here so that you shall understand that I forbid it. You can make fools of the whole world, you can have them kneeling at your feet to listen to your infernal nonsense—the whole world save one woman. I am ashamed to mention her name in your presence, but you know whom I mean."

Saton's lips seemed to move for a moment, but he still remained silent.

"Very well," Rochester said. "There shall be no excuse, no misunderstanding. The woman with whom I forbid you to have anything whatever to do, whom I order you to treat from this time forward as a stranger, is Pauline Marrabel."

Saton was still in no hurry to speak. He leaned a little forward. His eyes seemed to burn as though touched with some inward fire.

"By what right," he asked, "do you come here and dictate to me? You are not my father or my guardian. I do not recognize your right to speak to me as one having authority."

"It was I who turned you loose upon the world," Rochester answered. "I deserve hanging for it."

"I should be sorry," Saton said coldly, "to deprive you of your deserts."

"You have learned many things since those days," Rochester declared. "You have acquired the knack of glib speech. You have become a past master in the arts which go to the ensnaring of over-imaginative women. You have mixed with quack spiritualists and self-styled professors of what they term occultism. Go and practise your arts where you will, but remember what I have told you. Remember the person's name which I have mentioned. Remember it, obey what I have said, and you may fool the whole world. Forget it, and I am your enemy. Understand that."

"And you," Saton answered with darkening face, "understand this from me, Rochester. I do not for a moment admit your right to speak to me in this fashion. I admit no obligation to you. We are simply man and man in the world together, and the words which you have spoken have no weight with me whatever."

"You defy me?" Rochester asked calmly.

"If you call that defiance, I do," Saton answered.

Rochester came a step further into the room.

"Listen, my young friend," he said. "You belong to the modern condition of things, to the world which has become just a little over-civilized. You may call me a boor, if you like, but I want you to understand this. If I fail to unmask you by any other means, I shall revert to the primeval way of deciding such differences as lie between you and me, the differences which make for hate. I can wield a horse-whip with the strongest man living, and I am in deadly earnest."

"The lady whose name you have mentioned," Saton said softly—"is she also your ward? You are related to her, perhaps?"

"She is the woman I love," Rochester answered. "Our ways through life may lie apart, or fate may bring them together. That is not your business or your concern. When I tell you that she is the woman I love, I mean you to understand that she is the woman whom I will protect against all manner of evil, now and always. Remember that if you disregard my warning, in the spirit or in the letter, so surely as we two live you will repent it."

Saton crossed the room with noiseless footsteps. He leaned toward the wall and touched an electric bell.

"Very well," he said. "You have come to deliver an ultimatum, and I have received it. I understand perfectly what you will accept as an act of war. There is nothing more to be said, I think?"

"Nothing," Rochester answered, turning to follow the servant whom Saton's summons had brought to the door.

CHAPTER XIX

TROUBLE BREWING

Saton turned out of Bond Street, and climbed the stairs of a little tea-shop with the depressed feeling of a man who is expiating an offence which he bitterly repents. Violet was waiting for him at one of the tables shut off from the main room by a sort of Japanese matting hanging from the ceiling. He resigned his stick and hat with a sigh to one of the trim waitresses, and sat down opposite her.

"My dear Violet," he said, "this is an unexpected pleasure. I thought that Wednesday was quite one of your busiest days."

"It is generally," she answered. "To tell you the truth," she added, leaning across the table, "I was jolly glad to get away. I have a kind of fear, Bertrand, that we are going to be a little too busy."

"What do you mean?" he asked sharply.

She nodded her head mysteriously.

"There have been one or two people in, in the last few days, asking questions which I don't understand," she told him. "One of them, I am pretty sure, was a detective. He didn't get much change out of me," she added, in a self-satisfied tone, "but there's someone got their knife into us. You remember the trouble down in the Marylebone Road, when you——"

"Don't!" he interrupted. "I hate to think of that time."

"Well, I tell you I believe there is something of the sort brewing again," the woman said. "I'll tell you more about it later on."

The waitress brought their tea, which Violet carefully prepared.

"Two pieces of sugar," she said, "and no cream. You see I haven't forgotten, although it is not often we have tea together now, Bertrand. You are becoming too fashionable, I suppose," she added with a little frown.

"You know it isn't that," he answered hastily. "It's my work, nothing but my work. Go on with what you were telling me, Violet."

"You needn't look so scared," she said, glancing round to be sure that they were not overheard. "The only thing is that Madame must be told at once, and we shall all have to be careful for a little time. I shut up shop for the day as soon as I tumbled to the thing."

"I wonder if this is Rochester's doings," he muttered.

"The husband of the lady?" Violet enquired.

Saton nodded.

"He is my enemy," he said. "Nothing would make him happier than to have the power to strike a blow like this, and to identify us with the place in any way."

"I don't see how they could do that," she said meditatively. "I should be the poor sufferer, I suppose, and you may be sure I shouldn't be like that other girl, who gave you away. You are not afraid of that, are you, Bertrand? Things are different between us. We are engaged to be married. You do not forget that, Bertrand?"

"Of course I do not," he answered.

"Well," she said, "we won't talk about the past. You are safe so far as I am concerned—for the present, at any rate. But Madame must know, and your friends in Charing Cross Road."

"We will close the office to-morrow for a little time," Saton declared. "It's no use running risks like this."

"The old lady must have made a tidy pile out of it," Violet declared, flourishing an over-scented handkerchief. "If she takes my advice, she will go quiet for a little time. I can feel trouble when it's about, and I have felt it the last few days."

"It is very good of you, Violet, to have sent for me at once," he said. "I know you won't mind if I hurry away. It is very important that I see Madame."

"Of course," she agreed. "But when will you take me out to dinner? To-night or to-morrow night?"

"To-morrow night," he promised, eager to escape. "If anything happens that I can't, I'll let you know."

She laid her hand upon his arm as they descended the stairs.

"Bertrand," she said, "if I were you, I'd make it to-morrow night...."

He called a taximeter cab, and drove rapidly to Berkeley Square. In the room where she usually sat he found Rachael, looking through a pile of foreign newspapers.

"Well?" she said, peering into his face. "You have bad news. I can see that. What is it?"

"Helga has just sent for me," he answered. "She says that she has had one or two mysterious visitors to-day and yesterday. One of them she feels sure was a detective."

"Huntley has just telephoned up," Rachael said calmly. "Something of the same sort of thing happened at the office in the Charing Cross Road. Huntley acted like a man of sense. He closed it up at once, destroyed all papers, and sent Dorrington over to Paris by the morning train."

Saton sat down, and buried his face in his hands.

"Rachael," he said, "this must stop. I cannot bear the anxiety of it. It is terrible to feel to-day that one is stretching out toward the great things, and to-morrow that one is finding the money to live by fooling people, by charlatanism, by roguery. Think if we were ever connected with these places, if even a suspicion of it got about! Think how narrow our escape was before! Remember that I have even stood in the prisoner's dock, and escaped only through your cleverness, and an accident. It might happen again, Rachael!"

"It shall not," she answered. "I would go there myself first. It is well for you to talk, Bertrand, but you and I are neither of us fond of simple things. We must live. We must have money."

"We live extravagantly," he said.

"All my life I have lived extravagantly," she answered. "Why should I change now? I have but a few years to live. I cannot bear small rooms, or cheap servants, or bad cooking."

"We have some money left," he said. "Come with me into the country. We can live there for very little. Soon my book will be ready. Then the lectures will begin. There will be money enough when people begin to understand."

"No!" she said. "There is only one way. I have spoken of it to you before. You must marry that foolish girl Lois Champneyes."

"What do you know about her?" he asked, looking up, startled.

"I have made inquiries," Rachael answered. "It is the usual thing in the countries I know of. She will be of age in a short time, and she will have one hundred and seventy thousand pounds. Upon that you can live until our time comes, and you can afford to keep this house going."

"I do not want to marry," he said.

Her hand shot out towards him—an accusing hand; her eyes flashed fire as she leaned forward, gripping the arm of the chair with her other fingers.

"Listen," she said, "I took you from the gutter. I saved you from starvation. I showed you the way to ease and luxury. I taught you things which have set your brain working, which shall fashion for you, if you dare to follow it, the way to greatness. I saved your life. I planted your feet upon the earth. Your life is mine. Your future is mine. What is this sacrifice that I demand? Nothing! Don't refuse me. I warn you, Bertrand, don't refuse me! There are limits to my patience as there are limits to my generosity and my affection. If you refuse, it can be but for one reason, and that reason you will not dare to tell me. Do you refuse? Answer me, now, I will have no more evasions."

"She would not marry me," he said. "I have not seen her for days."

"Where is she?" Rachael demanded.

"In the country, at Beauleys," he answered. "The Rochesters have all left town yesterday or to-day, and she went with them."

"Then into the country we go," she declared. "It is an opportune time, too. We shall be out of the way if troubles come from these interfering people. I do not ask you again, Bertrand, whether you will or will not marry this girl. For the first time I exercise my rights over you. I demand that you marry her. Be as faithless as you like. You are as fickle as a man can be, and as shallow. Make love to her for a year, and treat her as these Englishmen treat their housekeepers, if you will. But marry her you must! It is the money we need— the money! What is that?"

The bell was ringing from a telephone instrument upon the table. Saton lifted it to his ear.

"There is a trunk call for you," a voice said. "Please hold the line."

Saton waited. Soon a familiar voice came.

"Who is that?" it asked.

"Bertrand Saton," Saton answered.

"Listen," the voice said. "I am Huntley. I speak from Folkestone. I am crossing to-night to Paris. Dorrington is already on ahead. Someone has been employing detectives to track us down. It commenced with that letter—the one for which you settled terms yourself. You hear?"

"I hear," Saton answered. "Was it necessary for you, too, to go?"

"I cannot tell," Huntley answered. "All I know is that I have done pretty well the last two years, and I am not inclined to figure in the police courts. If the thing blows over, I'll be back in a few weeks. Every paper of importance has been destroyed. I believe that you and Madame are perfectly safe. At the same time, take my tip. Go slow! I'm off. I've only a minute for the boat."

Saton laid down the receiver on the instrument.

"If it must be," he said, turning to Rachael, "I will go down to Blackbird's Nest to-morrow."

CHAPTER XX

FIRST BLOOD

Lois came walking down the green path that led to the wood, her head a little tilted back to watch the delicate tracery of the green leaves against the sky, her thoughts apparently far away. Suddenly she came to a standstill, the color rushed into her cheeks, her eyes danced with pleasure. Saton had come suddenly round the corner, and was already within a few feet of her.

"You?" she exclaimed. "Really you? I had no idea that you had left London."

He smiled as he took her hands.

"London was a desert," he said. "I have finished my work for a few days, and I have brought my writing down here."

"When did you come?" she asked.

"Last night," he answered. "I was just wondering how I could send a note up to you. Fortunately, I remembered your favorite walk."

"Did you really come to see me?" she murmured.

He laughed softly, and bent towards her. All her hesitation and mistrust seemed to pass away. She lay quietly in his arms, with her face upturned to his. He kissed her on the lips. All the time his eyes were watching the path along which he had come.

"Let us sit down," she said at last, gently disengaging herself from him. "There are so many things I want to ask you."

"And I too," he answered. "I have something to say—something I cannot keep to myself any longer."

He led the way to a fallen tree, a little removed from the footpath. They were scarcely seated, however, before he turned his head sharply in the direction from which he had come. His whole frame seemed to have become suddenly rigid with an intense effort of listening. He raised his finger with a warning gesture.

"Sit still," he whispered. "Don't say anything. There is someone coming."

Her hand fell upon his. They sat side by side in an almost breathless silence, safely screened from observation unless the passers-by, whoever they might be, should be unusually curious.

It was Pauline and Rochester who came—Pauline in a tailor-made gown of dark green cloth—Pauline, slim, tall and elegant. Rochester was bending toward her, talking earnestly. He wore a tweed shooting suit, and carried a gun under either arm.

"You see who it is?" Lois whispered.

Saton nodded. His face had darkened, his cheeks were almost livid. His eyes followed the two with an expression which terrified the girl who sat by his side.

"Bertrand," she whispered, "why do you look like that?"

"Like what?" he asked, without moving his eyes from the spot where those two figures had disappeared.

She shivered a little.

"You looked as though you hated Mr. Rochester. You looked angry—more than angry. You frightened me."

"I do hate him," Saton answered slowly. "I hate him as he hates me. We are enemies."

"Yet you were not looking at him all the time," she persisted. "You looked at Pauline, too. You don't hate her, do you?"

He drew a little breath between his clenched teeth. If only this child would hold her peace!

"No!" he said. "I do not hate Lady Marrabel."

"Is it because he has interfered between us," she asked timidly, "that you dislike Mr. Rochester so much? Remember that very soon I shall be of age."

"He has no right to interfere in my concerns at all," Saton answered, evasively. "Hush!"

The two had halted at a little wooden gate which led into the strip of field dividing the two plantations. Rochester was looking back along the footpath by which they had come. They could hear his voice distinctly.

"Johnson must have got lost," he remarked, a little impatiently. "I will leave my second gun here for him. It is quite time I took up my place. The beaters will be in the wood directly."

He leaned one of the guns against the stone wall, and with the other under his arm, opened the gate for Pauline to pass through. They crossed the field diagonally, and came to a standstill at a spot marked by a tiny flag.

All the time Saton watched them with fascinated eyes. The thoughts were rushing through his brain. He turned to Lois.

"Dear," he said, "I think that you had better run along home. I will come up to the shrubbery after dinner, if you think that you can get out."

"But there is no hurry," she whispered. "Can't we sit here and talk for a little time, or go further back into the wood? I know a most delightful little hiding-place just at the top of the slate pit—an old keeper's shelter."

Saton shook his head. He avoided looking at her.

"The beaters are in the other part of the wood already," he said. "Very likely they will come this way, too. If they see us together, they will tell Mr. Rochester. I don't want him to know that I am here just yet."

She rose reluctantly.

"Dear me," she said, sighing, "and I thought that we were going to have such a nice long talk!"

"We will have it very soon," he whispered, a little unsteadily. "We must, dear. Remember that I have only come down here so that we may see a little more of one another. I will arrange it somehow. Only just now I think that you had better run away home."

He kissed her, and she turned reluctantly away. She stole through the undergrowth back into the green path. Saton watched her with fixed eyes until she had turned the corner and disappeared. Then he seemed at once to forget her existence. He too rose to his feet, and stole gently forward, moving very slowly, and stooping a little so as to remain out of sight. All the time his eyes were fixed upon the gun, whose barrel was shining in the sunlight.

From the other side of the wood there commenced an intermittent fusilade. The shots were drawing nearer and nearer. Rochester stood waiting, his gun held ready. Pauline had retreated round the corner of the further wood, beyond any possible line of fire.

Saton had reached the gate now, and was within reach of the gun and the bag of cartridges, which were hanging by a leather belt from the gate-post. He turned his head, and looked stealthily along the path by which Rochester had come. There was no one in sight, no sound except the twittering of birds overhead, and the rustling of the leaves. He sank on one knee, and his hand closed upon the gun. The blood surged to his head. There was a singing in his ears. He felt his heart thumping as though he were suddenly seized with some illness. Rochester's figure, tall, graceful, debonair, notwithstanding the looseness of his shooting clothes, and his somewhat rigid attitude, seemed suddenly to loom large and hateful before his eyes. He saw nothing else. He thought of nothing else. It was the man he hated. It was the man who understood what he was, the worst side of him—the man whom his instincts recognised as his ruthless and dangerous enemy.

The rush of a rabbit through the undergrowth, startled him so that he very nearly screamed. He looked around, pallid, terrified. There was no one in sight, no sign of any life save animal and insect life in the wood behind.

The stock of the gun came to his shoulder. His fingers sought the trigger. Cautiously he thrust it through the bars of the gate. Bending down, he took a long and deliberate aim. The fates seemed to be on his side. Rochester suddenly stiffened into attention, his gun came to his shoulder, as with a loud whir a pheasant flew out of the wood before him. The two reports rang out almost simultaneously. The pheasant dropped to the ground like a stone. Rochester's arms went up to the skies. He gave a little cry and fell over, a huddled heap, upon the grass.

Saton, with fingers that trembled, tore out the exploded cartridge, seized another from the bag, thrust it in, and replaced the gun against the wall. His breath was coming in little sobs. Trees and sky danced before his eyes. Once he dared to look—only once—at the spot where Rochester was lying. His hands were outstretched. Once he half raised himself, and then fell back. From round the corner of the wood came Pauline. Saton heard her cry—a cry of agony it seemed to him. He bent low, and made his way back into the plantation, plunging through the undergrowth until he reached a narrow and little frequented footpath. He was deaf to all sounds, for the thumping in his ears had become now like a sledge-hammer beating upon an anvil. He was not sure that he saw anything. His feet fled over the ground mechanically. Only when he reached the borders of the wood, and crossed the meadow leading to the main road, he drew himself a little more upright. He must remember, he told himself fiercely. He must remember!

He paused in the middle of the field, and looked back. He was out of sight now of the scene of the tragedy. Nothing was to be seen or heard but the low, musical sounds of the late summer afternoon—the beat of a reaping-machine, the humming of insects, the distant call of a pigeon, the far-away bark of a farmhouse dog. The shooting had ceased. By this time they must all know, he reflected. He lit a cigarette, and inhaled the smoke without the slightest apprehension of what he was doing. He took a book from his pocket, held it before him, and glanced at the misty page of verse. Then he made his way out on to the highroad, sauntering like a man anxious to make the most of the brilliant sunshine, the clear air.

There was no one in sight anywhere along the white, dusty way. He crossed the road, and opened another gate. A few minutes' climb, a sharp descent, and he was safe within the gate of his own abode. He looked behind. Still not a human being in sight—no sound, no note of alarm in the soft, sunlit air. He set his teeth and drew a long breath. Then he closed the gate behind him, and choosing the back way, entered the house without observation.

CHAPTER XXI

AFRAID!

Saton wondered afterwards many times at the extraordinary nonchalance with which he faced the remainder of that terrible day. He wrote several letters, and was aware that he wrote them carefully and well. He had his usual evening bath and changed his clothes, making perhaps a little more careful toilet even than usual.

Rachael, who was waiting for him when he descended to dinner, even remarked upon the lightness of his step.

"The country suits you, Bertrand," she said. "It suits you better than it does me. You walk like a boy, and there is color in your cheeks."

"The sun," he muttered. "I always tan quickly."

"Where have you been to?" she asked.

"I have been walking with Miss Champneyes," he answered.

Rachael nodded.

"And your friend at Beauleys?" she asked, with a little sneer. "What if he had seen you, eh? You are very brave, Bertrand, for he is a big man, and you are small. I do not think that he loves you, eh? But what about the girl?"

A servant entered the room, and Saton with relief abandoned the conversation. She returned to it, however, the moment they were alone.

"See here, my son," she said, "remember what I have always told you. One can do without anything in this world except money. We have plenty for the moment, it is true, but a stroke of ill-fortune, and our income might well vanish. Now listen, Bertrand. Make sure of this girl's money. She is of age, and she will marry you."

"Her guardian would never give his consent," Saton said.

"It is not necessary," his companion answered. "I have been to Somerset House. I have seen the will. One hundred thousand pounds she has, in her own right, unalienable. For the rest, let her guardian do what he will with it. With a hundred thousand pounds you can rest for a while. We might even give up——"

Saton struck the table with his clenched fist.

"Be careful," he said. "I hate to hear these things mentioned. The windows are open, and the walls are thin. There might be listeners anywhere."

Her withered lips drew back into a smile. She was not pleasant just then to look upon.

"I forgot," she muttered. "We are devotees of science now in earnest. You are right. We must run no risks. Only remember, however careful we are, you are always liable to—to the same thing that happened before. It took a thousand pounds to get you off then."

Saton rose from his seat impatiently. He walked restlessly across the room.

"Don't!" he exclaimed. "Can't we live without mentioning those things? I am nervous to-night. Hideously nervous!" he added, under his breath.

He stood before the open window, his face set, his eyes riveted upon a spot in the distance, where the great white front of Beauleys flashed out from amongst the trees. Its windows had caught the dying sunlight, and a flood of fire seemed to be burning along its front. The flag floated from the chimneys. There was no sign of any disturbance. The quiet stillness of evening which rested upon the landscape, seemed everywhere undisturbed. Yet Saton, as he looked, shivered.

Down in the lane a motor-car rushed by. His eyes followed it, fascinated. It was one of the Beauleys cars, and inside was seated a tall, spare man, white-faced and serious, on whose knees rested a black case. Saton knew in a moment that it was one of the doctors who had been summoned to Beauleys, by telephone and telegraph, from all parts.

"You are watching the house of your patron," she said, drily.

"Patron no longer!" Saton exclaimed, rolling himself another cigarette. "We are enemies, declared enemies—so far as he is concerned, at any rate."

"You are a fool!" the woman said. "He might still have been useful. You quarrel with people as though it were worth the trouble. To speak angry words is the most foolish thing I know."

Saton glanced at the clock upon the mantelpiece.

"I am going out for an hour," he said.

"To Beauleys?" she asked, mockingly.

"Somewhere near there," he answered. "Good night!"

He strolled out, hatless, and with no covering over his thin black dinner-coat. He crossed the meadow, and climbed the little range of broken, rocky hills, from which one could see down even into the flower-gardens of Beauleys. He could see there no sign of disturbance, save that there were two motor-cars before the door. Slowly he made his way to the lodge gates, and passing through approached the house. There were many lights burning. A certain repressed air of excitement was certainly visible. Saton longed, yet dared not, to ask for news from the people at the lodge. At any rate, the blinds were still up, and the doctors there. Probably the man was alive. Perhaps, even, he might recover!

He struck off from the drive, and followed a narrow path, which led at first between two great banks of rhododendrons, and finally wound a circuitous way through an old and magnificent shrubbery. He reached a path whence he could command a view of the house, and where he was himself unseen. He looked at his watch. He was five minutes late, but as yet there was no sign of Lois. He composed himself to wait, watching the birds come home to roost, and the insects, whom the heat had brought out of the earth, crawl away into oblivion. The air was sweet with the smell of flowers. From a little further afield came the more pungent odor of a fire of weeds. The great front of the house, ablaze though it was with lights, seemed almost deserted. No one entered or issued from the hall door.

Half an hour passed. There was no sign of Lois. Then he saw her come, very slowly—walking, as it seemed to him, like one afraid of the ground upon which she trod. As she came nearer, he saw that her face was ghastly pale. Her eyes, which wandered restlessly to the right and to the left, were frightened, dilated. The thing had been a shock to her, of course.

He stepped a little way out from the shrubs, showing himself cautiously. She stopped short at the sight of him.

"Lois!" he called softly.

She looked at him, and a sudden wave of terror passed across her face. She made no movement towards him. He himself was wordless, struck dumb by her appearance. She gave a little cry. What the word was that she uttered, he could not tell. Then suddenly turning round, she fled away.

He watched her with fascinated eyes, watched her feet fly over the lawns, watched her, without a single backward glance, vanish at last through the small side door from which she had first issued. He wiped the moisture from his forehead, and a little sob broke from his throat. The vision of her face was still before him. He knew for a certainty what it was that had terrified her. She had started to keep her engagement, but she was afraid. She was afraid of him. Something that he had done had betrayed him. She knew! His liberty—perhaps his life—was in this girl's hands!

He crept out of the shrubbery and staggered down the drive, making his way homeward across the hills as swiftly as his uncertain footsteps would take him. It was dusk now, and he met no one. Yet his heart beat at every sound— the clanking of a chain, attached to the fetlock of a wandering horse, the still, mournful cry of an owl which floated out from the plantation, the clatter of the small stones which his own feet dislodged as he feverishly climbed the rocks. Above him, on the other side of the road, towered the hill where he had sat and dreamed as a boy, where Rochester had come and encouraged him to prate of his ambitions.

He looked away from its dark outline with a little groan. Up on the hillside flashed the lights of Blackbird's Nest. He stretched out his hands and groped onwards.

CHAPTER XXII

SATON REASSERTS HIMSELF

Rochester asked only one question during those few days when he lay between life and death. He opened his eyes suddenly, and motioned to the doctor to stoop down.

"Who shot me?" he asked.

"It was an accident," the doctor assured him, soothingly.

Rochester said no more, but his lips seemed to curl for a moment into the old disbelieving smile. Then the struggle began. In a week it was over. A magnificent constitution, and an unshattered nerve, triumphed. The doctors one by one took their departure. Their task was over. Rochester would recover.

"Who shot me?"

The doctor had seen no reason to keep silence, and this question of Rochester's had created something like a sensation as it travelled backwards and forwards. Rochester had been shot in the left side, in the middle of a field, where no accident of his own causing seemed possible. One barrel only of his gun had been fired, and to account for that a cock pheasant lay dead within a few feet of him. The shooting-party were all old and experienced sportsmen. The gun which Rochester had left leaning against the gate was discovered exactly as he had left it there, loaded in both barrels. There was not the ghost of a clue.

Only Lois kept to her room for three days, until she could bear it no longer. Then she walked out a little way toward the woods, and met Saton. He recognised her with a shock. He himself, especially now it was known that Rochester would live, had rapidly recovered from the fit of horrors which had seized him on that night. It was not so with Lois. Her cheeks were ghastly pale, and her eyes beringed. She walked like one recovering from a long illness, and when she saw Saton she screamed.

He held out his hand, and noticed with swift comprehension her first instinctive withdrawal.

"Bertrand!" she cried. "Oh, Bertrand!"

"What do you mean?" he asked, hoarsely.

"You know what I mean," she answered. "I don't want to touch you, but I must or I shall fall. Let me take your arm. We will go and sit down."

They sat side by side on the trunk of a fallen tree. A small stream rippled by at their feet. The meadow which it divided was dotted everywhere with little clumps of large yellow buttercups. She sat at a little distance from him, and she kept her eyes averted.

"Bertrand," she murmured, "what does it mean? Tell me what I saw that afternoon. You took up the gun. Was it an accident? But no," she added, "it is absurd to ask that!"

"You saw me?" he exclaimed quickly. "You believe that you saw me touch that gun?"

She nodded.

"I hated to go and leave you there," she said. "I waited about behind those thick blackthorn trees, hoping that you might come my way. I saw you creep up to the gun. I saw you raise it to your shoulder. Even then I had no idea what you were going to do. Afterwards I saw the smoke and the flash. I heard the report, and Mr. Rochester's cry as he fell. I saw you slip a fresh cartridge into the gun, and go stealing away. Bertrand, I have not slept since. Tell me, was it a nightmare?"

"It was no nightmare," he answered. "I shot him, and I wish that he had died!"

She looked at him with horror.

"Bertrand," she faltered, "you can't mean it!"

"Little Lois," he answered, "I do. You do not understand what hatred is. You do not understand all that it may mean—all that it may cause. He is my enemy, that man, and I am his. It is a duel between us, a duel to the death. The first blow has been mine, and I have failed. You will see that it will not be long before he strikes back."

"But this is horrible!" she muttered.

"Horrible to you, of course!" he exclaimed. "Hatred is a thing of which you can know nothing. And yet there it is. People might think that he was my benefactor. He gave me money to go out and find my level in the world, gave it to me with the bitter, cynical advice—advice that was almost a stipulation—that if I failed, I ceased to live. I did fail in every honest thing I touched," he continued, bitterly. "Then I tried a bold experiment. It was the last thing offered, the last wonderful chance. I took it, and I won. Then I returned. I paid him back the money which he had lent me—I did my best to seem grateful. It was of no use. He mistrusted me from the first. In his own house I was the butt for his scornful speeches. I was even bidden to leave. I ventured to speak to the woman with whom he is slavishly in love, and he came to me like a fury. If I had been a hairdresser posing as a duke, he could not have been more violent. He wanted me to promise never to speak to her again—her or you. I refused. Then he declared war, and, Lois, there are weak joints in my armor. You see, I admit it to you—never to him. When he finds his way there, he will thrust. That is why I struck first."

She shook her head sadly.

"Ah, but I do not understand!" she said. "He is very stern and very quiet, but he is a just man. I have never known him to find fault where there was none."

"There are faults enough in my life," Saton answered. "I have never denied it. But I have had to fight with my back to the wall. I shall win. I am not afraid of a thousand Mr. Rochesters. I am gathering to my hands—no, I will not talk to you about that! Lois, I am more anxious about you than Mr. Rochester. I am afraid that you will hate me for always now."

"No!" she said. "I cannot do that, I cannot hate you. But I do not wish to see you any more. As long as I live, I shall see you kneeling there, with your finger upon the trigger of that gun. I shall see the flash, I shall see him throw up his hands and fall. It was hideous!"

Saton passed his hand across his forehead. Her words had touched his keen imagination. The horror of the scene was upon him, too, once more.

"Don't!" he begged—"don't! Lois!"

"Well?" she asked.

"You will not speak of this to anyone?"

"No!" she answered, sadly, leaning a little forward, with her head resting upon her clasped hands. "I don't suppose that I shall. If he had died, it would have been different. Now that he is going to get well, I suppose I shall try to forget."

"To forget," he murmured, trying to take her hand.

She drew it away with a shiver.

"No!" she said. "That is finished. I had to see you. I had to talk to you. Go away, please. I cannot bear to see you any more. It is too terrible—too terrible!"

A born cajoler of women, he forced into play all his powers. He whispered a flood of words in her ear. His own voice shook, his eyes were soft. He pleaded as one beside himself. Lois—Lois whom he had found so sensitive, so easily moved, so gently affectionate—remained like a stone. At the end of all his pleadings she simply looked away.

"Do you mind," she asked, "leaving me? Please! Please!"

He got up and went. Defeat was apparent enough, although it was unexpected. Lois stole back to the house—stole back to her room and locked the door.

Saton walked home across the hills, with white face and set eyes. He looked neither to the right nor to the left, and when he arrived at Blackbird's Nest, he walked straight into the long, old-fashioned room on the ground floor, which he called his library, and where Rachael generally sat.

She was there, crouching over the fire, when he entered, and looked around with frowning face.

"Bertrand," she said, "I hate this country life. Even the sunshine mocks. There is no warmth in it, and the winds are cold. I must have warmth. I shall stay here no longer."

He threw a log on to the fire, and turned around.

"Listen," he said. "The girl Lois Champneyes—I have lost my hold of her. She knows something about the accident to Rochester."

"Bungler!" the woman muttered. "Go on. Tell me how you lost your power."

"I cannot tell," he answered. "I was in an unsettled mood. I think that I was a little afraid. She spoke of that afternoon. It all came back to me. I am sure that I was afraid," he added, passing his hand across his forehead.

She leaned toward him and her eyes glittered, hard and bright, from their parchment-like setting.

"Bertrand," she said, "you talk like a coward. What are you going to do?"

"To bring her here," he answered hoarsely. "She has gone back to Beauleys. She is passing up through the plantation, on her way to the house, perhaps, at this very moment. She wore white, and she carried her hat in her hand. There were rims under her eyes. She walks slowly. She is afraid—a little hysterical. You see her?"

He pointed out of the window. The woman nodded.

"Sit down," she muttered. "We shall see."

He sank into a low chair, with his face turned toward the window. No further words passed between them. They sat there till the sun sank behind the hills, and the dusk began to cast shadows over the land.

A servant came and said something about dinner. Rachael waved her away.

"In an hour, or an hour and a half," she said.

The shadows grew deeper. Rachael's face seemed unchanged, but Saton had grown so pale that his fixed eyes seemed to have become unnaturally large. Sometimes his lips moved, though the sounds which he uttered never resolved themselves into speech. At last Rachael rose to her feet. She pointed out of the window. Saton gave a little gasp.

"She is there?" he asked, breathlessly.

"She comes," Rachael answered. "See that you do not lose your power again. I am exhausted. I am going to rest."

She passed out of the room. Saton went and stood before the low window. Slowly, and with hesitating footsteps, Lois came up the path, lifted the latch of the little gate, and stood in the garden, close to a tall group of hollyhocks.

Saton went out to her.

"You have come to tell me that you are sorry?" he said.

"Yes!" she answered.

"You did not mean what you said?"

"No!"

"Come in," he whispered.

He laid his fingers upon her hand, and she followed him into the room. She was very pale, and she was breathing as though she had been running. He passed his arm around her waist.

"You are not angry with me any longer?" he whispered in her ear. "You will kiss me?"

"If you wish," she answered.

He looked into her eyes for a moment. Then he took her into his arms.

"Dear Lois," he whispered, "you must never be so unkind to me again."

CHAPTER XXIII

AN UNPLEASANT ENCOUNTER

Rochester and Pauline were driving through the country lanes in a small, old-fashioned pony carriage. Westward, the clouds were still stained by a brilliant sunset. The air was clear and brisk, chill with the invigorating freshness of the autumn evening. Already the stillness had come, the stillness which is the herald of night. The laborers had deserted the fields, the wind had dropped, a pleasant smell of burning weeds from a bonfire by the side of the road crept into the air. The silence was broken for a moment by the cry of a lonely bird, drifting homewards on wings that seemed almost motionless.

Rochester was quite convalescent now, and with the aid of a stick was able to walk almost as far as he chose. Pauline had remained at Beauleys, and her presence had divested those last few weeks of all their irksomeness. He stole a glance at her as she leaned back in the carriage. She was a little pale, perhaps, and her eyes were thoughtful, but the lines of her mouth were soft. There was no shadow of unhappiness in her face, none of that look which in London had driven him almost to madness.

His fingers closed upon hers. They were walking uphill, and the pony took little guiding.

"You are sure, Pauline," he asked, "that you are not bored yet with the country?"

"I am quite sure," she answered.

Something in her tone puzzled him. He looked at her again, long and fixedly. Her eyes met his, they answered his unspoken question.

"I suppose," she said, "that I should look happier. I have been content. I am content still. I suppose it is all one ought to expect from life."

"There are other things," he answered, "but not for us, Pauline—not yet."

"Life is a very perplexing matter," she declared.

He shook his head.

"There is no perplexity about it," he declared. "Its riddle is easily enough solved. The trouble is that the fetters which bind us are sometimes beyond our power to break."

"If we were free," she murmured, "you and I know very well whither we should turn. And yet, Henry, are you sure, are you quite, quite sure that there is nothing in life greater even than love?"

"If there is," he answered, "we will go in search of it, hand in hand, you and I together."

"Yes," she echoed simply, "we will go in search of it. But first of all we must find someone to light our torch."

He shook the reins a little impatiently, but they were not yet at the top of the hill, and the pony crawled on, undisturbed.

"Dear Pauline," he said, "sometimes lately I fancied that you have seemed a little morbid. I have lived longer than you. I have lived long enough to be sure of one thing."

"And that is?" she asked.

"That all real happiness," he said, "even the everyday forms of content, is to be found amongst the simple truths of life. Love is the greatest of them. Look at me, Pauline. Don't you think that even though we live our lives apart, don't you think that to me the world is a different place when you are near?"

She looked into his face a little wistfully. Then she let her hand rest on his.

"You are so steadfast," she said—"so strong, and so certain of yourself. Forgive me if I seem a little restless. One loses one's balance sometimes, thinking and thinking and wondering."

They were at the top of the hill, and the pony paused. Rochester stepped out.

"Come," he said, "I will take you for a little walk. We will leave Peter here."

He unlocked a gate with a key which he took from his pocket, and hand in hand they ascended a steep path which led between a grove of pine trees. Out once more into the open, they crossed a patch of green turf and came to another gate, set in a stone wall. This also Rochester opened. A few more yards, and they climbed up to the masses of tumbled rock which lay about on the summit of the hill.

"Turn round," he said. "You have seen this view many a time in the daylight. You can see it now fading away into nothingness."

They stood hand in hand, looking downwards. Mists rose from along the side of the river, and stood about in the valleys. The lights began to twinkle here and there. Afar off, like some nursery toy, they saw a train, with its line of white smoke, go stealing across the shadowy landscape.

Rochester's face darkened with a sudden reminiscence.

"It was here," he said, "that I first saw your friend the charlatan."

"My friend?" she murmured.

"More yours than mine, at any rate," he answered. "He sat with his back against that rock, and if ever hunger was written into a boy's face, it was there in his pale cheeks, burning in his eyes."

"He was very poor, then?" she asked.

"He was very poor," Rochester answered, "but it was not hunger for food, it was hunger for life that one saw there. He had been down at the Convalescent Home, recovering from some illness, and the next day he was going back to his work—work which he hated, which made him part of a machine. You know how many millions there are who live and die like that— who must always live and die like that. They are part of the great system of the world, and nine-tenths of them are content."

"You set him free," she murmured.

"I did," Rochester answered. "It was a mistake."

"You cannot tell," she said. "I know that you mistrust him. You are very, very English, dear Henry, and you have so little sympathy with those things which you do not understand—which do come, perhaps, a little near what you call charlatanism. Still, though you may deny it as much as you like, there are many, many things in the world—things, even, in connection with our daily lives, which are absolutely, wonderfully mysterious. There are new things to be learned, Henry. Bertrand Saton may be a self-deceiver. He may even deserve all the hard things you can say of him, but there are cleverer people than you and I who do not think so."

"Dear," Rochester answered, "I did not bring you here to talk of Bertrand Saton. To tell you the truth," he added, "I even hate to hear his name upon your lips."

There was no time for her to answer. From the shadow of the rock against which they leaned, he rose with a subtle alertness which seemed somehow a little uncanny—as though, indeed, he had risen from under the ground upon which they stood.

"I heard my name," he said. "Forgive me if I am interrupting you. I had no wish to play the eavesdropper."

Pauline took a quick step backwards. Even in that tense moment of surprise, Rochester found himself able to notice the color fading from her cheeks. He turned upon the newcomer, and there was something like fury in his tone.

"What the devil are you doing here, Saton?" he asked.

Saton's tone was almost apologetic.

"I did not know," he said, "that I was forbidden to walk upon your lands. I am often here, and this is my favorite hour."

Rochester laughed, a little harshly.

"You like to come back," he said. "You like to sit here, perhaps, and think. Well, I do not envy you. You sat here and thought, years ago. You built a house of dreams here, unless you lied. You come here now, perhaps, to compare it with the house of gewgaws which you have built, and in which you dwell."

Saton did not for a moment shrink. In his heart he felt that it was one of his inspired moments. There was confidence alike in his bearing and in his gentle reply.

"Why not?" he asked. "Why should you take it for granted that there is so much amiss in my life, that I have fallen so far away from those dreams? It may not be so," he continued. "Remember that the man who lives, and comes a little nearer toward knowledge, has nothing to be ashamed of. It is the man who lives, and eats and drinks and sleeps, and knows no more when his head presses the pillow at night than when the sun woke him in the morning, it is that man who is ignoble. You have spoken of the past," he added, turning face to face with Rochester. "Once more I will remind you of your own words. *The only crime in life is failure. If the crash comes, and the pieces lie around you, swim out to sea too far, and sink beneath the waves forever!* Wasn't that your advice? Not your exact words, perhaps, but wasn't that what you told the boy who sat here and dreamed?"

Rochester shrugged his shoulders slightly.

"Youth," he said, "may be forgiven much. Manhood must accept its own responsibilities."

Saton smiled grimly.

"Always the same," he said. "All the time you play with the truth, Rochester, as though it were a glass ball committed into your keeping, and yours alone. Don't you know that the one inspired period of life is youth—youth before it is sullied with experience, youth which knows everything, fears nothing— youth which has the eyes of the clairvoyant?"

Rochester frowned.

"Your tongue goes glibly to-night," he remarked. "Talk to the shadows, my friend. Lady Marrabel and I are going."

"I did not bid you come," Saton answered. "This is my spot, and my hour. It was you who intruded."

"The fact that this is my property——" Rochester began, gently.

"Is of no consequence," Saton answered. "You may buy the earth upon which we stand, but you cannot buy the person whose feet shall press it, or the thoughts that rise up from it, or the words that are breathed from it, or the hopes and passions which go trembling from it to the skies. Go away and jog homeward behind your fat pony, but——"

"Well, sir?" Rochester asked, turning suddenly.

Saton's eyes did not meet his. They were fixed upon Pauline's, and Pauline was as white as death.

"I take her, too, if you will," Saton said slowly. "Take her, too, if she will go."

"I am going this instant," Pauline cried, with a sudden nervous passion in her tone. "Come, Henry, come away. I hate this place. Come away quickly."

Rochester caught her hand. It was cold as a stone. She was pale, and she commenced to tremble.

"Take her," Saton said, "if she will go. Take her, because you are strong and she is weak. Lead her by the arm, guide her as you will, only be sure that you leave nothing with me."

He sat down upon the rock, and with folded arms looked away from them— even as though they had not existed—across to the world of shadows and vague places. Rochester passed his arm through Pauline's, and led her down the hill. Her hands were cold. She seemed to lift her feet as though they had been of lead. She did not look at him. Always she looked ahead. She moved slowly and heavily. When he spoke, her lips answered him languidly. Rochester felt an intense and passionate anger burning in his veins. The vague disquiet of an hour ago had settled down into something definite. She was his no longer! Something had come between them! Even though he might take her into his arms, might hold her there, and dare anyone in the world to take her from him, it was her body only, the shadow of herself. Something—some part of her seemed to have flitted away. He asked himself with a sudden cold horror, whether indeed it had remained by the side of that silent figure, blotted out now from sight, who sat upon the rocks while the darkness fell about him!

CHAPTER XXIV

LOIS IS OBEDIENT

Lois and her companion stopped on the summit of the hill to look at the rolling background of woods, brilliant still with their autumn coloring. The west wind had blown her hair into disorder, but it had blown also the color back into her cheeks. Her eyes were bright, and her laughter infectious. Her companion stooped down and passed his arm through hers, looking into her face admiringly.

"Lois," he said, "this is the first day I have seen you like your old self. I can't tell you how glad I am."

She smiled.

"I wasn't aware, Maurice," she said, "that I have been very different. I have had headaches now and then, lately. Fancy having a headache an afternoon like this!" she added, throwing back her head once more, and breathing in the fresh, invigorating air.

"You ought to have seen a doctor," her companion declared. "I told Lady Mary so the other day."

"Rubbish!" Lois exclaimed, lightly.

"Nothing of the sort," Captain Vandermere replied. "I was beginning to worry about you. I almost fancied——"

"Well?"

"It almost seemed," he continued, a little awkwardly, "as though you had something on your mind. You seemed so queer every now and then, little girl," he added, "I do hope that if there was anything bothering you, you'd tell me all about it. We're old pals, you know."

She laughed—not quite naturally.

"My dear Maurice," she said, "of course there has been nothing of that sort the matter with me! What could I have on my mind?"

"No love affairs, eh?" he asked, stroking his fair moustache.

She shook her head thoughtfully.

"No!" she said. "No love affairs."

He tightened his grasp upon her arm. He had an idea that he was being very diplomatic indeed. And Lady Mary had begged him to find out whatever was the matter with poor dear Lois!

"Well," he said, "I am glad to hear it. To tell you the truth, I have been very jealous lately."

"You jealous!" she exclaimed, mockingly.

"Fact, I assure you," he answered.

"Captain Maurice Vandermere jealous!" she repeated, looking up at him with dancing eyes—"absolutely the most popular bachelor in London! And jealous of me, too!"

"Is that so very wonderful, Lois?" he asked. "We have been pretty good friends, you know."

She felt his hand upon her arm, and she looked away.

"Yes," she said, "we have been friends, only we haven't seen much of one another the last month or so, have we?"

"It hasn't been my fault," he declared. "I really couldn't get leave before, although I tried hard. I shouldn't have been here now, to tell you the truth, Lois," he went on, "but Lady Mary's been frightening me a bit."

"About me?" Lois asked.

"About you," he assented.

"What has she been saying?"

"Well, nothing definite," Captain Vandermere answered, "but of course you know she's an awful good pal of mine, and she did write me a line or two about you. It seems there's some young fellow been about down here whom she isn't very stuck on, and she seemed to be afraid——"

"Well, go on," Lois said calmly.

"Well, that he was making the running with you a bit," Captain Vandermere declared, feeling that he was getting into rather deeper waters. "Of course, I don't know anything about him, and I don't want to say anything against anybody who is a friend of yours, but from all that I have heard he didn't seem to me to be the sort of man I fancied for my little friend Lois to get—well, fond of."

"So you decided to come down yourself," Lois continued.

"I decided to come down and say something which I ought to have said some time ago," Captain Vandermere continued, "only you see you are really only a child, and you've got a lot more money than I have, and you are not of age yet, so I thought I'd let it be for a bit. But you know I'm fond of you, Lois."

"Are you?" she asked, artlessly.

"You must know that," he continued, bending over her. "I wonder——"

"Are you aware that we are standing on the top of a hill," Lois said, "and that everybody for a good many miles round has a perfectly clear view of us?"

"I don't care where we are," he declared. "I have got to go on now. Lois, will you marry me?"

"Is this a proposal?" She laughed nervously.

"Sounds like it," he admitted.

She was silent for several moments. Into her eyes there had come something of that look which had sent Lady Mary into her room to write to Captain Vandermere, and bid him come without delay. The color had gone. She seemed suddenly older—tired.

"Oh, I don't know!" she said. "I think I should like to, but I can't!—no, I can't!"

They began to descend the hill. He kept his arm in hers.

"Why not?" he asked. "Don't you care for me?"

"I—I don't know," she answered. "I don't know whether I care for anybody. Wait, please. Don't speak to me for several moments."

Their path skirted the side of a ploughed field, and then through a little gate they passed into a long, straggling plantation. Directly she was under the shelter of the trees, she burst into tears.

"Don't come near me," she begged. "Leave me alone for a moment. I shall be better directly."

He disregarded her bidding to the extent of placing his arm around her waist. He made no attempt, however, to draw her hands away from her face, or stop her tears.

"Little girl," he said, "I knew that there was some trouble. It is there in your dear, innocent little face for anyone to see who cares enough about you to look. When you have dried those eyes, you must tell me all about it. Remember that even if you won't have me for a husband, we are old enough friends for you to look upon me as an elder brother."

She dried her eyes, and looked up at him with a hopeless little smile.

"You are a dear," she said, "and I am very fond of you. I don't know what's happened to me—at least I do know, but I can't tell anyone."

"Is it," he asked gravely, "that you care about this person?"

"Oh, I don't know!" she answered. "I hope not. I don't know, I'm sure. Sometimes I feel that I do, and sometimes, when I am sane, when I am in my right mind, I know that I do not. Maurice," she begged, "help me. Please help me."

His face cleared.

"I'll help you right enough, little girl," he answered. "Just listen to me. I'm not going to see you throw yourself away upon an outsider. Just remember that. On the other hand, I'm not going to bother you to death. Here I am by your side, and here I mean to stay. If that—no, I won't call him names!" he said, stopping short in his sentence—"but if anyone tries to make you unhappy, well, I shall have something to say. Come along, let's finish our walk. We'll talk about something else if you like."

She drew a little sigh of relief.

"You are a dear, Maurice," she repeated. "Come along, we'll go down the lane and over the hills home. I do feel safe, somehow, with you," she added, impulsively. "You are not going away just yet, are you?"

"Not for a fortnight, at any rate," he answered.

"And you won't leave me alone?" she begged—"not even if I ask to be left alone? You see—I can't make you understand—but I don't even trust myself."

He laughed reassuringly.

"I'll look after you, never fear," he answered. "I'll be better than a watchdog. Tell me, what's your handicap at golf now? We must have a game to-morrow."

They walked down the lane, talking—in a somewhat subdued manner, perhaps, but easily enough—upon lighter subjects. And then at the corner, just as they had passed the entrance to Blackbird's Nest, they came face to face with Saton. Vandermere felt her suddenly creep closer to him, as though for protection, and from his six feet odd of height, he frowned angrily at the young man with his hat in his hand preparing to accost them. Never was dislike more instinctive and hearty. Vandermere, an ordinarily intelligent but unimaginative Englishman, of the normally healthy type, a sportsman, a good fellow, and a man of breeding—and Saton, this strange product of strange circumstances, externally passable enough, but with something about him which seemed, even in that clear November sunshine, to suggest the footlights.

"You are quite a stranger, Miss Champneyes," Saton said, taking her unresisting hand in his. "I hope that you are going in to see the Comtesse. Only this morning she told me that she was finding it appallingly lonely."

"I—I wasn't calling anywhere this afternoon," Lois said timidly. "Captain Vandermere has come down to stay with us for a few days, and I was showing him the country. This is Mr. Saton—Captain Vandermere. I don't know whether you remember him."

The two men exchanged the briefest of greetings. Saton's was civil enough. Vandermere's was morose, almost discourteous.

"Let me persuade you to change your mind," Saton said, speaking slowly, and with his eyes fixed upon Lois. "The Comtesse would be so disappointed if she knew that you had passed this way and had not entered."

Vandermere was conscious that in some way the girl by his side was changed. She drew a little away from him.

"Very well," she said, "I shall be pleased to go in and see her. You do not mind, Maurice?"

"Not at all," he answered. "If I may be allowed, I will come with you."

There was a moment's silence. Then Saton spoke—quietly, regretfully.

"I am so sorry," he said, "but the Comtesse de Vestinges—my adopted mother," he explained, with a little bow—"receives no one. She is old, and her health is not of the best. A visit from Miss Champneyes always does her good."

Lois looked up at her companion.

"Perhaps," she said, "you will have a cigarette in the lane."

"I am sorry to seem inhospitable," Saton said smoothly. "If Captain Vandermere will come up to the house, my study is at his service, and I can give him some cigarettes which I think he would find passable."

"Thank you," Vandermere answered, a little gruffly, "I'll wait out here. Remember, Lois," he added, turning towards her, "that we are expected home to play bridge directly after tea."

"I will not be long," she answered.

She moved off with Saton, turning round with a little farewell nod to Vandermere as they passed through the gate. He took a quick step towards her. Was it his fancy, or was there indeed appeal in the quick glance which she had thrown him? Then directly afterwards, while he hesitated, he heard her laugh. Reluctantly he gave up the idea of following them, and swinging himself onto a gate, sat watching the two figures climbing the field toward the house.

CHAPTER XXV

A LAST WARNING

The laugh which checked Vandermere in his first intention of following Lois and Saton up the field, was scarcely a mirthful effort. Saton had bent toward his companion, and his tone had been almost threatening.

"You must not look at anyone like that while I am with you," he said. "You must not look as though you were frightened of me. You must seem amused. You must laugh."

She obeyed. It was a poor effort, but it sounded natural enough in the distance.

"Come," Saton continued, "you are not very kind to me, Lois. You are not very kind to the man whom you are going to marry, whom you have said that you love. It has been very lonely these last few days, Lois. You have not come to me. I have watched for you often."

"I could not come," she answered. "Lady Mary has been with me all the time. I think that she suspects."

"Surely you are clever enough," he answered, "to outwit a little simpleton like that. Has Rochester been interfering?"

"If he knew that I even spoke to you," she answered, "I think that he would send me away."

"It is not kind of them," he said, "to be so bitter against me."

She shrank from him.

"If they knew!" she said. "If they only knew that I even thought of marrying you, or—or—"

Saton shrugged his shoulders.

"Ah, well," he said, "they know as much as it is well for them to know! After all, you see, no harm has happened to your guardian. I saw him to-day, on his way home from hunting. He looked strong and well enough. Tell me, Lois," he continued, "has he had any visitors from London the last few days? I don't mean guests—I mean people to see him on business?"

"Not that I know of," she answered. "Why?"

Saton's face darkened.

"It is he, I am sure," he said, "who is interfering in my concerns. Never mind, Lois, we will not talk about that, dear. Give me your hand. We are engaged, you know. You should be glad to have these few minutes with me."

Her fingers which he clasped were like ice. He was puzzled at her attitude.

"A month ago," he said softly, "you did not find it such a hardship to spend a little time alone with me."

"A month ago," she answered, "I had not seen you on your knees with a gun, seen your white face, heard the report, and seen Mr. Rochester fall. I had not seen you steal away through the bracken. Oh, it was terrible! You looked like a murderer! I shall never, never forget it."

He laughed softly.

"These things are fancies," he said—"dreams. You will forget them, my dear Lois. You will forget them very soon."

They entered the house, and in the hall he drew her into his arms. She wrenched herself free, and crouched back in the corner, with her hands stretched out in front of her face.

"Don't!" she cried. "Don't! If you kiss me, I shall go mad. Can't you see that I don't want to come with you, that I don't want to be with you? You shall let me go! You must let me go!"

He stood frowning a few feet away. To tell the truth, he was honestly puzzled at her attitude. At last, with a little shrug of the shoulders, he threw open the door of the sitting-room.

"Rachael," he said, "Lois has come to see you for a few minutes."

Lois went timidly into the room. Rachael, with a shawl around her shoulders, was sitting in front of a huge fire. She turned her head and held out her long withered hand, as usual covered with rings.

"Sit opposite me, child. Let me look at you."

Lois sat down, gazing with fascinated eyes at the woman whose presence she found almost as terrifying as the presence of Saton himself.

"My son—I call Bertrand my son," she said, "because I have adopted him, and because everything I have, even my name if he will have it—will be his— my son, then, tells me that he has not seen you for several days."

"It is very difficult," Lois said, trembling.

"Why?" Rachael asked.

"My guardian, Mr. Rochester, does not allow Bertrand to come to the house," Lois said, hesitatingly, "and Lady Mary tries not to let me come out alone."

Rachael nodded her head slowly, her eyes glittered in the firelight. Wrapped in her black shawl, she looked like some quaint effigy—something scarcely human.

"Your guardian and his wife," she said, "are foolish, ignorant people. They do not understand such men as Bertrand. You will understand him, child. You will know him better when he is your husband, know him better, and be proud of him. Is it not so?"

"I—I suppose so," Lois said.

"I am glad that you came this afternoon," Rachael continued. "Bertrand and I have been talking. We think it well that you should be married very soon."

"I am not of age," Lois said, breathlessly.

"It does not matter," Rachael declared. "Your guardian can keep back your money, but that is of no consequence. It will come to you in time, and Bertrand has plenty himself. I am afraid that they might try and tempt you to be faithless to my son. You are very young and impressionable, and though I do not doubt but that you are fond of him, it is not easy to be faithful when you are alone, and with such people as Mr. Rochester and Lady Mary. I am going to London in a few days. I think it would be well if you went with me. Bertrand could get a special license, and you could be married at once."

"No!" she shrieked. "No! No!"

Rachael said nothing. Her lips moved, but no sound came. Only her eyes flashed unutterable things.

Upon the somewhat hysterical silence came the sound of Saton's voice—cold, decisive.

"Lois," he said, "what my mother has advised would make me very happy. Will you remember that I wish it? Will you remember that?"

"Yes!" she faltered.

"I shall make you a good husband," he added, coming a little nearer to her, sinking on one knee by her side, and taking her cold, unresisting hands into his. "I shall make you a good husband, and I think that you will be happy.

We cannot go on like this. I only see you now by stealth. It must come to an end."

"Yes!" she faltered.

"Next time we meet," he continued, "I will tell you what plans we have made."

She turned her head slowly, and looked at him with frightened, wide-open eyes.

"Why?" she asked. "Why do you want me to marry you? You do not care for me. You do not care for me at all. Is it because I am rich? But you—you are rich yourselves. I would offer you my money, but you cannot want that."

He smiled enigmatically.

"No!" he said. "Money is a good thing, but we have money ourselves. Don't you believe, Lois," he added, bending towards her, "that I am fond of you?"

"Oh! yes," she answered, "if you say so!"

"Of course I say so!" he declared. "I am very fond of you indeed, or I should not want to marry you. Come, I think that you had better say good-bye to my mother now. Your friend outside will be tired of waiting."

She rose to her feet, and he led her from the room. They walked down the field side by side, and Lois felt her knees trembling. She was white as a sheet, and once she was obliged to clutch his arm for support. As they neared the gate, they saw that Vandermere was talking to someone on horseback. Saton's face darkened as he recognised the tall figure. His first impulse was to stop, but with Lois by his side he saw at once that it was impossible. With the courage that waits upon the inevitable, he opened the gate and passed out into the lane.

"Good afternoon, Miss Champneyes!" he said, holding out his hand. "It was very good of you to come in and visit the Comtesse. She is always so glad indeed to see you."

The girl's fingers lay for a moment icy cold within his. Then she turned with a little breath of relief to Vandermere. They walked off together.

Rochester signalled with his whip to Saton to wait for a moment. As soon as the other two were out of earshot, he leaned down from his saddle.

"My young friend," he said, "it seems to me that you are wilfully disregarding my warning."

"I was not aware," Saton answered, "that Miss Champneyes was a prisoner in your house, nor do I see how I am to be held responsible for her call upon the Comtesse."

"We will not bandy words," Rochester said. "I have no wish to quarrel with you, but I want you always to remember the things which I have said. Lois Champneyes is very nearly of age, it is true, but she remains a child by disposition and temperament. As her guardian, I want you to understand that I forbid you to continue your friendship or even your acquaintance with her!"

The quiet contempt of Rochester's words stung Saton into a moment of fury.

"What sort of a creature am I, then," he exclaimed, "that you should think me unworthy even to speak to your ward, or to the women of your household? You treat me as though I were a criminal, or worse!"

Rochester tapped his riding boot with the end of his whip. Saton watched him with fascinated eyes. There seemed something a little ominous in the action, in the sight of that gently moving whip, held so firmly in the long, sinewy fingers.

"What you are," Rochester said, leaning a little down from his horse, "you know and I know. Let that be enough. Only remember that there comes a time when threats cease, and actions commence. And as sure as you and I are met here together this evening, Saton, I tell you that if you offend again in this matter, I shall punish you. You understand?"

Rochester swung his horse round and cantered down the lane. Saton stood looking after him with white, angry face and clenched hands.

CHAPTER XXVI

THE DUCHESS'S DINNER PARTY

The Duchess welcomed the little party from Beauleys in person, and with more than ordinary warmth.

"I am glad to see you all, of course," she said, "but I am really delighted to see you about again, Henry. Do tell me, now. I have heard so many contradictory reports. Did you shoot yourself, or was it one of your guests who did it? I don't know how it is, but poor Ronald always says that the men one asks to shoot, nowadays, hit everything except the birds."

"My dear Duchess," Rochester answered, "I certainly did not shoot myself. I have every confidence in my guests, and so far as we have been able to ascertain, there wasn't another soul in the neighborhood. Shall we say that I was shot by the act of God? There really doesn't seem to be any other explanation."

The Duchess was not altogether satisfied.

"To-night I am going to offer you a great privilege," she said. "I am going to give you a chance of finding out the answer to your riddle."

Rochester looked perplexed, and Lady Mary blandly curious. Pauline alone seemed as though by instinct to realize what lay beneath their hostess's words. Her face seemed suddenly to grow tense. She shrank back—a slight, involuntary movement, but significant enough under the circumstances.

"An answer to my riddle," Rochester remarked, smiling. "Really, I did not know that I had propounded one."

"Only a moment ago," the Duchess reminded him, "you spoke of being shot by the act of God. That, of course, was a form of speech. You meant that you did not know who did it. Perhaps we shall be able to solve that little mystery for you."

Rochester looked at his hostess as though for a moment he doubted her sanity. Tall and slim in his immaculate clothes, standing before the great wood fire which burned in the open grate, he leaned a little forward upon his stick, with knitted brows. Then his eyes caught Pauline's, and something which he was about to say seemed to die away upon his lips.

"Of course, you are unbelievers, all of you," the Duchess said, calmly, "but some day—perhaps even to-night—you may become converts. Did I tell you, Mary," she continued, turning away from Rochester, "that I met that extraordinary man Naudheim in London? He told me so many interesting things, and since then I have been reading. He introduced me to—to one of his most brilliant pupils—a young man, he assured me, whose insight was more highly developed, even, than his own. Of course, you understand that in these matters, insight and perception take the place almost of brains."

"My dear Duchess," Rochester interrupted, "what are you talking about?"

"The new science," the Duchess answered, with a note of triumph in her tone. "You will learn all about it some day, and you cannot begin too soon. The young man whom Professor Naudheim spoke so highly of is dining here to-night. Curiously enough, I found that he was almost a neighbor of both of ours."

There was an instant's silence. Pauline, who was prepared, was now perhaps the calmest of the trio. Rochester's face was dark with anger.

"You refer, Duchess, I suppose," he said—

The Duchess left him unceremoniously. She took a step or two forward with outstretched hands. The butler was announcing—

"Mr. Saton!"

The dinner was as successful as the Duchess's country dinners always were. She herself, a hostess of renown, led the conversation at her end of the table. Like all women with a new craze, she conscientiously did her best to keep it in the background, and completely failed. Before the third course had been removed, she was discussing occultism with the bishop of the diocese. Rochester, from her other side, listened with a thin smile. She turned upon him suddenly.

"Oh, I know that you're an unbeliever!" she said. "You're one of those people who go through life doubting everything. You shan't have him for an ally, Bishop," she said, "because your points of view are entirely different. Henry here doubts everything, from his own existence to the vintage of my champagne. You, on the other hand," she added, turning toward her other companion, "are forced to disbelieve, because you feel that any new power or gift that may be granted to us, and which we discover for ourselves, is opposed, of course, to your creed."

"It depends," the bishop remarked, "upon the nature of that power."

"Even in its elementary stages," the Duchess said, "there is no doubt that it is a power which can do a great deal for us towards solving the mysteries of existence. Personally, I consider it absolutely and entirely inimical to any form of religious belief."

"Why?" Rochester asked quietly.

"Because," the Duchess answered, "all the faith that has been lavished upon religion since the making of the world, has been a misapplied force. If it had been applied toward developing this new part of ourselves, there is no doubt that so many thousands of years could never have passed without our entering the last and greatest chamber in the treasure-house of knowledge."

The bishop, being a privileged guest, and a cousin of his hostess, deliberately turned his back upon her and escaped from the conversation. The Duchess looked past him towards Saton, who was sitting a few places down the table.

"There!" she exclaimed. "I have been braver than even you could have been."

Saton smiled.

"That sort of courage," he remarked, "is the prerogative of your sex."

"You have heard what I said," she continued. "Don't you agree with me?"

"Of course," he answered.

He hesitated for a moment, but the Duchess was looking at him. She evidently expected him to continue the subject.

"We are told," he said slowly, "that there is no such thing as waste in the physical world—that matter simply changes its form. I suppose that is true enough. And yet a change of form can be for the better or for the worse, according to our caprices. Strictly speaking, it is a waste when matter is changed for the worse. It is very much like this, I think, with regard to the subject which you were just then discussing. Faith, from our point of view, is a very real and psychical force. The faith which has been spent upon religion through all these ages, seems to us very much like the tragedy of an unharnessed Niagara."

The Duchess looked around her triumphantly. She was chilled a little, however, by Rochester's curling lip.

"Dear hostess," he whispered in her ear, "this sort of conversation is scarcely respectful to the bishop, even though he be a relative. You can let your young protégé expound his marvelous views after dinner."

The Duchess shrugged her ample shoulders.

"I wonder how it is," she declared, a little peevishly, "that directly one sets foot in the country, one seems to come face to face with the true Briton. What hypocrites we all are! We are broad enough to discuss any subject under the sun, in town, but we seem to shrink into something between the Philistine and the agricultural pedagogue, as soon as we sniff the air of the ploughed fields."

She rose a little pettishly, and motioned to Rochester to take her place.

"Five minutes only," she said. "You will find us all over the place. The cigarettes and cigars are in the hall. You can finish your wine here, and come out."

"Is there anything particular," Rochester asked grimly, "that we are permitted to talk about?"

"With this crowd," she whispered, "if I forbid politics and agriculture, I don't think you'll last the five minutes."

CHAPTER XXVII

THE ANSWER TO A RIDDLE

A few of the Duchess's guests left early—those who had to drive a long distance, and who had not yet discarded their carriage horses for motor-cars. Afterwards the party seemed to draw into a little circle, and it was then that the Duchess, rising to her feet, went over and talked earnestly for a few minutes with Saton.

"Some slight thing!" she begged. "Anything to set these people wondering! Look at that old stick Henry Rochester, for instance. He believes nothing—doesn't want to believe anything. Give him a shock, do!"

"Can't you understand, Duchess," Saton said, "how much harm we do to ourselves by any exhibition of the sort you suggest. People are at once inclined to look upon the whole thing as a clever trick, and go about asking one another how it is done."

The Duchess was disappointed, and inclined to be pettish. Saton realized it, and after a moment's hesitation prepared to temporize.

"If it would amuse you," he said, "and I can find anyone here to help me, I daresay we could manage some thought transference. All London seems to be going to see those two people at the Alhambra—or is it the Empire? You can see the same thing here, if you like."

The Duchess beamed.

"That would be delightful," she said. "Whom would you like to help you?"

"Leave me alone for a minute or two," Saton said. "I will look around and choose somebody."

The Duchess stepped back into the circle of her guests.

"Mr. Saton is going to entertain us in a very wonderful manner," she announced.

Rochester, who had been on his way to the billiard room, came back.

"Let us stay and see the tricks," he remarked to the bishop, who had been his companion.

The Duchess frowned. Saton shot a sudden glance at Rochester. A dull, angry color burned in his cheeks.

"Stay, by all means, Mr. Rochester," he said. "We may possibly be able to interest you."

There was almost a challenge in his words. Rochester, ignoring them save for his slightly uplifted eyebrows, sat down by the side of Pauline.

"The fellow's cheek is consummate!" he muttered.

"I need," Saton remarked quietly, "what I suppose Mr. Rochester would call a confederate. I can only see one whom I think would be temperamently suitable. Will you help me?" he asked, turning suddenly toward Pauline.

"No!" Rochester answered sternly. "Lady Marrabel will have nothing to do with your performance."

Rochester bit his lip the moment he had spoken. He felt that he had made a mistake. One or two of the guests looked at him curiously. The Duchess was literally open-mouthed. Saton was smiling in a peculiar manner.

"In that case," he remarked quietly, "if Mr. Rochester has spoken with authority, I fear that I can do nothing."

The Duchess was very nearly angry.

"Don't be such an idiot, Henry!" she said. "Of course Pauline will help. What is it you want her to do, Mr. Saton?"

"Nothing at all," he answered, "except to sit in a corner of the room, as far from me as possible, and answer the questions which I shall ask her, if she be able. You will do that?" turning suddenly towards her.

"Of course she will!" the Duchess declared. "Be quiet, Henry. You are a stupid, prejudiced person, and I won't have you interfere."

Pauline rose to her feet.

"I am afraid," she said, "that I can scarcely be of much use, but of course I don't mind trying."

Saton was standing a little away, with his elbow leaning upon the mantelpiece.

"If two of you," he said, helping himself to a cigarette, and deliberately lighting it, "will take Lady Marrabel over—say to that oak chair underneath the banisters—blindfold her, and then leave her. Really I ought to apologize for what I am going to do. Everything is so very obvious. Still, if it amuses you!"

Pauline sat by herself. The others were all gathered together in the far corner of the great hall. Saton turned to the bishop.

"This is only a repetition of the sort of thing which you have doubtless seen," he said. "Have you anything in your pocket which you are quite sure that Lady Marrabel knows nothing of?"

Silently the bishop produced a small and worn Greek Testament. Saton opened it at random. Then he turned suddenly toward the figure of the woman sitting alone in the distance. Some change had taken place in his manner and in his bearing. Those who watched him closely were at once aware of it. His teeth seemed to have come together, the lines of his face to have become tense. He leaned a little forward toward Pauline.

"I have something in my hands," he said. "I wonder if you can tell me what it is."

There was no answer. They listened and watched. Pauline never spoke. Already a smile was parting Rochester's lips.

"I think, Lady Marrabel," Saton said slowly, "that you can tell me, if you will. I think that you will tell me. I think that you must!"

Something that sounded almost like a half-stifled sob came to them from across the hall—and then Pauline's voice.

"It is a small book," she said—"a Testament."

"Go on," Saton said.

"A Greek Testament!" Pauline continued. "It is open at—at the sixth chapter of St. Mark."

Saton passed it round. The Duchess beamed with delight upon everybody. Saton seemed only modestly surprised at the interest which everyone displayed.

"We are only doing something now," he said, "which has already been done, and proved easy. The only trouble is, of course, that Lady Marrabel being a stranger to me, the effort is a little greater. If you will be content with one more test of this sort, I will try, if you like, something different—something, at any rate, which has not been done in a music-hall."

A gold purse was passed to him, with a small monogram inscribed. Again Pauline slowly, and even as though against her will, described correctly the purse and its contents.

Saton brushed away the little murmurs of surprise and delight.

"Come," he said, "this is all nothing. It really—as you will all of you know in a few years time—can be done by any one of you who chooses seriously to develop the neglected part of his or her personality. I should like to try something else which would be more interesting to you."

The Duchess turned towards him with clasped hands.

"Can't you," she said, "make her say how Mr. Rochester met with his accident?"

There was a little thrill amongst everyone. Saton stood as though absorbed in thought.

"Why not?" he said softly to himself.

Rochester laughed hardly.

"Come," he said, "we are getting practical at last. Let one thing be understood, though. If our young friend here is really able to solve this little mystery, he will not object to my making use of his discovery."

"By no means," Saton answered. "But I warn you that if the person is one unknown to Lady Marrabel or myself, I cannot tell you who it was. All that I can do is perhaps to show you something of how the thing was done."

"It will be most interesting!" Rochester declared.

There was a subdued murmur of thrilled voices. One or two looked at each other uneasily. Even the Duchess began to feel a little uncomfortable. Saton was suddenly facing Pauline. He was standing a little nearer, with the fingers of his right hand resting upon the round oak table which stood in the centre of the hall. His figure had become absolutely rigid, and the color had left his cheeks. His voice seemed to them to come from some other person.

"Listen," he said, bending even a little further toward the woman, who was leaning forward now from her chair, as though eager or compelled to hear what was being said to her. "A month—six weeks—some time ago, you were with Henry Rochester, a few minutes after his accident. He was shot—or he shot himself. He was shot by design or by misadventure. You were the first to find him. You came round the corner of the wood, and you saw him there, lying upon the grass. You heard a shot just before—two shots. You came round the corner of the wood, and you saw nothing except the body of Henry Rochester lying upon the ground."

"Nothing!" she murmured. "Nothing!"

There was an intense silence. The little group of people were all leaning forward with eyes riveted upon Pauline Marrabel. Even Rochester's expression had become a little tense.

"Think again," Saton said. "There was only a corner of the wood between you and that field when the shot was fired. You are walking there now, now, as the shots are fired. Bend forward. You can see through those trees if you try. I think that you do see through them."

Again he paused. Again there were a few seconds' silence—silence save for the quick breathing of the Duchess, who was crumpling her lace handkerchief into a little ball in her hands.

Then Pauline's voice came to them.

"There is a gun laid against a gate which leads into the field," she said—"a gun, and by its side a bag of cartridges. Someone has been hiding behind the wall. He has the gun in his hands. He looks along the path. There is no one coming."

A woman from the little group of people commenced to sob softly. Pauline's voice ceased. Someone put a hand over the mouth of the frightened woman.

"Go on," Saton said.

"The man has the gun in his hand. He goes down on his knees," Pauline continued. "The gun is pointed towards Mr. Rochester. There is a puff of smoke, a report, Mr. Rochester has fallen down. He is up again. Then he falls!—yes, he falls!"

Saton passed his hand across his forehead.

"Go on," he said.

"The man is taking the cartridge from the gun," Pauline said. "He slips in another from the bag. He has leaned the gun against the gate. He is stealing away."

Saton leaned towards her till he seemed even about to spring.

"You could not see his face?" he said.

There was no answer. Two of the women behind were sobbing now. A third was lying back, half unconscious. Rochester had risen to his feet. The faces of all of them seemed suddenly to reflect a new and nameless terror.

Saton moved slowly towards Pauline. He moved unsteadily. The perspiration now was standing in thick beads upon his forehead. He suddenly realized his risk.

"You could not see his face?" he repeated. "You do not know who it was that fired that gun?"

"I could not see his face," she repeated. "But I—I can see it now."

"You do not recognise it?" he said, and his voice seemed to come tearing from his throat, charged with some new and compelling quality. "You cannot recognise it? You do not know whether you have ever seen it before?"

Pauline rose suddenly to her feet. Her bosom was heaving, her face was like a white mask. Her hands were suddenly thrown high above her head.

She swayed for a moment, and fell over on her side.

"It is horrible!" she shrieked. "It was you who fired the gun!—You!"

She swayed for a moment, and fell over on her side like a dead woman—her arms thrown out, her limbs inert, as though indeed it were death which had stricken her.

Rochester, with a shout of anger, sprang towards her, sending Saton reeling against the table. He fell on his knees by her side.

"Bring water, some of you idiots!" he cried out. "Ring the bell! And don't let that cursed charlatan escape!"

CHAPTER XXVIII

SPOKEN FROM THE HEART

Pauline took the card from the hand of her servant, and glanced at it at first with the idlest of curiosity—afterwards with a fixed and steadfast attention, as though she saw in those copperplate letters, elegantly traced upon a card of superfine quality, something symbolical, something of far greater significance than the unexpected name which confronted her.

"I told you, Martin," she said, "that I was at home to nobody except those upon the special list."

"I know it, your ladyship," the man answered, "but this gentleman has called every day for a week, and I have refused even to bring his name in. To-day he was so very persistent that I thought perhaps it would be better to bring his card."

Pauline was lying upon a couch. She had been unwell for the last two or three weeks. Nothing serious—nerves, she called it. A doctor would probably have prescribed for her with a smile. Pauline knew better than to send for one. She knew very well what was the matter. She was afraid! Fear had come upon her like a disease. The memory of that one night racked her still—the memory of that, and other things.

Meanwhile, the servant stood before her in an attitude of respectful attention.

"I will see Mr. Saton," she decided at last. "You can show him in here, and remember that until he has gone, no one else is to be allowed to enter. Come yourself only if I ring the bell, or when you serve tea."

The man bowed, and went back to where Saton was waiting in the hall.

"Her ladyship is at home, sir," he announced. "Will you come this way?"

A certain drawn expression seemed suddenly to vanish from the young man's face. He followed the servant almost blithely. In a few seconds he was alone with her in the firelit drawing-room. The door was closed behind him.

Pauline was sitting up on the couch. For a moment they neither of them spoke. She, too, had been suffering, then, he thought, recognising the signs of ill-health in her colorless cheeks and languid pose.

He came slowly across the room and held out his hand. She hesitated, and shook her head.

"No!" she said. "I do not think that I wish to shake hands with you, Mr. Saton. I do not understand why you have come here. I thought it best to see you, and hear what you have to say, once and for all."

"Once and for all?" he repeated.

"Certainly," she answered. "It does not interest me to fence with words. Between us I think that it is not necessary. What do you want with me?"

"You know," he answered calmly.

She paused for a moment or two. She told herself that this was the most transcendental of follies. Yet it seemed as though there were something electrical in the atmosphere, as though something had come into the room unaccountable, stimulating, terrifying. All the languor of the last few days was gone.

"Am I to understand, then?" she said at last, speaking in a low tone, and with her face averted from him, "that you have come to offer me some explanation of the events of that night?"

"No!" he answered.

The seconds ticked on. She found his taciturnity maddening.

"Your visit had some purpose?" she asked.

"I came to see you," he answered.

"I am not well," she said, hurriedly. "I am not fit to see people or to talk at all. I thought that you must have some special purpose in coming, or I should not have received you."

"You wish to talk then, about that night?" he asked.

"No!" she answered—"and yet, yes!"

She sat upright. She looked him in the eyes.

"I have not dared to ask even myself this," she said, "but since you are here, since you have forced it upon me, I shall ask you and you will tell me. That night I had—what shall I call it?—a vision. I saw you shoot Henry Rochester. Now you are here you shall tell me if what I saw was the truth?"

"It was," he answered.

She drew back, shuddering.

"But why?" she asked. "He has never done you any harm."

"On the contrary," Saton answered, "he is my enemy. With all my heart and soul I wish him dead!"

"It is terrible!" she murmured.

"It is the truth," he answered. "The truth sometimes is terrible. That is why people so often evade it. Listen. I was only a boy, a sentimental boy, when I first knew Rochester. Perhaps he has posed to you as my benefactor. Certainly he lent me money. I tell you now, though, that upon every penny of that money was a curse. Whatever I did went wrong. However hard I fought, I was worsted. If I gambled, I lost. If I played for safety, something—even though it might be as unexpected as an earthquake—came to wreck my plans. It was like playing cards with the Devil himself. One by one I lost the tricks. When I was penniless, I had nothing left to think of but the only piece of advice your friend Henry Rochester gave me when he sent me out into the world. The sting of his voice was like a lash. Creatures of the gutter he called those who had failed, and who dared to live on. I tell you that until the time came when I looked down into the Thames, and hesitated whether or no I should take his cynical advice and make an end of myself, every action, every endeavor, and every effort I had made, had been honest. It was his words, and his words entirely, which drove me into the other paths."

"You admit, then—" she began.

"I admit nothing," he answered. "Yet I will tell you this. There are things in my life which I loathe, and they are there because of Rochester's words. Yet bad though I am," he continued, bitterly, "that man's contempt is like a whip to me whenever I see him. What, in God's name, is he? Because he has ancestors behind him, good blood in his veins, the tricks of a man of breeding, the carriage and voice of a gentleman, why, in Heaven's name for these things should he look upon me as something crawling upon the face of the earth—something to be spurned aside whenever it should cross his path? I have lived and spoken falsehoods. The greatest men in the world have lived and spoken falsehoods. But I am not a charlatan. I have mastered the rudiments of a great and mighty new science. I am not a trickster. I have a claim to live, as he has. There is a place in the world for me, too, as well as for him. You know what he has told me? You know with what he has threatened me? He has told me that if he even sees you and me together, that if I even dare to find my way into your presence, that he will horse-whip me. This because he has muscles and I have none. Yet you ask me why I desire to kill him! I have had only one desire in my life stronger than that, one thing in my life more intense than my hatred of this man."

"You are both in the wrong," she said. "Henry Rochester is a straight-living, God-fearing man, a little narrow in his views, and a little violent in his prejudices. You are a person such as he would not understand, such as he never could understand. You and he could never possibly come into sympathy. He is wrong when he utters such threats. Yet you must remember that there is Lois. He has the right there to say what he will."

"There is Lois, yes!" Saton repeated.

"You wish to marry her, don't you?" she asked.

The question seemed to madden him. Suddenly he threw aside the almost unnatural restraint with which he had spoken and acted since his entrance into the room. He rose to his feet. He stood before her couch with clenched hands, with features working spasmodically as the words poured from his lips.

"Listen," he said. "I have no money. I have lived partly upon the woman who adopted me, and partly by nefarious means. Science is great, it is fascinating, it is the joy of my life, but one must live. I have tasted luxury. I cannot live as a workingman. The woman who adopted me is all the time at my elbow, telling me that I must marry Lois because of her money. The child is willing. I have been willing."

"To marry her for her money—for her money only!" Pauline exclaimed, with scorn trembling in her tone.

"Absolutely for her money only!" Saton answered. "Now you know how poor a thing I am. Yet I tell you that all men have a bad spot in them. I tell you that I am dependent upon that woman for every penny I spend, and for the clothes I wear. When I tell her that I will not marry Lois Champneyes, she will very likely throw me into the street. What is there left for me to do? I have tried everything, and failed. I have no strength, I have a cursed taste for the easy ways of life. Yet this has come to me. I will not marry Lois Champneyes. I will break with this woman, notwithstanding all I owe to her, and I will go away and work once more, wherever I can earn enough to keep me. And I will tell you why. I haven't a good quality that I know of. I am as selfish as a man can be. I am a murderer at heart, an actor most of the time, but in one thing I am honest. I love you, Pauline Marrabel! I can't help it. It is the curse of my life, if you will, but it is the joy of it. Rochester knows it, and he hates me. I know that Rochester loves you, and I hate him. Listen. There is a man who believes in me—a great man. I'll go to him. I'll work, I'll study, I'll write. I'll live the thoughts I want to live. I'll shape my life along the firm straight lines. I'll make a better thing of myself, if you'll wait. Mind, I don't ask you to touch me now. If you offered me your hands, I wouldn't take them. I'm not fit. But there is just this one thing in me. I know myself and I know you. Give me the chance to climb!"

Time seemed to stand still while she looked at him. Yes, he had been honest! She saw him stripped of all the glamour of his unusual learning. She saw him as he was—small, false, a poor creature, who having failed on the mountains, had been content to crawl through the marshes. He seemed in those few moments to be stripped bare to her. He was not even a gentleman. He wore his manners as he wore his clothes. He belonged to her world no more than the servant who had announced him. She clenched her fingers. It was ignoble that her heart should be beating, that the breath should come sobbing through her parted lips. He was a creature to be despised!

She raised her head and told him so, fighting all the while with something greater and stronger which seemed to be tearing at her heart strings.

"If that is what you came here to say," she said, "please go."

He rose at once. She saw the anxious light with which his eyes had been filled, fade away. He turned almost humbly toward the door.

"You are quite right," he said. "I should not have come. I do not often have impulses. It is a mistake to listen to them. Yet I came because it was the one honest desire which I have had since I looked down into the water and turned away."

He walked toward the door. She stood with her finger pressing the bell. He seemed somehow to have lost what little presence he had ever possessed. His head was bowed; he walked as one feeling for his way in the dark. Never once did he look round. As he stood before the door, her lips were suddenly parted. A great wave of pity rose up from amongst those other things in her heart. She would have called out to him, but her butler was already there. The door had been opened.

She clenched her teeth, and resumed her place upon the sofa. She heard the front door closed, and she found herself watching him through the blind. She saw him cross the road very much as he had crossed the room—unseeing, stricken. She watched him until he crossed the corner of the square. Her eyes were misty with tears!

CHAPTER XXIX

THE COURAGE OF DESPERATION

Captain Vandermere had a friend from the country, and was giving him supper at the *Savoy*. He was also pointing out the different people who were worthy of note.

"That," he said, pointing to an adjoining table, "is really one of the most interesting men in London."

"He looks like an actor," his friend remarked.

"So he may be," Vandermere answered grimly, "but his is not the Thespian stage. He is a lecturer and writer on occultism, and in his way, I suppose, he is amazingly clever."

"Do you mean Bertrand Saton?" his friend asked, with interest.

Vandermere nodded.

"You have heard the fellow's name, of course," he said. "For the last month or so one seems to meet him everywhere, and in all sorts of society. The illustrated papers, and even the magazines, have been full of the fellow's photograph. Women especially seem to regard him as something supernatural. Look at the way they are hanging upon his words now. That is the old Duchess of Ampthill on his left, and the others are all decent enough people of a sort."

"I gather from your tone," his friend remarked, "that the young man is not a favorite of yours."

"He is not," Vandermere answered. "I don't understand the breed, and that's a fact. Apart from that, he has had the confounded impertinence to make love to—to a very charming young lady of my acquaintance."

"He isn't particularly good-looking," the friend remarked—"striking I suppose people would say."

"He has a sort of unwholesome way of attracting women," Vandermere remarked. "Look how they all manœuvre to walk out with him."

Saton was exercising his rights as lion of the party, and leaving early. The Duchess whispered something in his ear, at which he only laughed. Half-a-dozen invitations were showered upon him, which he accepted conditionally.

"I never accept invitations," he said, "except with a proviso. As a matter of fact, I never can tell exactly when I shall want to work, and when the feeling for work comes, everything else must go. It is not always that one is in the right mood."

"How interesting!" one of the women sighed.

"Must be like writing poetry, only far more exciting," another murmured.

"Tell me," a girl asked him, as he stooped over her fingers to say good night, "is it really true, Mr. Saton, that if you liked you could make me do things even against my will—that you could put ideas into my head which I should be forced to carry out?"

"Certainly."

"And you never make use of your power?"

"Very seldom," he answered. "That is the chicanery of science. It is because people when they have discovered a little are so anxious to exploit their knowledge, that they never go any further. It is very easy indeed to dominate the will of certain individuals, but what we really want to understand before we use our power, is the law that governs it. Good night, once more!"

"A wonderful man!" they sighed one to another as he passed out.

"I am one of the few," the Duchess remarked complacently, "who has seen a real manifestation of his powers. It is true," she added, with a little shudder, "there was a mistake toward the end. The experiment wasn't wholly successful, but it was wonderful, all the same—wonderful!"

Saton left the restaurant, and entered the small electric brougham which was waiting for him. He lit a cigarette and leaned back amongst the cushions, musing over the events of the evening with a complacent smile. The last few weeks seemed to have wrought some subtle change in the man. His face was at once stronger and weaker, more determined, and yet in a sense less trustworthy. His manner had gained in assertion, his bearing in confidence. There was an air of resolve about him, as though he knew exactly where he was going—how far, and in what direction. And with it all he had aged. There were lines under his eyes, and his face was worn—at times almost haggard.

He let himself into the little house in Berkeley Square with his latchkey, and turned at once into Rachael's room. She was sitting over the fire in a brilliant red dressing-gown, her head elaborately coiffured, her fingers and neck brilliant with jewels. Yet when she turned her head one saw a change. Age had laid its grip upon her at last. Her voice had lost its decision. Her hands trembled in her lap.

"You are late, Bertrand," she said—"very late."

"Not so very," he answered. "I have been supping at the *Savoy* with the Duchess of Ampthill and some friends."

She looked at him searchingly, looked at him from head to foot, noted the trim exactness of his evening attire, and his enamel links and waistcoat buttons, the air of confidence with which he crossed the room to mix himself a whiskey and soda. It was she who had been like that a few months ago, and he the timid one. They seemed to have changed places.

"Bertrand," she said, "you frighten me. You go so far, nowadays."

"Why not?" he answered.

"Huntley has been here to-night," she went on. "He tells me that you have opened even another place, and that all the old ones are going. He tells me that the offices are hard at work, too."

"Business is good," remarked Saton, drily.

"I thought that we were going quietly for a time," she said. "It was you who were so terrified at the risk. Do you imagine that the danger is over?"

"My dear Rachael," he answered, coming over to her, "I have come to the conclusion that I was over-timid. There is no success in life to be won without daring. Money we must have, and these places are like a gold mine to us. If things go wrong, we must take our chance. I am content. In the meantime, for all our sakes, it suits me to be in evidence everywhere. The papers publish my portrait, the Society journals record my name, people point me out at the theatres and at the restaurants. This is not vanity—this is business. I am giving a lecture the week after next, and every seat is already taken. I am going to say some daring things. Afterwards, I am going to Naudheim for a month. When I come back, I shall give another lecture. After that, perhaps these places will not be necessary any more. But who can tell? Money we must have, money all the time. Science is great, but men and women must live."

She looked at him with a grim smile.

"You amuse me," she said. "Are you really the half-starved boy who flung himself at my horses' heads in the Bois?"

"I am what the Fates have made of that boy."

She shook her head.

"You are going too fast," she said. "You terrify me. What about Lois?"

"Lois is of age in six weeks," he replied. "On the day she is of age, I shall go to Rochester and demand her hand. He will refuse, of course. I shall marry her at once."

"Why not now?" Rachael asked. "Why wait a day? The money will come later."

"I will tell you why," Saton answered. "Because I have ambitions, and because it would do them harm if people believed that I had exercised any sort of influence to make that girl marry me against her guardian's wishes. I do use my influence as it is, although," he added, frowning, "I find it harder every day. She walked with me in the Park this morning; she came to tea with me the day before."

"What do you mean when you say that you find it harder?" Rachael asked.

"I mean that I have lost some of my hold over her," he answered. "It is the sort of thing which is likely to happen at any time. She has very weak receptive currents. It is like trying to drive water with a sieve."

"You must not fail," she muttered. "I am nervous these days. I would rather you were married to Lois, and her money was in the bank, and that these places were closed. I start when the bell rings. Huntley himself said that you were rash."

"Huntley is a fool," Saton answered. "Let me help you upstairs, Rachael."

He passed his arm around her affectionately, and kissed her when they parted for the night. Then he came down to his little room, and sat for a time at his desk, piled with books and works of reference. He brooded gloomily for several moments over what Rachael had been saying. A knock at the door made him start. It was only a servant, come to see to the fire, but his hand had darted out toward a certain drawer of his desk. When the servant had retired, he opened it for a minute and looked in. A small shining revolver lay there, and a box of cartridges.

"Your idea, my friend Rochester!" he muttered to himself.

CHAPTER XXX

A SURPRISING REQUEST

The Duchess of Ampthill was giving a great dinner-party at her house in Grosvenor Square. She had found several new prodigies, and one of them was performing in a most satisfactory manner. He sat at her left hand, and though, unlike Saton, he had at first been shy, the continual encouragement of his hostess had eventually produced the desired result. His name was Chalmers, and he was the nephew of a bishop. He had taken a double first at Oxford, and now announced his intention of embracing literature as a profession. He wore glasses, and he was still very young.

"There is no doubt at all," he said, in answer to a remark from the Duchess, "that London has reached just that stage in her development as a city of human beings, which was so fatal to some of her predecessors in pre-eminence, some of those ancient cities of which there exists to-day only the name. The blood in her arteries is no longer robust. Already the signs of decay are plentiful."

"I wonder," Rochester inquired, "what you consider your evidences are for such a statement. To a poor outsider like myself, for instance, London seems to have all the outward signs of an amazingly prosperous—one might almost say a splendidly progressive city."

Chalmers smiled. It was a smile he had cultivated when contradicted at the Union, and he knew its weight.

"From a similar point of view," he said, "as yours, Mr. Rochester, Rome and Athens, Nineveh, and those more ancient cities, presented the same appearance of prosperity. Yet if you ask for signs, there are surely many to be seen. I am anxious," he continued, gazing around him with an air of bland enjoyment, "to avoid anything in the nature of an epigram. There is nothing so unconvincing, so stultifying to one's statements, as to express them epigrammatically. People at once give you credit for an attempt at intellectual gymnastics which takes no regard to the truth. I will not, therefore, weary you with a diatribe upon the condition of that heterogeneous mass which is known to-day as Society. I will simply point out to you one of the portents which has inevitably heralded disaster. I mean the restless searching everywhere for new things and new emotions. Our friend opposite," he said, bowing to Saton, "will forgive me if I instance the almost passionate interest in this new science which he is making brave efforts to give to the world. A lecture to-day from Mr. Bertrand Saton would fill any hall in London. And why? Simply because the people know that he will speak to them of new things. Look at this man Father Cresswell. There is no building in this great city which would hold the crowds who flock to his meetings. And why? Simply because he has adopted a new tone—because in place of the old methods, he stands in his pulpit with a lash, and wields it like a Russian executioner."

Lady Mary interrupted him suddenly from her place a little way down the table.

"Oh, I don't agree with you!" she said. "Indeed, I think you are wrong. The reason why people go to hear Father Cresswell is not because he has anything new to say, or any new way of saying it. The real reason is because he has the gift of showing them the truth. You can be told things very often, and receive a great many warnings, but you take no notice. There is something wrong about the method of delivering them. It is not the lash which Father Cresswell uses, but it is his extraordinary gift of impressing one with the truth of what he says, that has had such an effect upon everyone."

Rochester looked across at his wife curiously. It was almost the first time that he had ever heard her speak upon a serious subject. Now he came to think of it, he remembered that she had been spending much of her time lately listening to this wonderful enthusiast. Was he really great enough to have influenced so light a creature, he wondered? Certainly there was something changed in her. He had noticed it during the last few days—an odd sort of nervousness, a greater kindness of speech, an unaccustomed gravity. Her remark set him thinking.

Chalmers leaned forward and bowed to Lady Mary. Again the shadow of a tolerant smile rested upon his lips.

"Very well, Lady Mary," he said, "I will accept the truth of what you say. Yet a few decades ago, who cared about religion, or hearing the truth? It is simply because the men and women of Society have exhausted every means of self-gratification, that in a sort of unwholesome reaction they turn towards the things as far as possible removed from those with which they are surfeited. But I will leave Father Cresswell alone. I will ask you whether it is not the bizarre, the grotesque in art, which to-day wins most favor. I will turn to the making of books—I avoid the term literature—and I will ask you whether it is not the extravagant, the impossible, the deformed, in style and matter, which is most eagerly read. The simplest things in life should convince one. The novelist's hero is no longer the fine, handsome young fellow of twenty years ago. He is something between forty and fifty, if not deformed, at least decrepit with dissipations, and with the gift of fascination, whatever that may mean, in place of the simpler attributes of a few decades ago. And the heroine!—There is no more book-muslin and innocence. She has, as a rule, green eyes; she is middle-aged, and if she has not been married before, she has had her affairs. Everything obvious in life, from politics to mutton-chops, is absolutely barred by anyone with any pretensions to intellect to-day."

"One wonders," Rochester murmured, "how in the course of your long life, Mr. Chalmers, you have been able to see so far and truthfully into the heart of things!"

Chalmers bowed.

"Mr. Rochester," he said, "it is the newcomer in life, as in many other things, who sees most of the game."

The conversation drifted away. Rochester was reminded of it only when driving home that night with his wife. Again, as they took their places in the electric brougham, he was conscious of something changed, not only in the woman herself, but in her demeanor towards him.

"Do you mind," he asked, soon after they started, "just dropping me at the club? It is scarcely out of your way, and I feel that I need a whiskey and soda, and a game of billiards, to take the taste of that young man's talk out of my mouth. What a sickly brood of chickens the Duchess does encourage, to be sure!"

"I wonder if you'd mind not going to the club to-night, Henry?" Lady Mary asked quietly.

He turned toward her in surprise.

"Why, certainly not," he answered. "Have we to go on anywhere?"

She shook her head.

"No!" she said. "Only I feel I'd like to talk to you for a little time, if you don't mind. It's nothing very much," she continued, nervously twisting her handkerchief between her fingers.

"I'll come home with pleasure," Rochester interrupted. "Don't look so scared," he added, patting the back of her hand gently. "You know very well, if there is any little trouble, I shall be delighted to help you out."

She did not remove her hand, but she looked out of the window. What she wanted to say seemed harder than ever. And after all, was it worth while? It would mean giving up a very agreeable side to life. It would mean—Her thoughts suddenly changed their course. Once more she was sitting upon that very uncomfortable bench in the great city hall. Once more she felt that curious new sensation, some answering vibration in her heart to the wonderful, passionate words which were bringing tears to the eyes not only of the women, but of the men, by whom she was surrounded. No, it was not an art, this—a trick! No acting was great enough to have touched the hearts of all this time and sin-hardened multitude. It was the truth—simply the truth.

"It isn't exactly a little thing, Henry. I'll tell you about it when we get home."

No, it was no little thing, Rochester thought to himself, as he stood upon the hearthrug of her boudoir, and listened to the woman who sat on the end of the sofa a few feet away as she talked to him. Sometimes her eyes were raised to his—eyes whose color seemed more beautiful because of the tears in them. Sometimes her head was almost buried in her hands. But she talked all the time an odd, disconnected sort of monologue, half confession, half appeal. There was little in it which seemed of any great moment, and yet to Rochester it was as though he were face to face with a tragedy. This woman was asking him much!

"I know so well," she said, "what a useless, frivolous, miserable sort of life mine has been, and I know so well that I haven't made the least attempt, Henry, to be a good wife to you. That wasn't altogether my fault, was it?" she asked pleadingly. "Do tell me that."

"It was not your fault at all," he answered gravely. "It was part of our arrangement."

"I am afraid," she said, "that it was a very unholy, a very wicked arrangement, only you see I was badly brought up, and it seemed to me so natural, such an excellent way of providing a good time for myself, to marry you, and to owe you nothing except one thing. Henry, you will believe this, I know. I have flirted very badly, and I have had many of those little love-affairs which every woman I know indulges in—silly little affairs just to pass away the time, and to make one believe that one is living. But I have never really cared for anybody, and these little follies, although I suppose they are such a waste of emotion and truthfulness and real feeling, haven't amounted to very much, Henry. You know what I mean. It is so difficult to say. But you believe that?"

"I believe it from my soul," he answered.

"You see," she went on, "it seemed to me all right, because there was no one to point out how foolish and silly it was to play one's way through life as though it were a nursery, and we children, and to forget that we were grown-up, and that we were getting older with the years. You have been quite content without me, Henry?" she asked, looking up at him wistfully.

"Yes, I have been content!" he admitted, looking away from her, looking out of the room. "I have been content, after a fashion."

"Ours was such a marriage of convenience," she went on, "and you were so very plain-spoken about it, Henry. I feel somehow as though I were breaking a compact when I turn round and ask you whether it is not possible that we might be, perhaps, some day, a little more to one another. You know why I am almost afraid to say this. It has not been with you as it has been with me. I have always felt that she has been there—Pauline."

She was tearing little bits from the lace of her handkerchief. Her eyes sought his fearfully.

"Don't think, when I say that," she continued, "that I say it with any idea of blaming you. You told me that you loved Pauline when we were engaged, and of course she was married then, and one did not expect—it never seemed likely that she might be free. And now she is free," Lady Mary went on, with a little break in her voice, "and I am here, your wife, and I am afraid that you love her still so much that what I am saying to you must sound very, very unwelcome. Tell me, Henry. Is that so?"

Rochester was touched. It was impossible not to feel the sincerity of her words. He sank on one knee, and took her hands in his.

"Mary," he said, "this is all so surprising. I did not expect it. We have lived so long and gone our own ways, and you have seemed until just lately so utterly content, that I quite forgot that anywhere in this butterfly little body there might be such a thing as a soul. Will you give me time, dear?"

"All the time you ask for," she answered. "Oh! I know that I am asking a great deal, but you see I am not a very strong person, and if I give up everything else, I do want someone to lean on just a little. You are very strong, Henry," she added, softly.

He took her face between his hands, and he kissed her, without passion, yet kindly, even tenderly.

"My dear," he said, "I must think this thing out. At any rate, we might start by seeing a little more of one another?"

"Yes!" she answered shyly. "I should like that."

"I will drive you down to Ranelagh to-morrow," he said, "alone, and we will have lunch there."

"I shall love it," she answered. "Good night!"

She kissed him timidly, and flitted away into her room with a little backward glance and a wave of the hand. Rochester stood where she had left him, watching the place where she had disappeared, with the look in his eyes of a man who sees a ghost.

CHAPTER XXXI

BETWEEN LOVE AND DUTY

Rochester's hansom set him down in Cadogan Street just as a new and very handsome motor-car moved slowly away from the door. His face darkened as he recognised Saton leaning back inside, and he ignored the other's somewhat exaggerated and half ironical greeting.

"Lady Marrabel is 'at home'?" he asked the butler, who knew him well.

The man hesitated.

"She will see you, no doubt, sir," he remarked. "We had our orders that she was not 'at home' this afternoon."

"The gentleman who has just left——" Rochester began.

"Mr. Saton," the butler interrupted. "He has been with Lady Marrabel for some time."

Rochester found himself face to face with Pauline, but it was a somewhat grim smile with which he welcomed her.

"Still fascinated, I see, by the new science, my dear Pauline," he said. "I met your professor outside. He has a fine new motor-car. I imagine that after all he has discovered the way to extract money from science."

Pauline shrugged her shoulders.

"Those are matters which do not concern me," she said—"I might add, do not interest me. You are the only man I know who disputes Mr. Saton's position, and you are wrong. He is wonderfully, marvelously gifted."

Rochester bowed slightly.

"Perhaps," he said, "I judge the man, and not his attainments."

"You are very provincial," she declared. "But come, don't let us quarrel. You did not come here to talk about Mr. Saton."

"No!" Rochester answered. "I had something else to say to you."

His tone excited her curiosity. She looked at him more closely, and realized that he had indeed come upon some mission.

"Well," she said, "what has happened? Is it——"

She broke off in her sentence. Rochester stood quite still, as though passionately anxious to understand the meaning of that interrupted thought.

"It is about Mary," he said.

"Yes?" Pauline whispered. "Go on. Go on, please."

"It is something quite unexpected," Rochester said slowly—"something which I can assure you that her conduct has never at any time in any way suggested."

"She wants to leave you?" Pauline asked, breathlessly.

"On the contrary," Rochester said, "she wants what she has never asked for or expected—something, in fact, which was not in our marriage bond. She has been going to this man Father Cresswell's meetings. She is talking about our duty, about making the best of one another."

Pauline was amazed. Certainly no thought of this kind had ever entered into her head.

"Do you mean," she said, "that Mary wants to give up her silly little flirtations, and turn serious?"

"That is exactly what she says," Rochester answered. "I don't believe she has the least idea that what she proposes comes so near to tragedy."

"What have you answered?" Pauline asked.

"We have established a probationary period," he said. "We have agreed to see a little more of one another. I drove her down to Ranelagh yesterday afternoon, and we are going to dine together to-night. What am I to do, Pauline? I have come to ask you. We must decide it together, you and I."

She leaned a little forward in her chair. Her hands were clasped together. Her eyes were fixed on vacancy.

"It is a thunderbolt," she murmured.

"It is amazing."

"You must go back to her."

Rochester drew a little breath between his teeth.

"Do you know what this means?" he asked.

"Yes, I know!" she answered. "And yet it is inevitable. What have you and I to look forward to? Sometimes I think that it is weakness to see so much of one another."

"I am afraid," Rochester said slowly, "that I would sooner have you for my dear friend, than be married to any woman who ever lived."

"I wonder," she said softly. "I wonder. You yourself," she continued, "have always held that there is a certain vulgarity, a certain loss of fine feeling in the consummation of any attachment. The very barrier between us makes our intercourse seem sweeter and more desirable."

"And yet," he declared, leaning a little toward her, "there are times when nature will be heard—when one realizes the great call."

"You are right," she answered softly. "That is the terrible part of it all. You and I may never listen to it. We have to close our ears, to beat our hands and hide, when the time comes."

"And is it worth while, I wonder?" he asked. "What do we gain——"

She held out her hand.

"Don't, Henry," she said—"don't, especially now. Be thankful, rather, that there has been nothing in our great friendship which need keep you from your duty."

"You mean that?" he asked hoarsely.

"You know that I mean it," she answered. "You know that it must be."

He rose to his feet and walked to the window. He remained there standing alone, for several minutes. When he came back, something had gone from his face. He moved heavily. He had the air of an older man.

"Pauline," he said, "you send me away easily. Let me tell you one of the hard thoughts I have in my mind—one of the things that has tortured me. I have fancied—I may be wrong—but I have fancied that during the last few months you have been slipping away from me. I have felt it, somehow. There has been nothing tangible, and yet I have felt it. Answer me, honestly. Is this true? Is what I have told you, after all, something of a relief?"

She answered him volubly, almost hysterically. Her manner was absolutely foreign. He listened to her protestations almost in bewilderment.

"It is not true, Henry. You cannot mean what you are saying. I have always been the same. I am the same now. What could alter me? You don't believe that anything could alter me?"

"Or any person?" he asked.

"Or any person," she repeated, hastily. "Go through the list of our acquaintances, if you will. Have I ever shown any partiality for anyone? You cannot honestly believe that I have not been faithful to our unwritten compact?"

"Sometimes," he said slowly, "I have had a horrible fear. Pauline, I want you to be kind to me. This has been a blow. I cannot easily get over it. Let me tell you this. One of the reasons—the great reason—why I fear and dread this coming change, is because it may leave you more susceptible to the influence of that person."

"You mean Mr. Saton?" she said.

"I do," Rochester answered. "Perhaps I ought not to have mentioned his name. Perhaps I ought not to have said anything about it. But there the whole thing is. If I thought that any part of your interest in the man's scientific attainments had become diverted to the man himself, I should feel inclined to take him by the neck and throw him into the Serpentine."

She said nothing. Her face had become very still, almost expressionless. Rochester felt his heart turn cold.

"Pauline," he said, "before I go you will have to tell me that what I fear could not come to pass. Perhaps you think that I insult you in suggesting it. This young man may be clever, but he is not of our world—yours and mine. He is a *poseur* with borrowed manners, *flamboyant*, a quack medicine man of the market place. He isn't a gentleman, or anything like one. I am not really afraid, Pauline, and yet I need reassurance."

"You have nothing to fear," she answered quietly. "I am sorry, Henry, but I cannot discuss Mr. Saton with you. Yet don't think I am blind. I know that there is truth in all you say. Sometimes little things about him set my very teeth on edge."

Rochester drew a sigh of relief.

"So long as you realize this," he said, "so long as you understand, I have no fear."

Pauline looked away, with a queer little smile upon her lips. How little a man understood even the woman whom he cared for!

"Henry," she said, "I can only do this. I can give you my hands, and I can wish you happiness. Go on with your experiment—I gather that for the moment it is only an experiment?"

"That is all," he answered.

"When it is decided one way or the other," she continued, "you must come and tell me. Please go away now. I want to be alone."

Rochester kissed her hands, and passed out into the street. He had a curious and depressing conviction that he was about to commence a new chapter of his life.

CHAPTER XXXII

AT THE EDGE OF THE PRECIPICE

Naudheim's disapproval was very marked and evident. He scoffed at the great bowl of pink roses which stood upon the writing-table. He pushed scornfully on one side the elegantly shaped inkstand, with its burden of pens; the blotting-pad, with its silver edges; the piles of cream-laid foolscap. Most of all he looked with scornful disapprobation at his young host.

Saton was attired for his morning walk in the Park. During the last few weeks—or months, perhaps—a touch of foppishness had crept into his dress—a fondness for gray silk ties, a flower in his buttonhole, white linen gaiters drawn carefully over his patent boots. Certainly the contrast between this scrupulously dressed young man and Naudheim, bordered upon the absurd. Naudheim was shabby, unbrushed, unkempt. His collar was frayed, he wore no tie. The seams of his long black frock-coat had been parted and inked over and parted again. He wore carpet slippers and untidy socks. There were stains upon his waistcoat.

From underneath his shaggy gray eyebrows he shot a contemptuous glance at his host.

"My young friend," he said, "you are growing too fine. I cannot work here."

"Nonsense!" Saton answered, a little uneasily. "You can sweep all those things off the writing-table, if they seem too elaborate for you, and pitch the flowers out of the window if you like."

"Bah!" Naudheim answered. "It is the atmosphere. I smell it everywhere. This is not the house for thoughts. This is not the house wherein one can build. My young friend, you have fallen away. You are like all the others. You listen to the tin music."

"I think," Saton answered, "that the work which I have done should be my answer to you. We are not all made alike. If I find it easier to breathe in an atmosphere such as this, then that is the atmosphere which I should choose. We do our best work amidst congenial surroundings. You in your den, and I in my library, can give of our best."

Naudheim shook his head.

"You are a fool," he said. "As for your work, it is clever, fatally clever. When I read what you sent me last month, and saw how clever it was, I knew that you were falling away. That is why I came. Now I have come, I understand. Listen! The secrets of science are won only by those who seek them, like

- 168 -

children who in the time of trouble flee to their mother's arms. Never a mistress in the world's history has asked more from man than she has asked or has had more to give. She asks your life, your thoughts, your passions— every breath of your body must be a breath of desire for her and her alone. You think that you can strut about the world, a talking doll, pay court to women, listen to the voices that praise you, smirk your way through the days, and all the time climb. My young friend, no! I tell you no! Don't interrupt me. I am going to speak my say and go."

"Go?" Saton repeated. "Impossible! I am willing to work. I will work now. I simply thought that as the morning was so fine we might walk for a little time in the sunshine. But that is nothing."

Naudheim shook his head.

"Not one word do I speak of those things that are precious to me, in this house," he declared. "I tell you that its atmosphere would choke the life out of every thought that was ever conceived. You may blind others, even yourself, young man," he went on, "but I know. You are a renegade. You would serve two mistresses. I am going."

"You shall not," Saton declared. "This is absurd. Come," he added, trying to draw his arm through his visitor's, "we will go into another room if this one annoys you."

Naudheim stepped back. He thrust Saton away contemptuously. He was the taller of the two by some inches, and his eyes flashed with scorn as he turned toward the door.

"I leave this house at once," he said. "I was a fool to come, but I am not such a fool as you, Bertrand Saton. Don't write or come near me again until your sham house and your sham life are in ruins, and you yourself in the wilderness. I may take you to my heart again then. I cannot tell. But to-day I loathe you. You are a creature of no account—a foolish, dazzled moth. Don't dare to ring your bells. I need no flunkeys to show me the way to the door."

Naudheim strode out, as a prophet of sterner days might have cast the dust of a pagan dancing hall from his feet. Saton for a moment was staggered. His composure left him. He walked aimlessly up and down the room, swinging his gloves in his hand, and muttering to himself.

Then Rachael came in. She walked with the help of two sticks. She seemed gaunter and thinner than ever, yet her eyes had lost little of their fire, although they seemed set deeper in the caverns of her face.

"Naudheim has gone," she said. "What is wrong, Bertrand?"

"Naudheim is impossible," Saton answered. "He came in here to work this morning, looked around the room, and began to storm. He objected to the flowers, to the writing-table, to me. He has shaken the dust of us off his feet, and gone back to his wretched cabin in Switzerland."

She leaned on her sticks and looked at him.

"On the face of the earth," she said, "there does not breathe a fool like you."

Saton's expression hardened.

"You, too!" he exclaimed. "Well, go on."

"Can't you understand," the woman exclaimed, her voice shaking, "that we are on the verge of a precipice? Do you read the papers? There were questions asked last night in the House about what they called these fortune-telling establishments. Yet everything goes on without a change—by your orders, I am told. Oh, you fool! Huntley knows that he is being spied upon. In Bond Street, yesterday alone, three detectives called at different times. The thing can't go on. The money that we should save ready to escape at the end, you spend, living like this. And the girl Lois—you are letting her slip out of your fingers."

"My dear Rachael," he answered, "in the first place, there is not a thread of evidence to connect you or me with any one of these places, or with Huntley's office. In the second place, I am not letting Lois slip out of my fingers. She will be of age in three weeks' time, and on her birthday I am going to take her away from Rochester, whatever means I have to use, and I am going to marry her at once. You think that I am reckless. Well, one must live. Remember that I am young and you are old. I have no place in the world except the place I make for myself. I cannot live in a pig-sty amongst the snows like Naudheim. I cannot find the whole elixir of life in thoughts and solitude as he does. There are other things—other things for men of my age."

"You sail too near the wind. You are reckless."

"Perhaps I am," he answered. "Life in ten years' time may very well become a stranger place to those who are alive and who have been taught the truth. But life, even as we know it to-day, is strange enough. Rachael, have you ever loved anyone?"

The woman seemed to become nerveless. She sank into a chair.

"Of the past I do not speak," she said—"I choose never to speak."

He took up his hat.

"No!" he remarked. "One sees easily enough that there are things in your past, Rachael. Sometimes the memory may burn. You see, I am living through those days now. The fire has hold of me, and not all the knowledge I have won, not all the dim coming secrets, from before the face of which some day I will tear aside the veil, not all the experiences through which I and I alone have passed, can help me to-day. So perhaps," he added, turning toward the door, "I am a little reckless."

Rachael let him depart without uttering a word. She turned in her chair to watch him cross the square. He was drawing on his light kid gloves. His silk hat was a mirror of elegance. His gold-headed stick was thrust at exactly the right angle under his arm. He swaggered a little—a new accomplishment, and he had the air of one who is well aware that he graces the ground he treads upon.

The woman looked away from him, and with a slow, painful movement her head drooped a little until it reached her hands. A slight shiver seemed to pass through her body. Then she was still, very still indeed. It seemed to her that she could see the end!

CHAPTER XXXIII

"YOU DO NOT BELIEVE IN ME!"

Saton deliberately turned into the Park, and sauntered along under the trees in the wake of a throng of fashionable promenaders. He exchanged greetings with many acquaintances, and here and there he stopped to say a few words. He noted, as usual, and with a recurrence of his constant discontent, the extraordinary difference in the demeanor of the women and the men of his acquaintance. The former, gracious and smiling, accepted him without reservation. Their murmured words and smiles were even more than gracious. On the other hand, there was scarcely a man whose manner did not denote a certain tolerance, not unmixed with contempt, as though, indeed, they were willing to accept the fact that he was of their acquaintance, but desired at the same time to emphasize the fact that he was outside the freemasonry of their class—a freak, whom they acknowledged on sufferance, as they might have done a wonderful lion-tamer, or a music-hall singer, or a steeplejack. He knew very well that there was not one of them who accepted his qualifications, notwithstanding the approval of their womankind, and the knowledge stung him bitterly.

Presently he came face to face with Lois, walking with Vandermere. His face darkened for a moment. He had expressed his desire that she should see as little of this young man as possible, and here they were, not only walking together, but laughing and talking with all the easy naturalness of old acquaintanceship.

Saton drew a little breath of anger through his teeth as he paused and waited for them. He recognised the terms of intimacy upon which they were. He recognised that between them there was something which had never existed between Lois and himself, something which made their friendship a natural and significant thing. It was the freemasonry of class again, the magic ring against which he had torn his fingers in vain.

They saw him. The whole expression of the girl's face changed. All the animation seemed to leave her manner. For a moment she clung instinctively to her companion. Afterwards she looked at him no more. She came to Saton at once, and held out her hand without any show of reluctance, yet wholly without spontaneity. It was as though she was obeying orders from a superior.

"Only this morning," he said, "the Comtesse was speaking of you, Lois. She was so sorry that you had not been to see her lately."

"I will come this afternoon," Lois said quietly.

Vandermere, who had frowned heavily at the sound of her Christian name upon Saton's lips, could scarcely conceal his anger at her promise.

"I have never had the pleasure," he said, "of meeting the Comtesse. Perhaps I might be permitted to accompany Miss Champneyes?"

"You are very kind," Saton answered. "I am sorry, but the Comtesse is beginning to feel her age, and she receives scarcely anyone. I am afraid that the days are past when she would care to make new acquaintances."

"In any case," Vandermere said, turning to his companion, "weren't we going to Hurlingham this afternoon?"

"We were," she said doubtfully, "but I think——"

She looked towards Saton. His face was inexpressive, but she seemed to read there something which prompted her words.

"I think that we must put off Hurlingham, if you do not mind," she said to Vandermere. "I ought to go and see the Comtesse."

"It is very kind of you," Saton said slowly. "She will, I am sure, be glad to see you."

Vandermere turned aside for a moment to exchange greetings with some acquaintances.

"Lois," Saton said in a low tone, "you know I have told you that I do not like to see you so much with Captain Vandermere."

"I cannot help it," she answered. "He is always at the house. He is a great friend of Mr. Rochester's. Besides," she added, raising her eyes to his, "I like being with him."

"You must consider also my likes and dislikes," Saton said. "Think how hard it is for me to see you so very little."

"Oh, you don't care!" Lois exclaimed tremulously. "You know very well that you don't care. It is all pretence, this. Why do you do it? Why do you make me so unhappy?"

"No, Lois," he answered, "it is not pretence. I do care for you, and in a very few weeks I am coming to fetch you away to make you my wife. You will be glad, then," he went on. "You will be quite happy."

Vandermere turned back towards them. He had heard nothing of their conversation, but he saw that Lois was white, and he had hard work to speak calmly.

"Come," he said to Lois, "I think we had better go on. Good morning, Mr. Saton!"

Saton stood aside to let them pass. He knew very well that Lois would have stayed with him, had he bidden it, but he made no attempt to induce her to do so.

"Till this afternoon," he said, taking off his hat with a little flourish.

"Hang that fellow!" Vandermere muttered, as he looked at Lois, and saw the change in her. "Why do you let him talk to you, dear? You don't like him. I am sure that you do not. Why do you allow him to worry you?"

"I think," Lois answered, "that I do like him. Oh, I must like him, Maurice!"

"Yes?" he answered.

"Don't let us talk about him. He has gone away now. Come with me to the other end of the Park. Let us hurry...."

Saton walked on until he saw a certain mauve parasol raised a little over one of the seats. A moment afterwards, hat in hand, he was standing before Pauline.

"Has he come?" she asked, as he bent over her fingers.

Saton's face clouded.

"Yes!" he answered. "He came last night. To tell you the truth, he has just gone away in a temper. I do not know whether he will return to the house or not."

"Why?" she asked quickly.

Saton laughed to cover his annoyance.

"He does not approve of the luxury of my surroundings," he answered. "He declined to write at my desk, or to sit in my room."

"I don't wonder at it," she answered. "You know how he worships simplicity."

"Simplicity!" Saton exclaimed. "You should see the place where he writes himself. There is no carpet upon the floor, a block of wood for a writing-table, a penny bottle of ink, and a gnawed and bitten penholder only an inch or two long."

Pauline nodded.

"I can understand it," she said. "I can understand, too, how your rooms would affect him. You should have thought of that. If he has gone away altogether, how will you be able to finish your work?"

"I must do without him," Saton answered.

Pauline looked at him critically, dispassionately.

"I do not believe that you can do without him," she said. "You are losing your hold upon your work. I have noticed it for weeks. Don't you think that you are frittering away a great deal of your time and thoughts? Don't you think that the very small things of life, things that are not worth counting, have absorbed a good deal of your attention lately?"

He was annoyed, and yet flattered that she should speak to him so intimately.

"It may be so," he admitted. "And yet, do you know why I have i lu won to mix a little more with my fellows?"

"No!" she answered. "I do not know why."

"It is because I must," he said, lowering his tone. "It is because I must see something of you."

The lace of her parasol drooped a little. Her face was hidden now, and her voice seemed to come from a long way off.

"That is very foolish," she said. "In the first place, if my opinion of you is worth anything, I tell you frankly that I would rather see you with ink-stained fingers and worn clothes, climbing your way up toward the truth, working and thinking in an atmosphere which was not befouled with all the small and petty things of life. It seems to me that since it amused you to play the young man of fashion, you have lost your touch—some portion of it, at any rate—upon the greater things."

Saton was very angry now. He was only indifferently successful in his attempt to conceal the fact.

"You, too," he muttered. "Well, we shall see. Naudheim has brains, and he has worked for many years. He had worked, indeed, for many years when the glimmerings of this thing first came to me. He could help me if he would, but if he will not, I can do it alone."

"I wonder."

"You do not believe in me," he declared.

"No," she answered, "I do not believe in you—not altogether!"

Rochester and his wife drove down the Park. Saton followed her eyes, noticing her slight start, and gazed after them with brooding face.

"Rochester is becoming quite a devoted husband," he remarked, with a sneer.

"Quite," she answered. "They spend most of their time together now."

"And Lady Mary, I understand," he went on, "has reformed. Yesterday she was opening the new wing of a hospital, and the day before she was speaking at a Girls' Friendly Society meeting. It's an odd little place, the world, or rather this one particular corner of it."

She rose, with a little shrug of the shoulders, and held out her hand.

"I must go," she said. "I am lunching early."

"May I walk a little way with you?" he begged.

She hesitated. After all, perhaps, it was a phase of snobbery to dislike being seen with him—something of that same feeling which she had never failed to remark in him.

"If you please," she answered. "I am going to take a taximeter at the Park gates."

"I will walk with you as far as there," he said.

He tried to talk to her on ordinary topics, but he felt at once a disadvantage. He knew so little of the people, the little round of life in which she lived. Before they reached the gates they had relapsed into silence.

"It is foolish of me," he said, as he called a taximeter, "to come here simply in the hope of seeing you, to beg for a few words, and to go away more miserable than ever."

She shrugged her shoulders.

"It is certainly very foolish," she admitted.

"I don't see why," he protested, "you should disapprove of me so utterly."

"I do not disapprove," she told him. "I have not the right. I have not the desire to have the right. Only, since you will have me tell you, I am interested in your work. I like to talk about it, to hear you talk when you are enthusiastic. It does not amuse me to see you come down to the level of these others, who while their morning away doing nothing. You are not at home amongst them. You have no place there. When you come to me as a young man in Society, you bore me."

She stepped into the taximeter and drove away, with a farewell nod, abrupt although not altogether unkindly. Yet as she looked behind, a few seconds later, her face was very much softer—her eyes were almost regretful.

"It may hurt him," she said to herself, "but it is very good that he should hear the truth."

CHAPTER XXXIV

A WOMAN'S TONGUE

The man was harmless enough, to all appearance—something less than middle-aged, pale, and with stubbly brown moustache. He was dressed in blue serge clothes, and a bowler hat a little ancient at the brim. Neither his appearance nor his manner was remarkable for any particular intelligence. Yet the girl who looked him over was at once suspicious.

"What can I do for you?" she asked a little curtly.

He pointed to the crystal upon the table, and held out his hand.

"I want my fortune told," he said.

Violet shook her head.

"I do not attempt to read fortunes," she said, "and I do not, in any case, see gentlemen here at all. I do not understand how the boy could have shown you up."

"It wasn't the boy's fault," the visitor answered. "I was very keen on coming, and I gave him the slip. Do make an exception for once, won't you?" he went on. "I know my hand is very easy to read. I had it read once, and nearly everything came true."

Again she shook her head.

"I cannot do anything for you, sir," she said.

The man protested.

"But you call yourself a professional palmist," he said, "and you add crystal gazing to your announcement. I have seen it being carried along on Regent Street."

"It is quite true," Violet said, "that I sometimes try to amuse ladies, but I make no serious attempt to tell fortunes. And as I said before, I do not even receive gentlemen here at all. I am sorry that you have had your visit for nothing."

He rose to his feet with a shrug of the shoulders. There was nothing to be done but to accept defeat. And then, at the moment of defeat, something happened which more than reconciled him to his wasted visit. The door was opened abruptly, and Saton entered.

He realized the situation, or its possibilities, in an instant. His bow to Violet was the bow of a stranger.

"You are engaged," he said. "I will come again. I am sorry that your boy did not tell me."

"This gentleman came under a misapprehension," Violet answered. "I am sorry, but the same thing applies to you. I do not receive gentlemen here."

Saton bowed.

"I am sorry," he said.

The page-boy for whom Violet had rung, opened the door. The first comer passed out, with obvious reluctance. The moment that the door was closed, Violet turned towards Saton with a little exclamation.

"Well," she said, "of all the idiots I ever knew. Haven't I told you time after time that this place is infested with detectives? We get them here every day or so, trying to trap us, women as well as men. And yet you walk in as though the place belonged to you. The one thing they are so anxious to find out is who is running this show."

"I was a fool to come, Violet," Saton admitted, "and I am going at once. You think, then, that he was a detective?"

"I am sure of it," she answered. "I was sure of it, from the moment he came in."

"I will go," Saton said.

"Did you come to see me?" she asked, with a momentary softening in her tone.

Saton nodded.

"It must be another time," he said. "I will not stop now, or that man below will suspect."

"When will our next evening be, Bertrand?" she begged, following him to the door.

"I'll send you a telegram," he answered—"perhaps, to-morrow."

Saton descended the stairs quickly. On the threshold of the door he paused, with the apparent object of lighting a cigarette. His eyes travelled up and down the street. Looking into a shop-window a few yards away, was the man whom he had found with Violet.

He strolled slowly along the pavement and accosted him.

"I beg your pardon," he said. "Please don't think me impertinent, but I am really curious to know whether that young woman was honest or not. She refused to read my hand or look into the crystal for me, simply because I was a man. Did she treat you in just the same way?"

The detective smiled.

"Yes!" he said. "She was very much on her guard indeed. Declined to have anything to do with me."

"Well," said Saton, "I only went in for a joke. I'll try one of the others. There's a wonderful lady in Oxford Street somewhere, they tell me, with the biggest black eyes in London. Good day, sir!"

Saton walked off, and entered a neighboring tea-shop. From there he telephoned to Violet, who a few minutes later appeared.

"Sit down and have some tea," he said. "I want to talk to you."

"It's almost time, isn't it?" she asked, reproachfully.

"Never mind about that just now," he said. "You can guess a little how things are. Those questions in the House upset the Home Secretary, and I am quite convinced that they have made up their minds at Scotland Yard to go for us. You are sure that you have been careful?"

"Absolutely," she answered. "I have not once, to man or woman, pretended to tell their fortune. I tell them that the whole thing is a joke; that I will look into the crystal for them if they wish it, or read their hands, but I do not profess to tell their fortunes. What I see I will tell them. It may interest them or it may not. If it does, I ask them to give me something as a present. Of course, I see that they always do that. But you are quite right, Bertrand. Every one of our shows is being watched. Besides that fellow this afternoon I had two detectives yesterday, and a woman whom I am doubtful about, who keeps on coming."

"Three weeks longer," Saton remarked, half to himself. "Perhaps it isn't worth while. Perhaps it would be better to close up now."

"Only three weeks?" Violet asked eagerly. "Bertrand, what are you going to do then? What is going to become of me?"

Saton patted her on the hand.

"I will tell you a little later on," he said. "Everything will be arranged all right. The only thing I am wondering about is whether it wouldn't be better to close up at once."

"They've got a big piece of business on at the office," she remarked.

Saton frowned.

"I know it," he answered. "It's a dangerous piece of business, too. It's blackmail, pure and simple. I wonder Huntley dare tackle it. It might mean five years' penal servitude for him."

"He'd give you away before he went to penal servitude," Violet remarked. "You may make yourself jolly sure of that."

Saton passed his hand across his forehead.

"Phew!" he said. "How stuffy this place is! Violet, I wish you'd go round to Huntley, and talk to him. Of course, he gets a big percentage on the returns, and that makes him anxious to squeeze everyone. But I don't want any risks. We're nearly out of the wood. I don't want to be trapped now. And I've an enemy, Violet—a pretty dangerous enemy, too. I fancy that most of this activity at Scotland Yard and thereabouts lately, is due to him."

"I'll go," she said, drawing on her gloves. "Shall I telephone to you?"

He nodded.

"Telephone me at home," he said. "Tell Dorrington, or Huntley—whichever you see—that the affair must be closed up—either dropped or settled. The risk is too great. My other work is becoming more and more important every day. I ought not to be mixed up with this sort of thing at all, Violet."

"Why are you?" she asked.

"Money," he answered. "One must have money. One can do nothing without money. It isn't that you or any of the other places make such an amazing lot. It's from Dorrington, of course, that the biggest draws come. Still, on the whole it's a good income."

"And you're going to give it all up?" she remarked.

He nodded.

"I daren't go on," he said. "We've reached about the limit."

"How are you going to live, then?" she asked curiously. "You're not the sort of man to go back to poverty."

Saton considered for a moment. After all, perhaps it would pay him best to be straightforward with this girl. He would tell her the truth. If she were disagreeable about it, he could always swear that he had been joking.

"Violet," he said, "I will tell you what I am going to do. It does not sound very praiseworthy, but you must remember that my work, my real hard work, means a great deal to me, and for its sake I am willing to put up with a good deal of misunderstanding. I am going to ask you to break off our engagement. I am going to marry a young lady who has a great deal of money."

Violet sat perfectly still in her chair. For several seconds she did not utter a syllable. Her lips were a little parted. The color seemed suddenly drawn from her face, and her eyes narrowed. One realized then the pernicious effect of cosmetics. Her blackened eyebrows were painfully apparent. The little patch of rouge was easily discernible against the pallor of her powdered skin. She was suddenly ugly. Saton, looking at her, was amazed that he could ever have brought himself to touch her lips.

"Ah!" she remarked. "I hadn't thought of that. You want to marry some one else, eh?"

Saton nodded.

"It isn't that I want to," he declared, "only, as you know, I must have money. I can't marry you without it, can I, Violet? We should only be miserable. You understand that?"

"Yes, I understand!" she answered.

She was turning one of her rings round, looking down at her hands with downcast head.

"You're upset, Violet," he said, soothingly. "I'm sorry. You see I can't help myself, don't you?"

"Oh, I suppose so!" she answered. "Who is the young lady?"

"A Miss Lois Champneyes," Saton said. "She is a ward of a Mr. Henry Rochester, who has been my enemy all along. It is he, I believe, who has stirred up these detectives to keep watching us."

"Henry Rochester," she repeated. "Yes, I remember the name! He lives at the great house near Blackbird's Nest."

Saton nodded.

"He showed you the way to my cottage once there," he reminded her. "Well, I'm glad I've told you, Violet. I hope you understand exactly how much it means. It's Rachael's doings, of course, and I daren't go against her."

"No, I suppose not!" she answered.

They parted in the street. Saton called a taximeter and drove off. Violet walked slowly down Bond Street. As she passed the corner of Piccadilly, she was suddenly aware that the man who had visited her that afternoon was watching her from the other side of the street. She hesitated for a moment, and then, standing still, deliberately beckoned him over.

"You are a detective, are you not?" she asked, as he approached, hat in hand.

He smiled.

"You are a very clever young lady," he remarked.

"I don't want any compliments," she answered. "Did you come to my show this afternoon hoping just to catch me tripping, or are you engaged in a larger quest altogether?"

"In a larger quest," he answered. "I want some information, and if you can give it me, I can promise that you will be remarkably well paid."

"And the information?" she asked.

"I want," he said slowly, "to be able to connect the young man who came in and pretended to be a stranger, and who has just been having tea with you— I mean Mr. Bertrand Saton—I want to connect him with your establishment, and also with a little office where some very strange business has been transacted during the last few months. You know where I mean. What do you say? Shall we have a talk?"

She walked by his side along Piccadilly.

"We may as well," she said. "We'll go into the Café Royal and sit down."

CHAPTER XXXV

ON LOIS' BIRTHDAY

"

Lois is late this morning," Vandermere remarked, looking up at the clock.

"And on her birthday, too!" Lady Mary declared. "Young people, nowadays, are so *blasé*. Look at all those presents on the table for her, and here the breakfast gong has rung twice, and there is no sign of her."

Vandermere turned to his host.

"You haven't heard anything about that fellow Saton?" he asked. "You don't know whether he is in the neighborhood or not?"

"I have not heard," Rochester answered. "To tell you the truth, if he has as much sense as I believe he has, he is probably on his way to the Continent by now."

"I have an idea, somehow," Vandermere continued, "that Lois is afraid he'll turn up to-day."

"If Lois is afraid," Rochester remarked, "let me tell you in confidence, Vandermere, that I don't think you need be."

"My dear girl!" Lady Mary exclaimed, looking toward the staircase. "We were just going in to breakfast without you, and on your birthday, too!"

Lois came slowly down the broad stairs into the hall. It was impossible to ignore the fact that she was pale, and that she walked as one in fear. Her eyes were sunken, and spoke of a sleepless night. Her manner was almost furtive. She scarcely glanced, even, at the little pile of packages which stood upon the table.

"How nice of you all to wait!" she said. "Good morning, everybody!"

"Good morning, and many happy returns to you!" Lady Mary called out. "Will you look at your presents now or after breakfast?"

"I think after breakfast," she said. "Are there any letters?"

"They are on the table," Rochester said.

She glanced them through eagerly. When she had come to the last one, she drew a little breath of relief. A tinge of color came into her cheeks.

"You dear people!" she exclaimed, impulsively. "I know I am going to have ever such nice things to thank you for. May I be a child, and put off looking at them until after breakfast? Do you mind, all of you?"

"Of course not," Vandermere answered. "We want you to tell us how you would like to spend the day."

"I would like to ride—a long way away," she declared, breathlessly. "Or the motor-car—I shouldn't mind that. I should like to go as far away as ever we can, and stay away until it is dark. Could we start directly after breakfast?"

Rochester smiled.

"You can have the car so far as I am concerned," he said. "I have to go over to Melton to sit on the Bench, and your aunt and I are lunching with the Delameres afterwards. But if you can put up with Vandermere as an escort!"

"I'll try," she answered. "Dear Maurice, do order the car for half-an-hour's time, will you?"

He laughed.

"Why this wild rush?" he inquired.

"I don't know," she answered. "It is just a feeling, perhaps. I want to get away, a long way off, very soon. I can't explain. Don't ask me to explain, any of you. You are sure those are all the letters?"

"Certain," Rochester answered. "And, Lois," he added, looking up, "remember this. You speak and look this morning like one who has fears. I repeat it, you have absolutely nothing to fear. I am your guardian still, although you are of age, and I promise you that nothing harmful, nothing threatening, shall come near you."

She drew a little sigh. She did not make him any answer at all, and yet in a sense it was clear that his words had brought her some comfort.

"Don't expect us back till dinner-time," she declared. "I am going to sit behind with Maurice and be bored to death, but I am going to be out of doors till it is dark. I wish you did not bore me so, Maurice," she added, smiling up at him.

"I won't to-day, anyhow," he answered, "because if I talk at all I am going to talk about yourself."

As the day wore on, Lois seemed to lose the depression which had come over her during the early morning. By luncheon she was laughing and chattering, talking over her presents. Soon, when they were speeding on the road again, she felt her hand suddenly held.

"Lois," her companion said, "this is your birthday, and you are a free woman, free to give yourself to whom you will. It should be the happiest day of your life. Won't you make it the happiest day of mine?"

"Oh, if only I could!" she answered, with a sudden return of her old nervousness. "Maurice, if only I dared!"

He laughed scornfully.

"Dear Lois," he said, "you are impressionable, and you have let yourself become the victim of some very foolish fancies. You are a free agent. I tell you this now, and I tell you the truth. You are a free agent, free to give your love where you will, free to give yourself to whom you choose. And I come to you first on your birthday, Lois. You know that I love you. Give yourself to me, little girl, and never anything harmful shall come near you. I swear it, on my honor, Lois."

She drew a little sigh of content, and her arm stole shyly up to his shoulder. In a moment she was in his arms.

"Don't be angry with me, Maurice," she sobbed, "if I am a little strange just at first. I am afraid—I can't tell you what of—but I am afraid."

He talked to her reassuringly, holding her hands—most of the time, in fact, for the country was a sparsely populated one, with his arm around her waist. And then suddenly she seemed to lose her new-found content. Her cheeks were suddenly white. She looked everywhere restlessly about.

"What is the matter, dear?" he asked anxiously.

"I thought that I heard something!" she exclaimed. "What is the time?"

"Four o'clock," he answered, looking at his watch.

"Please tell the man to go back, straight back home," she said. "I am tired. I must get back. Please, Maurice!"

He gave the chauffeur instructions through the speaking-tube. The car swung round, and they sped on their way through the quiet lanes.

"Dear Lois," he said, "something has come over you. Your hands are cold, and you have drawn yourself away. Now please be honest and tell me all about it. If you have fears, all I can say is that you may dismiss them. You are safe now that you have given yourself to me, as safe as anyone in the world could be."

"Oh! If I could believe it!" she whispered, but she did not turn her head. Her eyes sought his no longer. They were fixed steadfastly on the road in front.

"You must believe it," he declared, laughing. "I can assure you that I am strong enough to hold you, now that I have the right. If any troubles or worries come, they are mine to deal with! See, we will not mince words. If that little reptile dares to crawl near you, I'll set my foot upon his neck. By God, I will!"

She took no notice of his speech, except to slowly shake her head. It seemed as though she had not heard him. By and bye he left off talking. There was nothing he could say to bring back the color to her cheeks, or the light to her eyes, or the confidence to her tone. Something had happened—he could not tell what—but for the moment she was gone from him. The little hands which his still clasped were as cold as ice. It seemed to him that they were unwilling prisoners. Once, when he would have passed his arm around her waist, she even shuddered and drew away.

The car rushed on its way, turned into the great avenue, and drew up in front of Beauleys. Lois stepped out quickly, and went on ahead. In the hall several people were standing, and amongst them Bertrand Saton!

Vandermere's face was dark as a thundercloud when his eyes fell upon the young man—carefully, almost foppishly dressed, standing upon the hearthrug in front of the open fire Rochester was there with Pauline, and Lady Mary was seated behind the tea-tray. There was a little chorus as the two entered. Lois went straight to Saton, who held out his hands.

"Dear Lois," he said softly, "I could not keep away to-day. I have been waiting for you, waiting for nearly an hour."

"I know," she answered. "I came as soon as I knew."

CHAPTER XXXVI

THE CHARLATAN UNMASKED

There seemed for the next few minutes to be a somewhat singular abstention from any desire to interfere with the two people who stood in the centre of the little group, hand-in-hand. Saton, after his first speech, and after Lois had given him her hands, had turned a little defiantly toward Rochester, who remained, however, unmoved, his elbow resting upon the broad mantelpiece, his face almost expressionless. Vandermere, too, stood on one side and held his peace, though the effort with which he did so was a visible one. Lady Mary looked anxiously towards them. Pauline had shrunk back, as though something in the situation terrified her.

Even Saton himself felt that it was the silence before the storm. The courage which he had summoned up to meet a storm of disapproval, began to ebb slowly away in the face of this unnatural silence. It was clear that the onus of further speech was to rest with him.

Still retaining Lois' hand, he turned toward Rochester.

"You have forbidden me to enter your house, or to hold any communication with your ward until she was of age, Mr. Rochester," he said. "One of your conditions I have obeyed. With regard to the other, I have done as I thought fit. However, to-day she is her own mistress. She has consented to be my wife. I do not need to ask for your consent or approval. If you are not willing that she should be married from your roof, I can take her at once to the Comtesse, who is prepared to receive her."

"A very pleasant little arrangement," Rochester said, speaking for the first time. "I am afraid, however, that you will have to alter your plans."

"I do not admit your right to interfere in them," Saton answered. "If you continue your opposition to my marriage with your ward, I shall take her away with me this afternoon."

Rochester shook his head.

"I think not," he answered.

"Then we shall see," Saton declared. "Lois, come with me. It does not matter about your hat. Your things can be sent on afterwards. Come!"

She would have followed him towards the door, but Rochester, leaning over, touched the bell, and almost at once two men stepped into the hall. One, Saton remembered in an instant. It was the man whom he had found with Violet—the man who was there to have his fortune told. The other was a stranger, but there was something in his demeanor, in the very cut of his clothes, which seemed to denote his profession.

Saton was suddenly pale. He realized in a moment that it was not intended that he should leave the room. He looked toward Rochester as though for an explanation.

"My young friend," Rochester said, "when you leave this place, you will leave it, unless I change my mind, in the company of those friends of mine whom you see there. I don't want to terrify you unnecessarily. These gentlemen are detectives, but they are in my employ. They have nothing to do with Scotland Yard. I can assure you, however, that there need not be ten minutes' delay in the issuing of a warrant for your arrest."

"My arrest?" Saton gasped. "What do you mean?"

Rochester sighed.

"Ah!" he said. "Why should you force me for explanations? Ask yourself. Once before you have stood in the dock, on the charge of being connected with certain enterprises designed to wheedle their pocket-money from over-credulous ladies. You got off by a fluke, but you did not learn your lesson. This time, getting off will not be quite so easy, for you seem to have added to your former profession one which an English jury seldom lets pass unpunished. I am in a position to prove, Bertrand Saton, that the offices in Charing Cross Road, conducted under the name of Jacobson & Company, and which are nothing more nor less than the headquarters of an iniquitous blackmailing system, are inspired and conducted by you, and that the profits are the means by which you live. A more despicable profession the world has never known. There are a sheaf of cases against you. I will remind you of one. My wife—Lady Mary here—left a private letter in the rooms of a Madame Helga. The letter was passed on at once to the blackmailing branch of your extremely interesting business, and the sum of, I think, five hundred pounds, was paid for its recovery. You yourself were personally responsible for this little arrangement. And there are many others. If all the poor women whom you have robbed," Rochester continued, "had had the common sense of my wife, and brought the matter to their husbands, you would probably have been a guest of His Majesty some time ago."

Such fear as had at first drawn the color from Saton's cheeks, and filled his eyes with terror, passed quickly away. He stood upright, his head thrown back, a faint smile upon his lips. He had some appearance, even, of manhood.

"Mr. Rochester," he said, "I deny your charges. I have no connection with the fortune-telling establishments to which you have alluded. I know nothing of the blackmailing transactions you speak of. You have been my enemy, my hopeless and unforgiving enemy. I am not afraid of you. If this is your great blow, strike. Let me be arrested. I will answer everything. Afterwards, you and I will have our reckoning. Lois," he added, turning to her, "you do not believe—say that you do not believe these things."

"I—do—not—believe—them—Bertrand," she answered slowly.

"You will come with me?"

"I—will—come—with—you," she echoed.

"By God, sir, she shan't!" cried Vandermere. "Take your hands off her, sir, or you shall learn how mountebanks like yourself should be treated."

Saton struck him full in the face, so that losing for a moment his balance upon the slippery floor, Vandermere nearly fell. In a moment he recovered himself, however. There was a struggle which did not last half-a-dozen seconds. He lifted Saton off his feet and shook him, till it seemed as though his limbs were cracking. Then he threw him away.

Rochester stepped forward to interfere.

"Enough of this, Vandermere," he said sternly. "Remember that the fellow's career is over. He may try to bluff it out, but he is done for. I have proofs enough to send him to prison a dozen times over."

Saton rose slowly to his feet. Unconsciously his fingers straightened his tie. He knew very well that life—or rather the things which life meant for him—was over. He had only one desire—the desire of the born *poseur*—to extricate himself from his present position with something which might, at any rate, seem like dignity.

"Do I understand," he asked Rochester, "that my departure from this house is forbidden?"

Rochester shook his head.

"No!" he answered. "For what you are, for the ignoble creature that you have become, I accept a certain amount of responsibility. For that reason, I bid you go. Go where you will, so long as your name or your presence never trouble us again. Let this be the last time that any one of us hears the name of Bertrand Saton. I give you that chance. Find for yourself an honest place in the world, if you can, wherever you will, so that it be not in this country. Go!"

Saton turned toward the door with a little shrug of the shoulders.

"You need have no fear," he said. "The country into which I go is one in which you will never be over-anxious to travel."

He passed out, amidst a silence which seemed a little curious when one considered the emotions which he left behind. Lois' pale face seemed all aglow with a sort of desperate thankfulness. Already she was in Vandermere's arms. And then the silence was broken by a woman's sobbing. They all turned towards her. It was Pauline who had suddenly broken down, her face buried in her hands, her whole frame shaking with passion.

Rochester moved towards her, but she thrust him aside.

"You are a brute!" she declared—"a brute!"

She staggered across the room towards the door by which Saton had departed. Before she could reach it, however, they heard the crunching of wheels as his car swept by the front on its way down the avenue.

Rochester pushed open the black gate which led from the road into the plantation at the back of the hill, and they passed through and commenced the last short climb. No word passed between them. The silence of the evening was broken only by the faint sobbing of the wind in the treetops, and the breaking of dried twigs under their feet. They were both listening intently—they scarcely knew for what. The far-away rumble of a train, the barking of a dog, the scurrying of a rabbit across the path—these sounds came and passed—nothing else.

They neared the edge of the plantation. There was only a short climb now, and a gray stone wall. Rochester passed his arm through his companion's. Her breath was coming in little sobs.

"We shall be there in a moment, Pauline," he said. "It is only a fancy of mine. Perhaps he is not here after all, but at any rate we shall know."

She said nothing. She seemed to be bracing herself for that last effort. Now they could see the bare rocky outline of the summit of the hill. A few steps more, and they would pass through the gate. And then the sound came, the sound which somehow they had dreaded. Sharp and crisp through the twilight air came the report of a revolver. They even fancied that they heard a little moan come travelling down the hillside.

Rochester stopped short.

"We are too late," he said. "Pauline, you had better stay here. I will go on and find him."

She shook her head.

"I am coming," she said. "It is my fault!—it is my fault!"

He held out his hand.

"Pauline," he said, "it may not be a fit sight for you. Sit here. If you can do any good, I will call to you."

She brushed him aside and began to run. With her slight start she outdistanced him, and when he scrambled up to the top, she was already on her knees, kneeling down over the crouching form.

"He is not dead," she cried. "Quick! Tell me where the wound is."

Rochester stooped down on the other side, and Saton opened his eyes slowly.

"I am a bungler, as usual!" he said.

Rochester opened his coat carefully.

"He has shot himself in the shoulder," he said to Pauline. "It is not serious."

Saton pointed to the rock.

"Lift me up a little," he said. "I want to sit there, with my back to it. Carefully!"

Rochester did as he was bid. Then he took his handkerchief and tried to staunch the blood.

"I don't know why you came," Saton faltered—"you especially," he added to Rochester. "Haven't you had all the triumph you wanted? Couldn't you have left me alone to spend this last hour my own way? I wanted to learn how to die without fear or any regret. Here I can do it, because it is easier here to realize that failure such as mine is death."

"We came to try and save you," said Rochester quietly.

"To save you!" Pauline sobbed. "Oh! Bertrand, I am sorry—I am very, very sorry!"

He looked at her in slow surprise.

"That is kind of you," he said. "It is kind of you to care. You know now what sort of a creature I am. You know that he was right—this man, I mean—when he warned you against me, when he told you that I was something rotten, something not worth your notice. Give me the revolver again."

Rochester thrust it in his pocket, shaking his head.

"My young friend, I think not," he said. "Listen. I have no more to say about the past. I am prepared to accept my share of the responsibility of it. You are still young. There is still time for you to weave fresh dreams, to live a new life. Make another start. No! Don't be afraid that I'm going to offer you my help. There was a curse upon that. But nevertheless, make your start. It isn't I who wish it. It is—Pauline."

Saton looked at her wonderingly.

"She doesn't care," he said. "She knows now that I am really a charlatan. And I needn't have been," he added, with a sudden fury. "It was only that cursed taste for luxury which seemed somehow or other to creep into my blood, which made me so dependent upon money. Naudheim was right! Naudheim was right! If only I had stayed with him! If only I had believed in him!"

"It is not too late," she whispered, stooping low over him. "Be a man, Bertrand. Take up your work where you left it, and have done with the other things. This slipping away over the edge, slipping into Eternity, is the trick of cowards. For my sake, Bertrand!"

He half closed his eyes. Rochester was busy still with his shoulder, and the pain made him faint.

"Go back to Naudheim," she whispered. "Start life from the very bottom rung, if he will have it so. Don't be afraid of failure. Keep your hands tight upon the ladder, and your eyes turned toward Heaven. Oh! You can climb if you will, Bertrand. You can climb, I am sure. Don't look down. Don't pause. Be satisfied with nothing less than the great things. For my sake, Bertrand! My thoughts will follow you. My heart will be with you. Promise!"

"I promise," he murmured.

His head sank back. He was half unconscious.

"We will stay with him for a moment," Rochester whispered. "As soon as he comes to, I will carry him down to the car."

In a moment or two he opened his eyes. His lips moved, but he was half delirious.

"Anything but failure!" he muttered to himself, with a little groan. "Death, if you will—a touch of the finger, a stroke too far to seaward. Oh! death is easy enough! Death is easy, and failure is hard!"

Her lips touched his forehead.

"Don't believe it, dear," she whispered. "There is no real failure if only the spirit is brave. The dead things are there to help you climb. They are rungs in the ladder, boulders for your feet."

He leaned a little forward. It seemed as though he recognised something familiar amongst the treetops, or down in the mist-clad valleys.

"Naudheim!" he cried hoarsely. "I shall go to Naudheim!"

EPILOGUE

THE MAN

About half-way up, where the sleighs stopped, Lady Mary gave in. Pauline and Rochester went forward on foot, and with a guide in front. Below them was a wonderful unseen world, unseen except when the snow for a moment ceased to fall, and they caught vague, awe-inspiring glimpses of ravines and precipices, tree-clad gorges, reaching down a dizzy height to the valley below. Above them was a plateau, black with pine trees. Higher still, the invisible mountain tops.

"It is only a few hundred yards further," Rochester said, holding his companion by the arm. "What a country, though! I wonder if it ever stops snowing."

"It is wonderful!" she murmured. "Wonderful!"

And then, as though in some strange relation to his words, the storm of whirling snow-flakes suddenly ceased. The thin veil passed away from overhead like gossamer. They saw a clear sky. They saw, even, the gleam of reflected sunshine, and as the mist lifted, the country above and beyond unrolled itself in one grand and splendid transformation scene: woods above woods; snow-clad peaks, all glittering with their burden of icicles and snow; and above, a white chaos, where the mountain-peak struck the clouds.

They paused for a moment, breathless.

"It is like Naudheim himself," she declared. "This is the land he spoke of. This is the place to which he climbed. It is wonderful!"

"Come," Rochester said. "We must be up before the darkness."

Slowly they made their way along the mountain road, which their guide in front was doing all he could to make smooth for them. And then at the corner they found a log hut, to which their guide pointed triumphantly.

"It is there!" he exclaimed—"there where they live, the two madmen. Beyond, you see, is the village of the woodhewers."

Rochester nodded. They struggled a few steps upwards, and then paused to look with wonder at the scene below. The one log cabin before which they were now standing, had been built alone. Barely a hundred yards away, across the ravine, were twenty or thirty similar ones, from the roofs of which the smoke went curling upwards. It seemed for a moment as though they had climbed above the world of noises—climbed into the land of eternal silence. Before they had had time, however, to frame the thought, they heard the crashing of timber across the ravine, and a great tree fell inwards. A sound like distant thunder rose and swelled at every moment.

"It is the machinery," their guide told them. "The trees fall and are stripped of their boughs. Then they go down the ravine there, and along the slide all the way to the river. See them all the way, like a great worm. Day and night, month by month—there is never a minute when a tree does not fall."

Again they heard the crashing, and another tree fell. They heard the rumble of the slide in the forest. The peculiar scent of fresh sap seemed like a perfume in the air. Then suddenly the snow began to fall again. They could not see across the ravine.

The guide knocked at the door and opened it. Rochester and Pauline passed in....

There was something almost familiar about the little scene. It was, in many respects, so entirely as she had always imagined it. Naudheim, coatless, collarless, with open waistcoat, twisted braces, and unkempt hair, was striding up and down the room, banging his hands against his side, dictating to the younger man who sat before the rude pine table.

"So we arrive," they heard his harsh, eager tones, "so we arrive at the evolution of that consciousness which may justly be termed eternal—the consciousness which has become subject to these primary and irresistible laws, the understanding of which has baffled for so many ages the students of every country. So we come——"

Naudheim broke off in the middle of his sentence. A rush of cold air had swept into the room. He thrust forward an angry, inquiring countenance toward the visitors. The young man sprang to his feet.

"Pauline!" he exclaimed.

He recognised Rochester, and stepped back with a momentary touch of his old passionate repugnance, not unmixed with fear. He recovered himself, however, almost immediately, Rochester gazed at him in amazement. It would have been hard, indeed, to have recognised the Bertrand Saton of the old days, in the robust and bearded man who stood there now with his eyes fixed upon Pauline. His cheeks were weather-beaten but brown with health. He wore a short, unkempt beard, a flannel shirt with collar but no tie, tweed clothes, which might indeed have come, at one time or another, from Saville Row, but were now spent with age, and worn out of all shape.

Pauline's heart leaped with joy. Her eyes were wet. It had been worth while, then. He had found salvation.

"We hadn't the least right to come, of course," she began, recognising that speech alone could dissolve that strange silence and discomposure which seemed to have fallen upon all of them. "Mr. Rochester and Lady Mary and I are going to St. Moritz, and I persuaded them to stay over here and see whether we couldn't rout you out. What a wonderful place!" she exclaimed.

"It is a wonderful place, madam!" Naudheim exclaimed glowering at them with darkening face. "It is wonderful because we are many thousands of feet up from that rotten, stinking little life, that cauldron of souls, into which my young friend here had very nearly pitched his own little offering."

"It was we who sent him to you," Pauline said gently.

"So long as you have not come to fetch him away," Naudheim muttered.

Pauline shook her head.

"We have come," she said, "because we care for him, because we were anxious to know whether he had come to his own. We will go away the moment you send us."

"You will have some tea," Naudheim growled, a little more graciously. "Saton, man, be hospitable. It is goat's milk, and none too sweet at that, and I won't answer for the butter."

Saton spoke little. Pauline was content to watch him. They drank tea out of thick china cups, but over their conversation there was always a certain reserve. Naudheim listened and watched, like a mother jealous of strangers who might rob her of her young. After tea, however, he disappeared from the room for a few moments, and Rochester walked toward the window.

"It is very good of you to come, Pauline," Saton said. "I shall work all the better for this little glimpse of you."

"Will the work," she asked softly, "never be done?"

He shook his head.

"Why should it? One passes from field to field, and our lives are not long enough, nor our brains great enough, to reach the place where we may call halt."

"Do you mean," she asked, "that you will live here all your days?"

"Why not?" he answered. "I have tried other things, and you know what they made of me. If I live here till I am as old as Naudheim, I shall only be suffering a just penance."

"But you are young," she murmured. "There are things in the world worth having. There is a life there worth living. Solitude such as this is the greatest panacea the world could offer for all you have been through. But it is not meant to last. We want you back again, Bertrand."

His eyes were suddenly on fire. He shrank a little away from her.

"Don't!" he begged. "Don't, Pauline. I am living my punishment here, and I have borne it without once looking back. Don't make it harder."

"I do not wish to make it harder," she declared, "and yet I meant what I said. It is not right that you should spend all your days here. It is not right for your own sake, it is not right——"

She held out her hands to him suddenly.

"It is not right for mine," she whispered.

Rochester stepped outside. Again the snow had ceased. In the forest he could hear the whirl of machinery and the crashing of the falling timber. He stood for a moment with clenched hands, with unseeing eyes, with ears in which was ringing still the memory of that low, passionate cry. And then the fit passed. He looked down to the little half-way house where he had left his wife. He fancied he could see someone waving a white handkerchief from the platform of pine logs. It was all so right, after all, so right and natural. He began to descend alone.

Saton brought her down about an hour later. Their faces told all that there was to say.

"Bertrand is going to stay here for another year," Pauline said, answering Lady Mary's unspoken question. "The first part of his work with Naudheim will be finished then, and we think he will have earned a vacation."

Saton held out his hands to Rochester.

"Mr. Rochester," he said, "I have never asked you to forgive me for all the hard things I have said and thought of you, for my ingratitude, and—for other things."

"Don't speak of them," Rochester interrupted.

"I won't," Saton continued quickly. "I can't. That chapter of my life is buried. I cannot bear to think of it even now. I cannot bear to come in contact with anything which reminds me of it."

Rochester took his hand and grasped it heartily.

"Don't be morbid about it," he said. "Every man should have at least two chances in life. You had your first, and it was a rank failure. That was because you had unnatural help, and bad advice. The second time, I am glad to see that you have succeeded. You have done this on your own. You have proved that the real man is the present man."

Saton drew Pauline towards him with a gesture which was almost reverent.

"I think that Pauline knows," he said. "I hope so."

Early in the morning their sleigh rattled off. Saton stood outside the cottage, waving his hand. Naudheim was by his side, his arm resting gently upon the young man's shoulder. A fine snow was falling around them. The air was clean and pure—the air of Heaven. There was no sound to break the deep stillness but the tinkle of the sleigh-bells, and behind, the rhythmic humming of the machinery, and the crashing of the falling trees.

"Naudheim is a great master," Rochester said.

Pauline smiled through her tears.

"Bertrand isn't such a very bad pupil."

THE END

Milton Keynes UK
Ingram Content Group UK Ltd.
UKHW021332290324
440175UK00006B/640